For our esteemed
Monsignor Renwald and
very dear friend of many
years,

Lourdes High

PAPA,

I CAN

HARDLY WAIT

A Novel
by
Lourdes High

International Standard Book Number (ISBN):
0-930534-02-6

Published by
Brock Publishing Company
Post Office Box 1685
Chico, California 95927

First Printing 1977

Cover Art: Pat Lemmon

To Our Lady, and to my grandchildren for whom
Papa, I Can Hardly Wait was written

Author's Note

My singular preoccupation with Fatima over many years — strengthened by the interest of my Portuguese parents and sister — not only took me there, but led me to write *Papa, I Can Hardly Wait*. Only when the truth could be made more explicit have I used that creativity inherent in the novel. I have kept to the known facts, using Portuguese sources and taking care to weave into the story the historic events that occurred in Fatima, Portugal, in 1916 and 1917, involving three children: Francisco Marto, his sister Jacinta, and his cousin Lucia.

Accounts of their conversations and spiritual lives, their struggles with hostile government officials, with members of the clergy, and families and neighbors, as well as the phenomena of the "sun miracle" have been well documented by innumerable witnesses, both friend and nonfriend (including Lucia now a Carmelite nun in her native country). Reams of prose in many languages have repeated this preponderance of evidence. I have chosen to do the same through the novel in the happy expectancy that the message of Fatima, which so inflamed the hearts of three young shepherds, may also uplift and inflame other hearts with the love of God . . . and his mother.

PAPA,

I CAN

HARDLY WAIT

by
Lourdes High

Chapter One

Spring, 1916

At the foot of the *cabeço*, a hill that he loved more than
any other, the boy dropped his staff and eyed the band of
sheep — the whole twenty-five of them — filing right past
him on to the slope. He knew that once up there the lambs
and their mothers would fan out a little, fretting around rocks
and pushing their noses into the hard red clay but still getting
enough to eat on this day in late, late spring, every bit as
much as they'd ever get down here in *Chousa Velha* — a
pasture scribbled with rocks and spring grass where Cousin
Lucia wanted them. Half of the sheep belonged to her father,
Uncle Antonio.

1

"Look here, Lucia," he ought to tell her — if she and Jacinta ever got here — "can't you smell all that stuff up on the *cabeço*? Well, the sheep can. Rosemary, bluebells, white *margaridas* . . . wild roses small as almond blossoms." But never, never, would he open his mouth like that to Lucia — not that she would listen to him, anyway. Hastily he searched for the little reed pipe in the pocket of his long trousers. Why, the tune was already popping in his head and bursting at his lips.

Very soon he would be eight years old, June 11, 1916. He knew he was big for eight. Only yesterday, Papa had put an arm around his shoulder. "Francisco Marto, you stand as tall as ten," he'd said, with that wonderful smile that crinkled the corners of his eyes deep down. He was always saying things like that. One day he'd heard a Portuguese-American lady ask Papa why the children in the *serra* were so polite, so grown-up. "Maybe it's because we have a great love for children," he had answered. "Maybe it's because at a very early age our children learn to help their brothers and sisters, to share in all the work, and God knows there's always plenty to do."

Responsibility, Papa called it; children learned it as soon as they could talk. Papa had been a soldier in far-off places like Africa and seen crocodiles, monkeys, and lots of lions. He knew everything. That must be why people sometimes called him "The Thinker." But most of the time it was *Ti* Marto; he was like a good uncle to everybody. This morning at the sheep corral, just as he and Jacinta were about to take off to meet Lucia, Papa had hoisted a sack of barley seed to his shoulder. His big amber eyes squinting at the mountains over to the west, he'd said, "Look — *ohla*, Francisco, you and your sister, where are you taking the sheep today?"

"Chousa Velha." It was the pasture Lucia had chosen. "Tomorrow we will go here," she'd say one day. "Tomorrow we will go there," she'd say on another. And there they went because she always decided everything. This field be-

longed to her father, and from the delightful, wind-smelling *cabeço* above it you could see the whole world — almost.

"*Eia!*" Papa had stopped frowning at the lowering sky. "That's a good place; if it rains you can always climb up to that olive grove, you know the one."

Francisco could see the olive trees now (already, the sheep were not too far from there) and the old windmill at the summit. Above, the sky was still dark, the same gray as the granite that bound these hills of the *Serra de Aire* in the highlands of central Portugal. Francisco had never been away from here, not even to the old city of Leira fifteen miles to the north, although he often crossed a highway that went there where occasionally he would watch a horseless carriage speed by. Lisbon, the capital, over eighty miles to the south, was little more than a name, one not even as sweet-sounding as his own hamlet of Aljustrel with its narrow winding road sandwiched by walls of stone on either side. Close behind these rock-piled fences (much like those that rambled over the reddish-brown hills enclosing small fields and pastures) stood about twenty-one one-level stone houses, not large, some white-washed, stuccoed, or plain stone. All had red-tiled roofs; "S" shaped slots of Moorish design marked the chimney tops. Windows were few and small, protection against the wet, bitter northwest winds of winter and the heat of summer. Nearby were the families' patios, out-houses, small sheds and barns, animal corrals, and undersized fields. Here at the uppermost part of Aljustrel, Francisco lived with his parents, Manuel and Olimpia Marto, the youngest son of a family of eight living children. He had four brothers and three sisters, one of whom — the youngest — he thought should be here by now.

While blowing on the *pifaro* — the little reed pipe — he decided that as usual Jacinta and Lucia had stopped to talk. Jacinta would be asking questions, and Lucia would be answering right back. She always knew what to say, but were those two scared of everything. "Look! *Ohla*! Francisco caught a wild rabbit,'' or, "Run, run, here he comes with a snake on his staff!" Anyway, he could take care of the sheep without them, not that he was crazy about poking sheep from one place to another. At first, sheepherding had been Jacinta's idea, not his; just because she had to be near her *querida* — her dearest Lucia. Well, now that Brother João's turn had come to skip off to school, he guessed the staff belonged in his hands. School was a fox trap. The very word was enough to shake the *pifaro*, and quivering, the tune fluttered, soared thinly with the melody of a mournful Portuguese *fado*, yet managed to sing happily of a turtle dove in spring. Jacinta loved to sing it as well as a hundred others, and now to its rhythm he swayed, his eyes on the windmill above. Like windmills across the other hills, its four sail-like arms hung motionless — begging for wind. The music quickened . . . nightingales and turtle doves . . . sunsets with Our Lord's Lamp falling fast behind mountains, splashing and scattering gold and purples on every hill until windmills and trees wildly danced. Here the notes swelled, strutted, sped — just the kind that made a fast spinning wheel bobbin of Jacinta; and now scuttled him atop a great pitted rock to see the two girls in long somber skirts and bright shoulder-length kerchiefs — Jacinta only half as big as Lucia — sauntering down the steepness from the pasture *Valinhos*.

Jacinta had heard the music. Tiny as a humming bird, she danced over the rough ground toward him, singing and snapping her fingers until he could no longer make out the wide-set golden eyes, the dimples, the brown braids. No one, but no one, could sing and dance like Jacinta. All kinds of fancy twirls and steps she could make up.

But now out of nowhere, a gusty northwest wind, as if trapped in the windmill's arms, pushed fast and hard. "It's going to rain," Lucia's high thin voice called out. "Francisco, the sheep! Where are they?"

Say, it was hardly raining, just some light wet stuff. And the sheep? Oh, oh! Well — Retrieving his staff, he pointed toward the olive orchard; and racing uphill past a scattering of spindly oaks, he halted for a moment at the sight of a yellow chain of canaries winging throught the silvery branches of a young olive tree.

Now close to the crest of the *cabeço*, he could see the hamlets of *Casa Velha* and *Eira de Pedra*, his own house at the top of the Aljustrel road, and Lucia's not too far away, almost at the other end. But best of all was the great sweep of land spread out like a picture; hills topped by windmills, farms a lot bigger than any he'd ever seen close, and far beyond — big ranges of mountains. Grabbing a handful of pebbles, he threw them singly toward some tall pines in a green valley, noting that the girls had stopped to pick wildflowers. And Lucia in such a hurry! The wind had blown itself out, so he'd take a run up to the ridge, but now, as soon as he got there, the wind was back and this time with rain. Turning on his heel, his glance fell on a big rock slanted slightly toward him. Stepping closer, he leaned past it, one hand on another boulder that also jutted out of a smallish cavity filled with rocks of all sizes, some of them piled together as if by a giant hand.

After a brief inspection, he looked at the two girls now dashing up the *cabeço*. "Hey! See what I found — over here." He had an unusual voice for his age, low-pitched with rough-edged notes. Well, he was staying right here. Propping the staff against a rock, he shook off an old leather shepherd's pouch, a *surrão*, which today replaced the usual cotton bag carrying his and Jacinta's lunch.

"What, what did you find?"

Francisco laughed. Lucia's voice really sounded scary. "Don't worry, it's not a snake or anything like that. Come and see; it's a cave."

Her straight black brows knitted together, Lucia's gaze made an unbroken orbit of the enclosure, noting the huge craggy rocks, the slabs of granite. Still frowning, she looked directly at Francisco, her head to one side. "How did you ever find it? We've been up up here before, but this is the very first time . . . '' She squeezed past him and searched through the light rain for the sheep. ''They're all right,'' she said, her back to him. ''This ought to be a good place to watch them.''

Was that all she was going to say? A good place to watch them! Why, this place was different . . . lots more fun than being in *Chousa Velha*. Guess she'd forgotten about wanting the sheep down there. Some night, maybe, he'd come up here. There must be owls and swallows and . . . His thoughts were cut off by Jacinta, teetering on a boulder batting her long eyelashes at Lucia, her grin minus a couple of front teeth. ''I love it here,'' she lisped; ''it's like a little house.'' Fingering her skirt, she wobbled and lost her footing.

''Jacinta!'' Lucia tried to break the fall. ''Are you hurt?''

''No.'' Jacinta brushed her skirt, then catching the look of concern in her cousin's eyes, hugged her close. ''I love you!'' Lucia laughed outright and caught her in her arms. She was used to these endearments of Jacinta. But, now what was Francisco doing? As usual, he wasn't paying any attention to her and Jacinta, no more than he ever did when all the kids played tag, hide and seek, forfeits. He never cared who won, his side or whatever. Sometimes she just had to take him by the arm and put him out of the game. Then off he'd go without a word, sit on a rock and toot his pipe while everybody else ran to hide behind the well in her back yard, or up in the trees, sometimes even in the house under the beds. He really was different.

''You know something, Lucia?'' Jacinta was still clinging to her. ''You know the happiest day of my life?''

''The day your godmother gave you a locket; no, the day your mother gave you a spanking!''

''No, no, the day Mama finally said, 'To the pastures you may go with Lucia.' '' Her upraised voice and her waving hands, indicating hills and winding trails, bore a close resemblance to her mother's.

Lucia fell silent. The happiest day of my life . . . The square serious face with its full lips and dark brows grew thoughtful. Never, never could she forget that day. A sharp sweetness of remembrance brought a slight flush to the olive cheeks.

Jacinta was quick to see the wistfulness in her cousin's face. "Lucia, what is it?" She looked so beautiful, her *querida* Lucia, eyes shining like that.

Quietly, Lucia answered, "Jacinta, the happiest day of my life was the day of my first Holy Communion."

"When was that?"

"Three years ago."

"And you still remember!"

"I do."

"Can you see the Baby Jesus when you go to Holy Communion? I couldn't see Him in the procession; that's why I didn't throw any flowers. I looked and looked, but I couldn't see Him in the big white Host."

"I've told you before, Jacinta. He is hidden in the big Host but he is the same One we receive in Holy Communion. He is the Hidden Jesus in both — the Hidden Jesus. You understand?"

"Do you talk with the little Jesus when you go to Holy Communion?"

"Yes, everytime I receive Him."

"I want to receive Him too!"

"But you can't. You're too little. You've got to be ten."

"You were six."

Lucia sighed. They'd been over all this before. "I knew my catechism, that's why." A new thought struck her. "Maybe I could teach you —"

"And Francisco, too?"

Lucia didn't answer; looking across at him hunched over a rock, she wasn't so sure. He was always doing such queer things, like now. For a moment she regarded him impatiently: the tanned face with its fine regular features under the long stocking cap that covered a light-brown crew-cut. His large dark eyes were focused on his hands, so it seemed to her, sliding unhurriedly across the rough surfaces of the rock. "What are you doing?"

His hands stopped. "Nothing." He continued staring down at the grainy texture with its marblings of black. Hundreds of crystals would be gleaming when the sun fell on them . . . like dew drops . . . like window panes caught by the reds of sunset.

Lucia shrugged and looked up; her eyes took in the arms of the gangly old oak directly above. "This isn't a cave," she declared, noting the clearing sky. "It's, it's a grotto." It was this fat rock sticking out like an old boot that had kept out the rain.

Slumping to the ground, Francisco flexed his bare toes against a rock. Cave or not, it sure looked a lot like the one on the hill facing Lucia's house. Anyway, he was starving, the hole in his stomach hurting and getting bigger every minute. Sun was peeking in, too. He peeled off his short homespun jacket and reached for the *surrão*: two sardines, one for him and one for Jacinta, a handful of olives, a good-sized hunk of bread. Breaking off half, he swallowed hard, smelling the same yeasty aroma that floated through the yard whenever Mama baked her barley loaves in the brick oven out in the patio. On days like Easter and Saint Anthony's Feast Day, the bread was deliciously different; then it was white, sometimes made with eggs and sugar. They shared it with the poor — people who couldn't buy shoes.

As soon as they had finished eating, Lucia held up a rosary. And there goes Jacinta, too, right after hers, he thought. Lucia never forgets, like that very first day when the three of them had set out with the sheep. "Do you have your rosaries with you?" she had asked. "*Por favor* — please get them. We'll say the rosary every day after we eat." And so they had, except that sometimes they shortened it. He hoped that today would be one of those days. On the big beads you just said two words: Our Father. The same went for all the Hail Marys.

As if she had read his thoughts, Lucia wheeled toward him. "I can't understand you," she said sharply. "Why don't you like to say the rosary? That's a lot better than throwing rocks, boring holes, and, and catching lizards, and snakes, and foxes —"

"And you know what else he does, Lucia? He takes bread and stuff, and puts it in the rock holes for birds and squirrels and things to eat."

Lucia knelt. For some reason, her eyes didn't look so scrappy now, he thought, as he slid to his knees beside her.

"When I say the rosary, Francisco, I like to think about Jesus, when He was a Baby in His mother's arms, how much He suffered for us when He grew up. Sometimes, I don't even think about each mystery. I just say the words, feeling Him very close."

He nodded, keeping his eyes averted.

Sidling past him, Jacinta knelt close to Lucia. "Do you say the rosary, all of you together?" Lucia had four older sisters, a big brother and a little one.

"Sometimes. Mama always says it with us." She also read to them from the Bible and other religious books, especially on winter evenings and in Lent.

But most of the time Uncle Antonio wasn't there, Francisco thought. Oh, well, the sky was blue as bluebells now; it was time to get out. If Jacinta would quit asking questions they could get on with the rosary. But, no, there she was at it again.

"Lucia, did you know that Mama didn't like what the new priest said about dancing?"

"Neither did you!" Francisco fell back on his heels. He'd jump right out of this cave, except that Lucia . . . Why, she wasn't even two whole years older than he. Sure, he knew how Mama felt about dancing; she loved it. Lots of

times when she saw the *pifaro* in his mouth, she would hum
and toss her head, her fingers snapping, her eyes sparky. She
wasn't like Aunt Maria Rosa, Lucia's mother, who was too
heavy — to even raise herself to her toes.

It was right after the new pastor's sermon that Aunt
Maria Rosa had faced Mama in front of Saint Anthony's
Church in Fatima. "The *senhor prior* is absolutely right!"
Her pointing finger and narrowed eyes had framed each
word. "After this my daughters will do their dancing at home
— nowhere else." Right under her gray watchful eyes.

Tossing her head, Mama had broken away from her and
the other ladies standing around them. Almost on the run for
the whole half-mile home, she had caught up with Papa at the
back door. Usually she stayed after Mass because Saint Anthony's was the parish church for many hamlets, and so
there were many to see and to visit. Behind the church was
the priest's tall house; a long flight of stairs rose above a
garden bordered by a low brick wall. Close by was the cemetery, the school (only for boys), the post office, and dark
little stores including a tavern — all in a kind of lopsided
square.

"Look, woman, don't get so upset, " Papa had said,
eyes twinkling as Mama slammed the door behind them.
"Maybe the new *senhor prior* is right. Let the young people
dance at home; isn't that what he said? But not at the
festas."

"And what is the difference I'd like to know!"

"Sometimes there is no difference, but sometimes there
is, and then it is not good."

Hands on her hips, Mama had looked puzzled, but Papa
with a wave of his hand made it clear that he was all finished
with dancing. "Francisco, tell me, how would you like to
make your First Confession — Holy Communion, too? This
new priest . . . say! Maybe Jacinta could also make hers."

Before he could answer Papa, Mama's voice had
jumped right through the trap door in the low wooden ceiling.

"Jacinta! Confession and Holy Communion! Don't let her hear you say that. Don't you realize she's only six? Another thing: Don't forget who teaches the catechism around here."

"I know, I know, but Jacinta is bright, like Lucia." Then his eyelids had drooped a little, his white teeth suddenly flashing in a big smile. "Jacinta's not only bright but every bit as pretty as her Mama."

"Humm. And terribly spoilt, too. Everybody spoils her, especially you." But honey had melted her voice and made her dark eyes shine. "Don't forget, Manuel Marto, that our old pastor, Father Pena, was dead set against Lucia making her First Confession and Holy Communion. 'It's not customary at such an early age,' he said. Do I remember his words! I was right there beside Maria Rosa when he said them, and she wasn't a bit happy with him, I can tell you. In fact . . ."

"You're still miffed at Maria Rosa, but tell me, while you're remembering so well, how about that Jesuit missionary, the one from Lisbon . . ."

"Father Cruz? Ah, yes, he talked Father Pena into letting Lucia receive the sacraments . . ."

"Right. She knew her catechism, even better than the older ones, he said. Mayby this new Father Ferreira won't be so old-fashioned as Father Pena."

And rubbing his hands together, Papa had said, "Francisco, you haven't answered me yet. At seven, even younger, children know right from wrong."

"Oh, I quite agree with that," Mama said fast, "but as for the 'old fashioned,' nobody could beat this new priest. No dancing!" Removing her Sunday kerchief which resembled a turban, two ends knotted at the top, a third one, shoulder length, at the back, Mama had tripped toward her bedroom, a song on her lips. Just then his two big sisters, Florinda and Teresa, had come in with Jacinta, so without answering Papa, he had slipped out of the room.

At last, the rosary finished, Francisco leaped into the bright clearing, just short of a covey of birds in fulltilt flight. Except for the chatter of gossipy robins, the *cabeço* lay serene under a wide, clear blue sky. He began piling stones, when without any warning, the calm was shattered by a swift swishing sound, like miles of leaves rustling in the wind, their echoes whistling from the pines in the valley beyond.

"What was that!" Jacinta had dropped a handful of pebbles.

"Look — over there, way up high." Lucia pointed eastward.

He saw it then: something like a big ball, full of light, gliding toward them over the green valley. Without saying a word — not one peep, either, from Jacinta or Lucia — he kept his eyes fixed on the advancing globe. Brighter than any crystal on a rock was this, with Our Lord's Lamp shimmering through it.

Beside the two girls he waited.

Chapter Two

All his life Francisco had heard about angels. They were good spirits, beautiful spirits, created by God. They were his messengers; they also took good care of you, just like his guardian angel whose song he often played and sometimes sang. Like birds, they had lovely wings. In church he had seen angels with halos; he'd also seen them in black and white pictures, on colored holy cards. Although this shining splendid young man had no wings, no halo, it was easy to see, as his blurry eyes grew used to the glimmering flow of light, that that was exactly what he was — an angel.

Francisco leaned closer. With both hands he rubbed his eyes, tried to open them, tried again, and finally met for an instant the Angel's straight glance. "I am your friend," it seemed to say. "Don't be afraid."

No, I'm not afraid . . . but all that light! I can hardly see . . . well, now little by little I can: your eyes, nose, mouth. Ai! The whole brightness of you. Are you saying something? . . . If you are, I can't hear you, not a word. Maybe angels don't have to talk, maybe they don't have voices.

But the girls so close beside him clearly heard the Angel's voice.

"Do not be afraid. I am the Angel of Peace. Pray with me."

And with these words he was no longer above the rock which was about three feet high and the one from which Jacinta had tumbled but lying full-length, his form a fragile cloud, transparent, gilded by a light brighter than the sun. His forehead against the earth, he prayed:

"My God, I believe, I adore, I hope, and I love You. I beg pardon of You for those who do not believe, do not adore, do not hope and love You."

The Angel spoke the words three times; three times Francisco heard the girls repeating those words.

"Pray this way." The Angel, resplendent and handsome, and very young, was standing now. "The hearts of Jesus and Mary listen to your prayers."

Francisco stood motionless, eyes fixed on the Angel, seeing him soundlessly disappear, his visit no longer than their short rosaries. Without a glance at the girls already prostrated, he fell face to the ground, his voice taking on the prayer the girls were repeating. With them he said it over and over:

"My God, I believe, I adore, I hope, and I love You. I beg pardon of You for those who do not believe, do not adore, do not hope and love You."

At last he pushed himself to his knees, both hands at his back. The girls still lay on the ground, faces in their hands. "My poor back," he groaned, gripping the rock beside him. How could they stay down like that so long? He was dead tired, like he'd been running up and down a hundred hills. His heart, too, was running wild; yet, how come he could stay here forever? — all this sweet new joy tearing right through him. He sat on one of the rocks, staring down at the girls, then stood again, hands still on his back. "How — how — can you?" The words had to be pushed out. He watched Lucia and Jacinta struggling to their feet, bright stars and angel music in their eyes.

"The — the Angel," he stammered. "I — never — heard him."

They said nothing, just stood very still, with eyes that looked right through him, seemed like.

The sun was already flecking rose on wisps of white clouds and reddening the western sky when they came down the *cabeço* with the sheep. Flurries of birds flashed by; a slight spring chill braced the air. Like sleepwalkers they trudged along, up and down, past stone walls and the pasture of *Valinhos*, the girls behind Francisco. On reaching Aljustrel where the sheep gamboled home over the familiar road, Lucia stopped, waiting for an old mule cart with wood to trundle by. Standing close to the stone fence on the Marto side of the road she faced the other two. Pale, their eyes never leaving her, they stood rigid as the rocks in the wall.

"Listen," Lucia's voice broke into halting whispers; "one day on the *cabeço*, a long time ago when I was with Maria Justine, and her sister and Maria Mattias, we all saw something white above the trees — way off. Later, it came again, just like before . . . three times, but I never told anyone." She was ready to fall she was so tired, but she must warn them. "The whiteness was like what we saw today, shiny, bright — a shape, kind of. The girls told my mother and everybody. They laughed. Mama was too mad."

Francisco barely nodded. Nobody will believe us she was trying to say. As if he'd ever tell! As they neared his house (he could hardly push one foot ahead of the other, but he'd better; the sheep were already at the corral gate and João yelling crazy at him), he turned into the wide gateless front yard, Jacinta at his side. She wasn't even saying goodby to Lucia, who now, head slightly bent, shuffled down the road.

She just hoped Jacinta wouldn't talk. Francisco was a little strange about some things, but you could count on his mouth staying shut. Funny that he hadn't heard the Angel, especially when he talked so loud, each word clear as a bell. She took a deep breath, full of remembering. "My God, I believe, I adore, I hope, and I love You . . ." She had told

Francisco this morning that sometimes when she said the rosary she could feel Jesus near. Now she was bursting with love for Him, love for everyone, everywhere!

"Lucia." Startled, she looked up to see her newly-married sister, Maria dos Anjos — Maria of the Angels — standing in front of her gate, a blue water jug on her head. "Mama's been wondering what happened to you. Have you any idea what time it is? The sheep —"

Lucia tried to hurry, turning into her yard across the street. The sheep would be fussing at the corral gate, and Mama!

About three months later, in the dawn of a hot summer day, Francisco awoke with a start as if someone had sung out his name. That's just the way it sounded. He listened. *Ohla!* Must have been old cock-a-hoop himself, now crowing to the highest mountain. The tiny bedroom — his single, brass bed with its thin mattress packed tightly but comfortably with corn leaves, took almost three sides of the room — was dark, except for the grey-blue at the small open window. João shared a larger room with his two older brothers. Wide awake, Francisco blessed himself, then hunched toward the wall, pushed his finger lazily along a familiar broken line of plaster, screwed his eyes, tried to sleep. No one was up yet; he rolled back, feeling happy, with something way down inside of him kind of humming — like waiting for a new tune to jump out of the *pifaro*.

At last he heard the boots, soon followed by a patter of bare feet. Papa and Mama. Papa on the way to the kitchen, walking straight as a soldier, hair straight and thick above his large ears, his small moustache with a little red in it, trim and neat. First thing, he'd open the wooden box with the matches. Then he'd light the candles in the old green bottle next to the oil lamp way above the black sooty hearth. With the poker, Papa would loosen the ashes and blow into the reddening coals, throwing in twigs of oak and pine. There was usually something simmering in that big round-bellied pot hanging on a rod above the fire — *sopa*, a soup of vegetables, sometimes just kale and potatoes. Milk, eggs, cheese, bread, were always plentiful. And when the pig was slaughtered there was a wonderful sausage — *linguiça* — made with garlic and Mama's own spices. Very special.

Special like the day on the *cabeço* when the Angel had sped across the valley on his way from heaven. They had never given their secret away. A few days after the tiredness had left them, they'd gone back to the cave, the three of them, and again prayed exactly like the Angel, their heads down to the ground. It was only then he'd heard what the Angel had said. "The hearts of Jesus and Mary listen to your prayers." The hearts — both hearts. Glancing at the crucifix high on the wall, Francisco slipped to his knees and laid his head against the bed.

In the kitchen his mother's voice hummed deliberately low. ". . . must have been weeks and weeks ago when I told you about that spell of Jacinta's. Not like her at all it was, moping around, quiet as a mouse. 'I'm all right,' she'd say if I asked her why she was so quiet. I'd really forgotten all about it until yesterday. Don't you remember that time? It lasted about two or three days."

Snuffing the candles with one breath, her husband reached for the lamp. The morning light, he saw, was light gray in the window near the ceiling. What was Olimpia getting at? "No, I don't remember." He adjusted the long wick and lit it. Replacing the blackened chimney, he set the lamp on the heavy wooden table in front of her, suddenly noting the little gold circles in her ears as they reflected the pale flickering amber from the lamp. Even this early in the morning she made a pleasant picture: the two parts of dark hair smoothly brushed from their center, the large lively eyes in the small face as busy as her hands now sorting the olive-green leaves of kale. He stirred the fire. As soon as the *sopa* was warm . . . there was plenty to do before sun-up.

But Olimpia was intent on pursuing her story. "What started me thinking about that quietness of Jacinta's a while back was Mrs. Borge's visit yesterday." With a long paring knife, Olimpia snipped the stems and dropped them into a bucket. Water was too precious to waste on stalks, even if the cisterns were full. "She and her *cachopos* haven't been here in months, but even before they walked in, Jacinta scooted off." Olimpia set the knife down, trying to catch her husband's eye. "And where do you think she went? Right down to Lucia's before I could yell her back. It really put the mustard up my nose."

"I agree she shouldn't have done that, but what's that got to do with —" Her husband's voice trailed off. The humorous lines around his eyes deepened as the lids drooped a little, the way they sometimes did when he was amused or reminiscing. It must have been, he mused, the gold earrings sparkling from the lamp that had triggered the old memory. She'd been wearing them the first time he had seen her, a young vivacious Olimpia, slim and graceful as a gazelle. Some women had a certain charm, some didn't. Back from Mozambique — fourteen whole months there! — he'd fallen in love with her, the young widow of José Fernandes Rosa. Although she had been four years older, he'd taken her and her two little sons to his heart. Antonio and Manuel were as dear to him as the seven who had come to bless their home. One little one they had lost to heaven, their first Teresa.

"Uh — what was that you were saying?"

"I was wondering where you'd gone to!" Olimpia piled the leaves into a big pot. "I've been trying to tell you that ever since that time when Jacinta acted so terribly quiet, she never leaves Lucia's side. "Oh, yes — *sim*!" forestalling his objection. "I know she's always been full of sweet honey for Lucia, but . . ."

"What other kind is there?" He laughed, trying to divert her, but she forged ahead. "Nothing like lately — Lucia's constant shadow. I really got after her yesterday, and I had a good mind to talk to Lucia, too." She felt baffled by something she didn't quite understand, and her husband's blank face wasn't helping any. "Manuel, I know how you feel about Lucia . . ."

"All the children love her; Jacinta's no exception. Lucia," he said the name gently, "has a way with all of them; she teaches them songs, tells them stories, makes up games. I've watched her lots of times."

Olimpia wasn't listening. "This constant sticking to Lucia, like yesterday!" Indignation at Jacinta's flight still rankling, she went to the windowless pantry where she kept her bread in a low wooden chest. The room was big enough for earthen jugs of water, oil and wine, and big tubs for bathing and washing clothes.

Ti Marto pulled at one of his ears. Must be this heat spell; puts people on edge sometimes. He took a white crockery bowl from a shelf; his finger told him the *sopa* was about right. On Olimpia's return with a loaf in each hand, he said, "I think you're trying to make quick oaks out of acorns, you're just making too much out . . .

"Too much!" Carefully, Olimpia laid the two crusty loaves on the table. Well, she had news for him. "Now let me tell you something. Francisco has gotten just as bad — quiet, quiet! — sometimes as if he had stepped into another world. And mind you!" The thought had just struck her. "It's only been since those days when Jacinta . . ."

She stopped, catching his surprise. "Manuel Marto, I know exactly what you are going to say." Arms akimbo, Olimpia stood very erect; her tones fell as she minicked him. "Eia! Francisco? Quiet? Why, don't you know he's naturally a very quiet boy. He has always been quiet, like the quietness of a growing tree, but he's a thinker!" Carried away, she finished in a tenor remarkably like his. "He's full of spirit, too, and so brave! not afraid of animals, tame or wild."

Supressing a grin, he countered, "That's all true, not spouting everything he knows, nor getting ruffled about every little thing. He's a great boy — born with a smile!"

"Born with a smile! Why, he yelled as loud as all the others. Either he's not well . . ."

"You know he's never been sick in his life!"

"Then he's got some kind of secret."

"Secret! Look here, woman, what's got into you? It's got to be the heat! Just because he likes to steal out into the *serra* after dark by himself . . ."

"All right, all right!" She had gone too far; should never have brought up Francisco's name in the first place. Maybe she *was* imagining too much. Manuel was usually right, but that business of yesterday hadn't really been the first time. It musn't happen again.

Finished with his *sopa*, and now munching a piece of bread, Francisco felt his father's hand on his head. "Isn't it a little early for the sheep?" His hand tugged playfully at the long cap's tassle. "Everything good?"

"Sim, senhor!"

Looking into the smiling brown eyes, *Ti* Marto returned the smile and cleared his throat with a loud raspy grunt as he threw a quick glance at Olimpia bent over a wooden counter. "Well, well, Francisco, I'm glad everything is so fine with you," repressing the urge to add, "never saw you look better, as if you had a very happy secret." Before he had even turned on his heel, he heard Olimpia's resounding "humph!" Stepping from the threshold to a flat stone wide as the door, he lifted a mattock used for heavy weeding, hearing the sheep's dry gutteral coughs. A little breeze, just a cool one, would help. Even the moulting chickens scurrying about pecking and scratching looked shriveled. Heat was not only hard on people but on animals, he thought, walking toward the lean-to at the rear of the house where he kept tools, wood, and supplies of grain.

Hearing the barking, he looked back to see Francisco fondling *Segunda* who had been caught in a wide yawn at his whistle. "Wake up," Franciso was shouting, and sprinting toward the fence, the little dog streaking behind him, he jumped over a breach in the half-space of broken rock. If that boy had some mysterious secret, then he'd like to have one like it. Well, it was time for the other boys to come out, but the older they got the longer they wanted to sleep.

Out on the road, Francisco had almost stepped on a green lizard. "Get down, *Segunda*!" He slapped at her, holding the lizard high. "Get down! *Ohla, Senhor* Lizard, how would you like to go with me?" Francisco knew that warm as it already was, the lizard wouldn't cock a jeweled eye until the day got good and hot; now he lay limp, eyes closed. Slipping him into his pocket, he looked up to see the faint pink rays creeping behind the top of a high hill. Like a tree deeply rooted, he stood; waiting and watching the sky deepen with rose until, like a great red ball, the sun appeared. Our Lord's Lamp! Jacinta liked Our Lady's better, but not he. Hurling a stone, he ran downhill, *Segunda* barking joyously at his side. It was going to be a wonderful day; he'd known it ever since Mr. Rooster had called him.

Later on, he and the two girls would take off for a pasture after stopping at the "mud hole" to let the sheep drink. Of course, the Carreira pond wasn't exactly a muddy hole. It was big enough so that people brought their oxen, burros, and sheep to drink in its shallow water. Even women scrubbed their clothes on the flat rocks. It was here that he and Jacinta often met Lucia in the mornings before setting off with their sheep.

They hadn't been out with them very long when Lucia complained, "It's too hot, let's go home."

At the Martos', Jacinta stood uncertain, eyes warily studying the quiet empty yard. "No visitors?" She was remembering her mother's words, "Next time I won't be so easy on you."

"Doesn't look like it," Francisco assured her with a grin.

"Jacinta and I'll be at the well," Lucia told him. "We'll wait for you there." The well in the depths of her back yard sheltered by fruit trees overlooked a valley of fields; hay, corn, groves of olives. Covered with flat rocks, the well was large enough to stand a whole family.

Francisco now drove the sheep, dusty and panting, into the corral. A mid-summer sun was beating down hard, throwing a reddish glare over the silent, deserted yard. The only animal in sight was a yellow cat curled in the shadow of the kitchen door. Francisco hooked his staff on the gate, ran both hands over his face and hair, wiped them on his trousers. In this big, big world, his eyes were the only ones wide open. Not a sound now, not a thing moving, except those silly flies skimming close to the ground. Wait a minute. He'd almost forgotten *Senhor* Lizard. Ai! This had to be good; it always worked. Almost as much fun as that day when he and João had thrown a hundred rocks at those kids from Boleiros.

———————

Chapter Three

Summer and Fall, 1916

Francisco's bare feet hardly touched the hot stones as he skimmed down and around the road to Lucia's house. By now she and Jacinta would be sitting on the big slabs of stone guarding the well close to the fig trees. Already, he could see their eyes popping, hear the squeals, especially Jacinta's. Although the hot sun on his back sent streams of sweat down his whole body, he never stopped until he reached Lucia's front yard. With a sidelong glance at the house, he turned right, the green lizard in his hand. First, he'd have to sneak past those two almond trees and the threshing shed. Now he could see them, Jacinta stretched out, chin in hand, listening to Lucia, not that she wouldn't be saying plenty herself. This was the time to get down like a cat, one paw down, then a standstill and run . . . easy now, very easy . . . Eia! You'd think he had dropped a firecracker between them instead of one poor little lizard.

"Throw him in the well!" Jacinta had him by the shirt tail.

"Why do you think the well is covered?" Lucia grimaced. "To keep Francisco and pests from falling in." Why was he always doing things like this, and on such a hot day! You'd think . . . Wiping her face, she drew Jacinta down beside her. "It's just too hot to play."

Francisco was now inclined to agree. He was burning up
— a red hot pepper, that's what he was. And, besides, he had
to have a drink right now. Ready to reach for the long rope
tied to the galvanized bucket near him, he stopped, hand in
mid-air.

Today the Angel gave no warning. Unlike the first time,
he appeared suddenly without sounds of rustling leaves and
whistling wind; shining brilliantly he stood in front of one of
the fig trees.

"What are you doing? Pray, pray a great deal!"

Francisco blinked, closed his eyes, opened them again;
again hearing no words except that lovely music which had
begun even at dawn and now drew him to his knees.

Today the Angel had more to say. His words were just
as strong, precise, easy to understand. "The hearts of Jesus
and Mary have plans for you — plans of mercy."

Lucia nodded, the olive-tinted face serious and intent.

"Offer again and again prayers and sacrifices to the
Most High."

"How shall we do that, how shall we make sacrifices?"

"All that you can, offer as an act of reparation . . ."

Lucia nodded again; she knew what reparation meant —
making up for sin. More than that, it was giving love back to
Love unwanted — outraged.

"Do this," the Angel continued, "for the sins which so
greatly offend God; do it for the conversion of sinners."

Lucia recalled that at his first visit the Angel had said, "I
am the Angel of Peace." Now she better understood what he
had meant as he now added, "Pray for peace for our country.
I am its guardian — the Angel of Portugal." She knew that
there was a terrible big war on, bigger than any there ever
had been, everybody said. Portugal, France, England, Russia, Germany — other countries too. Her brother Manuel
wanted to enlist.

The Angel had one more thing to say before disappearing. "Above all try to accept the sufferings which the Lord

will send you.''

Sufferings? The word at this moment of sweetness seemed meaningless.

They were alone again and on their knees praying as fervently as on the first day on the *cabeço*. The sun was still hot, but a slight breeze stirred the five-fingered leaves of the fig trees crusted with cobwebs. A child's plaintive cry sounded from the road. Dogs barked. New stirrings came from the house. The siesta was about over.

"Lucia —" Francisco was standing now. "What — what — did the Angel tell you?" Again it was hard to talk. "*Fazem a favor* — please tell me.''

Her voice was so low he could barely hear. "Didn't you . . .?''

"No, I only heard you. "What — this time — what did he say?''

She made no answer; her eyes were closed. "Jacinta?'' He looked down at her, eyes closed, too, hands clasped in prayer before her. "Tomorrow,'' she said, without looking at him.

That night after blowing out the candle beside their bed, Olimpia leaned over her husband. She knew from the long trembling sigh which inevitably ended with a series of mini-like puffs that he was asleep. But try to tell him that! The speed with which he could go off never ceased to amaze her. She shook his shoulder slightly. "Manuel, wake up — just for a minute.''

"I wasn't asleep. What is it?''

"Remember, what I told you this morning about Jacinta and Francisco?''

"What — oh, that! Just the hot weather. Mama, get to bed.'' He was snoring again.

She bent closer, her face close to his. "Didn't you see them tonight? Hardly ate a thing, quiet as two thieves they were.''

"What did you say?" He was wide awake now. "Thieves! Have you ever seen any?"

"Quiet as two thieves, that's what I said!"

"Look here, woman. Stop worrying. This hot spell won't last forever. Those *cachopos*, both of them, are just fine," he said firmly, recalling the bright expectant look he had seen on his youngest son's face that morning.

Blessing herself, Olimpia got into bed beside him. Usually, she was bone-tired enough to fall asleep shortly after Manuel, but tonight sleep seemed far away. Hot and close it was! Must be the heat like he'd said. Staring into the darkness, her thoughts went from one child to the other. She'd had nine children: their fourth — Teresa — had gone to heaven when only two years old. She'd often wondered what she would have been like . . . no two were ever alike. Take Francisco and Jacinta. One, the "quietness of a tree," the other — lightning.

Only a few days ago, Jacinta had jumped into the house. "Mama! Someone stole Francisco's new handkerchief, the one with the picture of Our Lady of Nazaré on it. When we were playing, one of the boys must have taken it, but Francisco says he doesn't care."

She knew he must have cared because he was so pleased when his godmother had given it to him. With a big smile, he'd said, "Thank you, thank you!" And seeing how happy he was, his godmother had hugged him close. Later when asked about the handkerchief, he'd said, "Oh, that's all right. Let him have it." Now anyone else! Olimpia turned on her side . . . Antonio and Manuel — her first two sons. If only this war would end. Millions of boys dying, and for what? If Antonio . . .Short buzzing sounds, like a saw, cut off her worry. Manuel was on his back. She had but to touch his shoulder and he would turn over, muttering a little but still blissfully asleep. She put out her hand. The room grew suddenly still and in the muggy silence sleep finally came to the wife of *Ti* Marto.

But in the little room across the way, there was no sleep for her youngest son. The Angel's beauty hovered about him. Eyes opened or closed he could see him vividly, feel from head to toe a heart-swelling joy that brought close the presence of God. What had the Angel said today? Pray more? Jacinta had promised to tell him. "Tomorrow," she'd said. He could hardly wait. What time was it now? Too dark to be morning. Why, he wasn't any sleepier now than when *Senhor* Rooster had called him this morning.

Early the next day, Jacinta avoided him, even when they came out on the road with the sheep. "Look, here, Jacinta. I didn't sleep a wink last night thinking about the Angel. Now I want to know what he said."

She barely nodded, avoiding his eyes, lifting a small lamb and cradling it in her arms as she silently strolled off. He kept at her side. "I have to know what he said. You promised. 'Tomorrow,' you said. Remember?"

"I did? Well, it's too hard to talk — not now. Later." She set the lamb down and hurried on.

"Later!"

"Maybe Lucia can tell you."

"Lucia, what did the Angel say?" They were at *Chousa Velha* now, and the sheep were really fretting today at the stubby, brownish grass around the rocks and ready to take the trail at the foot of the *cabeço*. He had waited to ask her from the time they had met her at the *barreiro* — the mud-hole — hoping that she would say something, but like Jacinta her mouth was clamped tight. He tried again.

"What did the Angel tell you?"

Frowning, Lucia looked at him. She had her lunch bag in one hand and now she clutched it tightly with the other. "He said . . . he . . ."

"Yes?"

" 'Pray a great deal. The Hearts of Jesus and Mary have — have plans of mercy for you.' " She lifted her head, her eyes now focused on the hill above. With effort she turned her attention to him. " 'Offer prayers and sacrifices constantly to the Most High . . .' "

"The Most High? What does that mean?"

"God."

"Plans? What kind of plans?"

"I don't know." She turned toward the hill.

His bare feet bridging the trail, he stopped her "I —"

"Not now." This wasn't like Francisco. Asking, asking. Later when she could, she would tell him everything, but not now.

Her voice hadn't been sharp, but he knew she wasn't going to say another word. He stood helplessly watching her ascent. As Jacinta approached, he held her back with both hands.

"For sinners," she said slowly. "We must offer up our sufferings . . ."

"Sufferings? What sufferings?"

"Please!"

He let her go, but she had seen his face. "I'm sorry." She slipped her hand into his, and now there were tears on her cheeks.

"It's so hard to talk . . ."

"Or anything else," he answered. But he'd wanted to know so badly.

Under a polished sky of blue, they ascended hand in hand, followed by the sheep, now ready for the shade of the olive trees. When they came to the big rocks, Lucia was already on her knees.

Two days later, she said, "Francisco, I'm sorry about the other day, but . . ." She paused; even now she still found it hard to talk. At home she'd managed to do her chores, even escape the notice of Carolyn, her thirteen-year-old sister, but even more luckily, Mama.

"Tell me now."

And so she gave him the whole account, word for word.

"The Guardian Angel of Portugal! So countries . . . they have guardian angels like us!"

"Who guard us day and night," she added with a quick laugh as she quoted from the song they often sang. "But we must pray hard for peace and offer up everything we can for the conversion of sinners. We must pray hard for our country."

So following this second appearance of the Angel, they began earnestly to offer up everything unpleasant that came their way. They didn't look for sufferings, for sacrifices, not yet. The whole day — you didn't have to look too much! — was really full of crosses. Big brothers and sisters yelling, "Do this, don't do that." And, of course, no grumbling at the sight of a watery egg in your bowl. Help cheerfully, and be obedient, which was especially hard for Jacinta and even Francisco. Lucia was a good teacher. "All that you can, offer up as an act of reparation," she reminded them.

Thus, the summer of 1916 went by. No one suspected the daily sacrifices they offered, the time Francisco and Lucia and Jacinta spent in prayer up on the *cabeço*. "Pray, pray a great deal," the Angel had urged. Francisco was learning fast; he was glad now to be with Lucia and Jacinta; to be with them seemed as easy as praying.

Olimpia — seeing her two youngest children occasionally playing with other children, and Jacinta sometimes singing and dancing to Francisco's tunes, began to forget that she had ever been troubled or puzzled at their behavior. She now saw them through her husband's eyes, so she thought: normal, sometimes fagged by the heat, but no different than other *cachopos*.

As for Lucia's mother, deeply worried at this particular time with family problems, Lucia appeared no different. She went off early to pasture with her two little cousins, returned punctually in late afternoon, always ready for an extra chore, played zestfully with the children who flocked around her as soon as she got home. Besides, she had always been a religious child; yet for all her lovingness (none of the other children had ever done so much snuggling in her arms), there was a certainty about her youngest daughter which Maria Rosa interpreted as a streak of stubbornness. "She doesn't have to tell you she doesn't agree with you; her eyes tell the story." Most of the family agreed.

As the hot summer faded, with acorns falling everywhere and squirrels as busy as the windmills on the hills, a chill crispness bit into the early mornings. Sometimes velvet hollows of mauve and blue lay in the mountains as brief but hard showers struck the autumn-littered *serra*. It was on one of these days, on the *cabeço* again that Francisco and the two girls saw the Angel for the third and last time. He came to them in blazing splendor as he had come that first time in the spring above the valley.

This time he held a Chalice and a Host. Leaving them both suspended, he knelt before them and, bowing deeply, said three times:

"Most Holy Trinity, Father, Son, and Holy Spirit. I adore You and offer You the most precious Body, Blood, Soul and Divinity of Jesus Christ, present in all the tabernacles of the earth, to make up for the outrages, sacriliges, and indifference with which He if offended. And through the infinite merits of His Most Sacred Heart and intercession of the Immaculate Heart of Mary, I beg of You the conversion of poor sinners."

Standing, he took the Chalice and Host into his hands and turned toward them.

"Take and drink the Body and Blood of Jesus Christ, horribly insulted by ungrateful men. Make reparation for their crimes and console your God." Placing the Host on Lucia's tongue, he then held out the Chalice to Francisco and Jacinta.

Following this Communion, the Angel again prostrated himself and again repeated the same prayer three times.

Francisco also prayed, as the words from the girls came to him.

A long time later, Francisco broke the silence as he had on the two previous occasions. "Lucia, the Angel gave you Holy Communion, but what was it he gave me and Jacinta?"

Swiftly, Jacinta exclaimed, "Didn't you see the drops of Blood falling from the Host into the Cup?"

"Yes."

"It was the same. Holy Communion, too — the Hidden Jesus."

So that was why he had felt like that — as if he had swallowed all the sunlight in the world. "You know when I drank from the Cup, I felt God in me, but I didn't know . . . I didn't know how it was." A great yearning welled in him. Maybe Papa would yet have that talk with Father Ferreira about going to Confession and Holy Communion. Maybe, sweet Lord, I won't have to wait until I'm ten.

———————

Chapter Four

Spring, 1917

Over six months had gone by since the Angel's last visit. Today was Sunday, May 13, and after an April of steady showers, the *serra* was at its fullest bloom. The Spring would be brief; so nature doubled its effort, lavish with bold bright greens and bursting buds. Now, small fields of ripening barley and wheat would be by the end of June yellow and ready for harvest. This morning, a bird on a short northwest flight from the *cabeço* where the Angel had twice appeared, would have found Francisco busy on the broad side of another hill that gently sloped into a hollow-like field called the *Cova da Iria*. Here Uncle Antonio, who owned most of the acreage, grew corn and beans, peas and potatoes, in spite of the hard clay which surprisingly retained enough moisture to grow good crops. Sometimes fifty sacks of potatoes the whole year, Francisco had heard him say.

At this moment, Francisco was having problems with his house, and Jacinta wasn't helping a bit. He had been elected architect and builder. "He's good at things like that," Lucia had said. She and Jacinta would be his helpers. But now, Jacinta, red kerchief at the back of her head, looked down in mock dismay, although he knew she meant every word. "That wall is too crooked — it looks like it's going to fall over." Vigorously, she brushed her light-colored jacket and the striped blue and white cotton skirt from which she had just dropped a few rocks.

Studying them, Francisco said, "These rocks are way too big; that's the trouble with this wall." He threw his cap over a low branch above his head. "Look, why don't you go tell Lucia that what we need are smaller ones."

"I'll tell her." Jacinta dashed off.

Even six months later she was still tiny and "very bright" as her father often confided to Olimpia who in turn thought: He sees something good in everybody, and with our children always something extra good. Francisco is so brave, so thoughtful; Jacinta's very, very bright, and so on up the line to our oldest.

It was true that he tried to think well of everyone, but he also sensed something unique about his two youngest children as he did about his niece, Lucia. Often that winter when Jacinta sat on his lap as the family huddled around the open fire (like all other homes the kitchen was the only room with heat), he was struck by the radiance he saw in the luminous eyes, also noting the same shining quality in the quiet glance of his youngest son. For lack of better words, he told himself that it was a look of beautiful innocence.

Now waiting for the girls to return, Francisco climbed the oak where he had hung his cap, careful with the white shirt, long-sleeved and buttoned at the collar. Like the long cotton pants, it had been made for the recent celebration of Easter. Sunday clothes were always those worn to Mass, sheep or no sheep. Swinging wide on a limb, he came down hard on both feet, wiggling his toes in the big shoes, carefully bought to insure long wear. Around his feet, the bright green grass caught his sudden fancy. Although not very thick, it was long enough to be brushed by a light wind that sent it running downhill in myriads of ripplets. His gaze traveled with it, speeding down past rocks and rosemary and wild flowers of all colors, even encircling the black trunk of a lone almond tree. Why, only a while back he'd seen that tree, little by little, burst into a magic of pink silk . . . The grass continued down on its way, finally reaching the *Cova* and halting at a large oak with broad green leaves. The oak was a *carrasquira* and differed in size and variety from the loose cluster of small oaks about a hundred yards east of it. *Azinheiras*, those holm oaks ranged from three to four feet high. Close by, the potatoes belonging to Uncle Antonio looked good, already at least half a foot out of the ground.

Francisco now heard the church bells from Fatima ringing for the noon Mass, fading into the silence of the surrounding hills. The sun was shining bright and almost in the middle of the blue, blue sky. He took a long breath. Where was the *pifaro*? In the other pants, of course. Not that he had played it much lately. Maybe because of the professor; he wasn't sure of that. It had all happened quick, back in February. Even now he had goose pimples when he thought about it. Papa had sent him to school. Papa! Even though he had always known it would be exactly like a fox trap, he had never dreamed it could be so bad.

On that very first day when he had followed João into the big, dark room lined with blackboards, the bearded professor had latched on to him as if no one else needed teaching. "This is no time of the year for you to be starting school!" And every day after that, the professor had yelled things like: "Stupid, stupid boy! What's the matter with your eyes . . . can't you see those letters? And your tongue — do you have one?" It was pretty awful. More than once he'd seen the small eyes narrowed to pin points with fury above the arm that shook him. But the hardest part was João who sat nearby, his face kind of pink under the straight black hair each time the boys shouted with laughter at the professor's smart words. Poor João . . . guess this was the kind of sufferings the Angel had meant. "All that you can," he had said, "offer up for the conversion of sinners." He had, just about every minute. He was glad that João never said anything at home about the professor.

Of course, Papa knew that the professor was no lover of religion. People who worked for the government usually weren't. He'd heard Papa talk about revolutions, one right after another, and how they had killed King Carlos, burned churches, drove nuns out of their convents, sent hundreds of priests to prison. If only the government could see an Angel, see God everywhere, like now; when the whole *serra* hummed and smelled like flowers; when sometimes the dark blue of heaven blazed with the candles of Angels . . .

The girls were back. "Here they are," Lucia said breathlessly, dropping a load of extra small rocks at his feet. She was ten years old, a year and three months older than Francisco, but she was no taller than he. She still had the same kind of gravity and blunt honesty that often irked her elders, except her *Ti* Manuel who enjoyed the humor that this candor gave her.

"Are these the right size?" she asked, her eyes on the unfinished house.

"I guess so — yes." He'd almost forgotten about the crooked old wall, checking the urge to tell her about the "running grass" as he saw her frowning study of the half-built house. But there was no time to say anything, anyway, because some kind of light was flashing through the tree and over the ground. "Lightning?" Couldn't be. Above, the sky was cloudless.

At the word lightning, Jacinta clapped her ears as if she had already heard fierce crackling. "I'm scared!" she cried as the light flashed by them again.

Lucia took her hand. Lightning storms sometimes came fast; sometimes pine trees were split in half. "We'll go home. Get the sheep — quick! Francisco!"

Driving them, Francisco hurried down the slope, joining the girls in the *Cova* where they waited for him under the big oak at the spot where he'd seen the grass stop. There the light again struck, zigzagging all about them. Running eastward toward the section of small oaks, they came to a quick stop in front of one of them, a tree about three feet high. A soft white mistiness enclosed them that was familiar, except that its light was even brighter than that of the Angel's.

Rubbing his eyes, blinking, then rubbing them again and again as he had at the sight of the Angel, Francisco tried to look through the glowing light. Nothing. As if coming from hills away, Lucia's light voice was asking a question, just as if she must be seeing something . . . someone. Then slowly, gradually, like the graceful young almond tree which had finally unfurled its delicate blossoms before him, he began to see the dim contours of a dainty little lady in dazzling white. She stood above the small tree, her feet on its top branches. That much he could see. Her white mantle began there; made of folds and folds of light, it went on up to cover her hair. He was also able now to see a small globe at her waist, a sparkling white rosary in her fingers. He closed his eyes, tight. It was these crazy tears that blurred her face. Drying them with both hands, he looked again, this time faintly glimpsing a face incredibly lovely. But it was the Lady's eyes, softly regarding him — a world of warmth and love in them — that drew him closer. They were the most beautiful eyes he had ever seen. They weren't smiling; there was even a little sadness in them as now she, too, bent a little toward him. She was telling him something, but not with words. Words he could not use, either. They were way deep, deep down. But she knew! She had asked him a question; not whispered nor said it aloud, and in the same way he had given his answer . . .

Gently, the Lady had looked at Francisco, and now with the same gentleness she addressed Lucia and Jacinta.

"Do not be afraid. I will not harm you."

Blinking rapidly, her eyes half-closed, Lucia smiled. *Pois*, no — well, no, she wasn't afraid, not now. It really had been that strange lightning that had frightened them, especially Jacinta.

"Where did you come from?" Angels were beautiful, but this little lady!

"I came from heaven."

From heaven — like the Angel, but, look! There was a difference in the way their words came through. His: like a trumpet, so that she had been able to repeat each one exactly as he had said it. Hers: so soft, low, and — something else? She clasped her hands, took a step closer, then for a second pressed her smarting eyes, her whole being flooded with a longing that cried for more.

"Will I go to heaven?"

"Yes."

"Jacinta, too?"

"Yes."

"And Francisco?"

Lucia heard the Lady's answer (as if one word told all), not once looking toward him. She couldn't have, had she tried. But there was something else that she would like to know — about two girls who had died recently. They used to come to her house to learn to sew and weave. Were they in heaven now?

One was in heaven, the other was still in purgatory.

She would pray hard for her. By now, Lucia was fairly certain that she had know this little Lady for a very long time. Even before she had learned to say the rosary, hadn't they been the dearest of friends? There must be a reason for this visit. "What is it you want?"

"I would like you to come here — this same place — six months in a row at this same hour, on the thirteenth of each month. In October, I will tell you who I am and what I want. Now I have something to ask you."

Lucia waited.

"Will you offer your sacrifices to God and accept all the sufferings He may send you?"

"We will!"

"Will you do this in reparation for the sins which offend God? For the conversions of sinners, for offences against the Immaculate Heart of Mary?"

At each visit the Angel had linked the hearts of Jesus and

Mary. The first time: "The hearts of Jesus and Mary listen — pay attention to your prayers." The second time: "The hearts of Jesus and Mary have plans for you, plans of mercy." And at the last visit, before giving them Holy Communion, he had spoken about the infinite merits of the Sacred Heart and the intercession of the Immaculate Heart of Mary. Over and over, Lucia had thought about his words. The heart at the foot of the cross had also bled with love and sorrow. Mary was like us, yet she was the Mother of God. "We will!" she said the second time.

"Then you will have much to suffer, but God will be your comfort." They would be loved and tenderly comforted, even joyously. Leaning slightly forward the Lady extended her arms. Streams of light flowed from her palms toward them, sending them to their knees in ecstasy, the words on their lips flames of love. "Most Holy Trinity, I adore You. My God, my God, I love You." (Years later, Lucia wrote that in that light they had seen themselves in God more clearly than possible in the brightest of mirrors.)

At last, looking up, they saw her, still standing there, the gentleness of her eyes softly regarding them, her arms still out to them. They pressed closer.

"Say the rosary every day. Say it to obtain peace for the world and to end the war." The words were barely intelligible; yet Jacinta heard their meaning as clearly as Lucia.

Unlike the Angel who had immediately disappeared before them after each visit, the Lady turned slowly, moving away and up toward the side of the early morning sun, her back toward them. When they could no longer see her, Francisco sprang to Lucia's side. "What did she say?" In his first exuberance it was hardly a question. "She was so beautiful . . . and look over there!" The sheep had remained near, away from Uncle Antonio's new peas. As Jacinta now pirouetted around him, singing, "What a beautiful, beautiful lady," he repeated, "Lucia, what did she say?"

"Didn't you?" Jacinta had stopped her dance. "You

didn't hear her, either!''

"No, but I saw her!''

Lucia had been watching them, her face wreathed in smiles.

"Tell Francisco everything,'' Jacinta said. "I want to hear it all over again.''

They sat at the foot of the tree. The dimples in Lucia's cheeks were as deep as Jacinta's. "I never felt this way — not after seeing the Angel. Remember? We could hardly talk. But now!''

Jacinta moved closer. "Start right at the beginning.''

Lucia began, then stopped, remembering that she had a message for Francisco, now that she knew he hadn't heard the Lady. She wasn't quite sure how he would take it. Well, she'd tell him later. She began again, but Jacinta kept interrupting, finally exclaiming, "And don't forget to tell Francisco about us, you know, about heaven.''

Giving him a side glance — he was all eyes, all smiles — Lucia stood, brushing her skirt with extra care. Better tell him right now. "Francisco, the Lady said — she said that we are going to heaven, but first you must say many rosaries.''

"Is that what she said?'' He was up and facing her. "You mean, well look! I could say a hundred right now!'' Their laughter sent a cheeky, uncertain squirrel spinning in retreat.

"And that Light!'' Jacinta crossed her hands over her breast. "That Light from the Lady's hands!'' They grew silent. After a few moments, Lucia broke the silence. "That Light was God! I could feel it right here.''

Presently, she turned to Francisco, her eyes like his, momentarily watching a tiny bird gyrating and spinning off into the green branches of the *azinheira*. "You know, Francisco, that the Angel asked us to pray, to offer our sacrifices and our sufferings in reparation for the conversion of sinners?''

"*Sim.*'' He hadn't had any sufferings, not really, until

he'd met the professor.

"This time, the Lady said the same thing, except that she also asked if we would offer up our sufferings for the sins committed against the Immaculate Heart of Mary. Jacinta, you heard her?"

"I heard what you said, too. You said it real loud. 'We will!' you said."

Lucia looked questioningly at Francisco. He looked so serious now; perhaps he hadn't understood. "I said, 'We will' for all of us . . . ?"

"Oh." He began to smile and the smile felt like Papa's. "Certainly!" Just the way he would say it. Of course, Lucia couldn't know what had happened between him and the Lady during that very special moment when she had leaned toward him wordlessly, just like him, and had asked him the same thing. Quick, in his heart, he had answered right back: "Sweet Lady, I will!"

With a ripple of laughter, Lucia mimicked him, "Certainly!" And then to Jacinta, "What — what are you saying?"

"That must have been Our Lady. That's what I said!"

A shadow fell over Lucia's face. She pressed her fingers to her lips. "Sh! She never told us who she was."

"I know, but . . ."

"Didn't you hear her say? 'Later, I will tell you who I am.' You heard her, didn't you?"

"You know something? I heard her!" Eyes sparkling, Jacinta tossed back her braids, broke into a little dance as she tripped off. "What a beautiful, beautiful Lady you are." She made a song out of the words. "I know you are Our Lady and I do love you!"

"Jacinta!" Lucia hurried after her. "Come back here!" Jacinta had never given away the visits of the Angel but there had been something about him that had kept their tongues tied, even after the first few days were over. but this time she felt like singing and dancing, too. "Listen!" She put her hand on Jacinta's arm. "We must not tell anyone — you hear? — about what happened here today. Not even your mother."

Oblivious of Lucia's distress, Jacinta flung her arms to embrace the turquoise blue sky, the green wide hill above. "I'm sure it was Our Lady, but don't worry, I won't tell anybody."

Why would Lucia think Jacinta would tell, Francisco wondered. Not a word had she whispered about the Angel, not one. Ai! With all that lightning, he'd forgotten about his cap. *Sim, senhor*! The sheep were still safe — far away from Uncle Antonio's sweet corn and peas. Arms swinging, he sprinted toward the hill. It sure was Our Lady!

Chapter Five

"It sure was Our Lady!" Francisco repeated softly, locking the gate behind the sheep. "Jacinta was right." At the long front of the house — where one door opened into the parlor and the other into his bedroom — she was crying at the top of her voice, "Mama, where are you?"

Both doors were closed, the panes in the small windows beside them black in the white-stuccoed wall, for by now the waning light shadowed the house, the stone fence, the buildings at the rear of the yard.

Still standing at the corral, Francisco heard the wheels grinding, and as the wagon lumbered through the wide gateless wall and stopped, he saw Jacinta like the shadow of a bird fly toward it. Her voice was even higher than the squeals and shrills from the wagon.

"Mama, I've got something to tell you!"

She surely wasn't, or was she? "Not even your mother," Lucia had warned. He ambled toward the wagon.

Papa was pulling a pig from a screened wooden box. "Look at him, Francisco!" He was laughing, both hands around the screaming, squirming pig. "Strong and slippery," he added, walking off with him. Bristly, that's what he was, *Ti* Marto thought; not quite young enough to be fine-haired-smooth, but by fall he would be worth the long trip to Batalha. Not that Olimpia had complained much about the rough road. It was a good chance to see many things — the great church, which someone had told him was one of the greatest Gothic churches in Europe — to visit and gossip at the market where everything from a pair of boots to a pair of oxen could be bought. And he surely needed two young ones badly. Maybe at Pedreira . . . a good market there, too . . . later. Humm! What was Olimpia yelling about? Not that he could hear her. All the animals were now shredding the air over the newcomer; even the chickens always bedded at this time were cackling their heads off.

But Olimpia had only called, "I'll fix the barley for the pig right away," and then, in a lower tone; "Jacinta, stop pulling my skirt!"

"Mama, in the *Cova da Iria* . . ."

"Jacinta!" It was really too late for him to stop her. Mama was bending over her. "You're trembling. Are you sick?"

"No, I'm not sick. I saw Our Lady in the *Cova da Iria* today!"

So Lucia was right after all. And Jacinta saying not to worry about her telling!

"You saw Our Lady in the *Cova da Iria*!" Mama threw back her head, laughing until the kerchief slipped past her earrings. "Ai, ai, what a little saint we have that Our Lady comes to see her." Shaking her head she hurried off, thinking, I must be tired to be laughing like that, with so much yet to be done. And are my feet killing me! Where are those girls? The house is pitch dark. When I was their age . . . "Jacinta, stop! I told you to stop pulling my skirt."

"Ask Francisco. He didn't see her at first."

"Francisco? Now, look here, young lady, it's all right to 'play saints,' but I haven't time to hear about it, not now."

They stepped into a kitchen as dark as the lamp waiting on the shelf. Olimpia lit it and in the yellow light Francisco thought that she looked pointedly at him before peering into the black kettle. The coals beneath were pink. "At least," she said dryly, "the girls have the water on; they can't be too far away." On the table she found the potatoes, peeled and cut and in the water to keep their color, the kale piled and ready. "Here," she handed Francisco a small pot. "I told your father I'd fix the pig's supper right away; please fill this with barley, just halfway.'' He took the clay pot; stood looking at Jacinta, but her eyes were busy dodging him and following Mama. "Go, now,'' Olimpia said, "while I fix the onions and garlic. Before you know it, the boys will all be trooping in."

He ran to the lean-to. The yard was quiet, settled for the night — now that the newcomer had toned down. He could hear voices in the back field — Papa and the boys. Digging the pot into the grain, he wondered if the Lady had said anything about their keeping her visit a secret. Was that why Lucia had been so afraid Jacinta might tell? He hadn't thought about that. Returning, he saw the stars, one by one, kindling; soon the blue sky would darken and sparkle. And heaven — why, it hadn't taken any time for the little Lady to get there . . . From the hill beyond, the one with the four windmills at its top, he heard the trilling notes of a nightingale. He waited, smiled as he heard the answer sweetly pierce the air, then jumped from the flat stone into the kitchen.

"Jacinta,'' Mama's voice was high and sharp. "I told you I didn't want to hear another word. Please stir that fire.'' She took the pot from him and began pouring hot water and milk into the barley, stirring and patting down the brownish lumps with a wooden spoon.

"But you should have seen her, Mama. She was brighter than the sun!''

Lifting the poker — Jacinta hadn't heard one word Mama had said about fixing the fire — Francisco pushed it through the embers until they blazed into one flame.

"Look, Mama, it was like this. First we saw this lightning; that's what we thought it was, so we ran and ran until we got down to the big oak. You know, the one across from those little ones?''

"How would I know? . . . for heaven's sake, Jacinta, stop it.''

"Well, Francisco saw her too. Ask him.''

"Francisco?"

Mama's eyes were boring right through his back. "Turn around! Was this some kind of game — Lucia?"

Francisco set the poker down carefully.

"I'm waiting."

"It wasn't a game." He had turned and was looking straight at her now. "I saw her, too."

"What's wrong with you two!" If Lucia had put them up to this . . .

A whoopla now sounded at the door, as João, white teeth flashing, his short black hair stiff and straight, streaked through the kitchen, hotly pursued by his brothers, José and Manuel. Watchful of the milk pail in his hand, nineteen-year-old Antonio, the oldest, followed. "If there's any work to do," he grinned, "João can outrun the fastest rabbit in the *serra*."

There were assenting murmurs and some laughter from the late comers as Francisco and Jacinta slipped out unnoticed. Both girls had arrived, Florinda with a jug of water on her head. There was a healthy tanned outdoor look, a wholesome simplicity about all of them. Although the boys were not tall, they were handsome and straight as pine props with a tightwire springiness about them. The girls, Florinda and Teresa, were pretty brunettes in their early teens with that fine posture peculiar to the girls of the *serra*, used to carrying bundles on their heads. The two, now avoiding their mother's eyes — they hadn't meant to be so late! — bustled about, setting out bowls and spoons, getting bread and cheese from the pantry chest as the pungent odors of garlic and onion filled the kitchen.

"Smells good!" Papa was at the door with Antonio da Silva, a relative. "Antonio, you're just in time to eat with us," he was saying. "We're a little later than usual; that trip to Batalha set us back."

Inside, the little man bowed, removed his cap and glanced hesitantly around the kitchen, even though he'd been there many times.

"You haven't been to see us for a long time," Olimpia greeted him. "Manuel is right; we're a little late tonight so you're just in time for supper."

The weather-lined face with its strong nose and thin jaws assumed an afflicted cheerfulness belying the merry glint in the small brown eyes. "Thank you, thank you, but I really shouldn't be bothering you."

"It's no bother at all; you know there is always enough here for an extra mouth."

"One extra mouth! When you already have so many. I really shouldn't . . ."

Before he could remonstrate further, *Ti* Marto raised his hand. Why did people carry on like this? he thought. "No, no," when they really meant "yes, yes." "Antonio, sit down, right here, I've got to wash." At one corner of the kitchen, close to the pantry, the boys were already lined up waiting for José to fill the big tin basin.

Olimpia beamed at her guest, sighing contentedly. Now that her shoes were resting under the table she was at rest, too. Manuel liked to see his family shod, especially on Sundays and Holy Days, but the coolness of the wooden floor felt good tonight, good and familiar. The girls had already strained the milk. Everything was as it should be, her family, all eight here; even Francisco and Jacinta had returned, hopefully forgetting that silly story.

Supper was over; the frugal meal, hearty and tasteful, had not taken long. João lay sprawled under the table, lids swollen with sleep. Only a few coals glowed in the hearth as the lamplight sketched shadows and drew tiny white moths to the window. A warm, satisfying comfort had set in as the talk about the war, high prices of seed, oxen, sheep, the poor health of Antonio da Silva's family, had all been exhausted. Francisco and Jacinta had hardly listened. Beside her mother Jacinta had seemed to be asleep until the hum of words had ceased. "Mama," she whispered, just as the faint hoot of an owl stirred Antonio da Silva to his feet. "I must be going," he said.

"Wait, Antonio, wait. You might as well hear this, too." Olimpia's voice was markedly patient although she was smiling faintly.

Antonio sat down promptly, a broad smile on his leathery face at seeing Jacinta, her small face flushed and eager, climb her stool. She was still dressed in the light-colored jacket and long striped skirt she had worn to early Mass. Her dark, glossy hair, usually neatly braided, now fell loose from one braid around her face. She pushed it back, the words tumbling fast.

"She was beautiful, beautiful, this white lady! She was all light, right in the middle of it. She had a gold chain around her neck and . . ."

There was scraping of feet under benches and stools. Whatever had brought this on?

"Where did you see this lady?" Teresa's voice was studiously polite.

"In the *Cova da Iria*, near Uncle Antonio's peas, on the top of a little tree."

"On the top of a tree!" Manuel's voice exploded, bringing a few guffaws from the boys and more shuffling of feet.

"What's the matter?" Half awake, João crawled out from under the table.

"João," Manuel explained with arched brows and a great grin, "your little sister has seen a very classy lady on the top of a tree, all dressed in gold!"

"No, no, Manuel, it was white — whiter than, than milk. She didn't talk to me, just Lucia. Francisco saw her too!"

"Not Francisco!" Antonio gravely regarded his little brother with exaggerated concern. "Look — *ohla*! Who was minding the sheep? All the time you're staring at this lovely *senhora*."

While all eyes swiveled toward him, Francisco stared at

the floor.

"Wait until Aunt Maria hears about you playing around those peas," José said seriously.

"Oho! She'll really fix you kids!" João was wide awake now.

"Sh! quiet, all of you." Papa stood, looked at the boys, sat again, no smile on his face.

"She had a white robe, it came to her feet and, and over this a long, long *mantilha*; there was a gold light along the edge . . ."

This time the laughter burst convulsively through clenched fingers; this time Papa's "Sh" meant he had had enough.

"She had a rosary, shining, shining. But her eyes! They looked at me so soft . . ." Jacinta paused.

Like a velvet flower. Francisco was still looking at the floor.

"You could tell from the way she looked at me and Lucia and Francisco how much she loved us," Jacinta continued. "Before she left, she put her arms out like this, and from her hands . . ." Suddenly she stopped again and looked down the table at the far end where Francisco sat, but he wasn't looking at her. Jumping off the stool, she ran to her father, climbed into his lap, then putting her face close to his, she laughed. "You know something, Papa? The Lady told us she is going to take me to heaven — Lucia and Francisco, too. That's what she said! And, Mama, she told us to say the rosary every day. Oh, yes, I almost forgot. She's coming to see us again lots of times. Next month on the thirteenth."

The giggling began again. What an actress! "I don't believe a word of it," José murmured, still deadly serious as he looked at his mother. She bit her lip. Why had she ever let Jacinta tell such a story? In a way it was like blasphemy. And to think that she had asked Antonio da Silva to listen! Well, she'd put an end to the whole thing right now. And in the morning, first thing, she'd go down and see Maria Rosa.

Lucia might be good at making up games, but this one was going too far. Meanwhile she would change the subject.

She managed a crisp, casual voice. "Don't forget; the thirteenth of June is our big feast day! Father Ferreira has already asked us to make preparations." They all knew. The procession, with the solemn Holy Communion class dressed in white, the wonderful music and singing, fireworks, carts draped in brightly colored paper, sweets, and white bread. All this in honor of the patron of their church — Saint Anthony. "Saint Anthony was born in . . ." Olimpia sighed, pretending a deep yawn.

"In Lisbon," her husband finished for her, "instead of Rome as the Italians seem to think." Chuckling, he stood (she hadn't fooled him a bit), still holding Jacinta in his arms.

Taking his cue, Antonio da Silva lifted his *boné* by the tassle from the floor, bowed slightly in Olimpia's direction. "A very good supper. Thank you very much and good night." Immediately, the girls began gathering the crockery and tin spoons. At the door he turned, eyeing them all quizzically. "Now who could that possibly have been all dressed in white and standing above a tree but Our Lady herself!" The tone of his voice matched the mirth in the deep-set little eyes and took the boys' laughter with him into the night.

Seated by the hearth, after giving the customary blessing to his children, *Ti* Marto drew his youngest son to him. Looking closely at the brown eyes thoughtfully raised to his, he smoothed the short hair with a clumsy gesture, noting the shapely head with its well-shaped ears, the fine sensitive mouth. What a little man he was. He would be taller and broader than any of the others when he grew up. Even his voice with its husky music was a pleasure for the ears. "The little pig really gobbled up his supper, didn't he?" he asked lightly.

"He was hungry," Francisco answered. He'd watched Papa feed him, but he knew something else was on Papa's mind.

"Francisco, tell me something. Was Jacinta, were you very close to that lady?" There it was out. It was hard to believe that Jacinta had acted that well.

Francisco moved closer into the circle of his father's arm. The others had all laughed, like Antonio da Silva. Mama had been angry, too. "Papa, if I had put out my arm, up like this, I could have almost touched her." Would Papa believe him?

"Did she say she was coming again, like Jacinta said?"

"That's what Lucia said."

"What do you mean?"

"I never heard the Lady; I never heard her voice."

"You mean, you never . . ."

"No, but I saw her! Not very good, especially at first. The light was so bright it blinded me. Lucia didn't want us to say anything about seeing her. Do you, do you believe me?"

From the sudden strong pressure of the arm around him, he knew that Papa believed, really believed. For a second, he rubbed his face against the big warm shoulder. The tears that had been so close all evening felt wet and good.

"Go to bed now." Papa's laughing eyes, the lids drooping a little, were moist, too. "You've had a big day, my little son."

Ready for bed, Olimpia found her husband still sitting by the hearth, although he had already covered the coals. "Wasn't that something?" She began pulling pins from her long thick hair. "The way she stood up on that stool, her arms out like a statue. I could hardly get supper going, she was so full of this 'white lady' business. She actually thinks it's all true. Even now, before going to bed, she was still at it. Lucia said this, Lucia said that, and I don't think I heard everything. You ask Lucia. Can you imagine! Well, I intend to see Maria Rosa first thing in the morning. Lucia's told one story too many!"

"No, no, don't do that, just wait a little longer. Lucia wouldn't make up *that* kind of story. She's too truthful, sometimes even for the likings of some people. I also find it hard to believe that Jacinta" — he was not about to drag in Francisco's name since she hadn't mentioned it — "is making up this story."

"What! You mean to sit there and tell me — Francisco's in this thing, too! — that you believe they saw Our . . ." She couldn't make herself finish the word. "They're anything but saints, and you know it."

With a long sigh, her husband pushed himself to his feet. "Is there anything God can't do? He still works his miracles when and where He pleases."

"But this is different . . ."

"How so? Our Lady has appeared before. I think that if she hadn't, the world would be in an even bigger mess than it is right now. Not saints, maybe, but innocent little children."

The next day, later than she had planned, and unheedful of her husband's wishes, Olimpia left for her sister-in-law's house. What on this green earth was the matter with Manuel, falling for a story like that? Well, she knew exactly how Maria Rosa would feel. With her there would be no pussy footing; she was a stickler for the truth — sometimes, it had seemed to her, just a little too severe with the children over matters that hardly seemed bothering so much about. But this thing was quite different and must be nipped in the bud before the whole parish got wind of it.

But, by now, many had already heard the story. Somehow, it had spread, not only by the bemused Antonio da Silva who had heard it firsthand, but by some of the amused Marto boys. "What has come over Lucia?" the neighbors gasped as they passed along the story. "She had better tell the truth, or else! Her mother will never stand for such nonsense. Not Maria Rosa!"

Chapter Six

That wasn't all her neighbors said about Maria Rosa in the following days after raking over her youngest daughter. No wonder our *cachopitos* all hang around Lucia, enchanted with her songs, her games and stories which she probably has them act out, just as she has now done with her little cousins. A bright one like Jacinta would eat up something like that. Our Lady on a tree! All in white and gold. Antonio da Silva said it was something to see when she got up on a stool to show them. No wonder, Olimpia had said more than once that Lucia had Jacinta eating right out of her hand.

Of course, Maria Rosa would stop all this foolishness quickly, although some of her daughters were saying that Lucia was sticking by her story, broom or no broom. Strict and like iron was Maria Rosa, with a new sack of troubles now to add to all the others: a son enlisting in the army when he was so badly needed at home, a husband who had mortgaged and lost most of his fields but those in the *Cova da Iria* as that extra cup of wine had caught up with him. Not that matters had always been like this. When Maria Rosa had married the handsome Antonio dos Santos he had been a man of property, and while she was no beauty, her smart eyes, like her smiling mouth — few smiles these days! — had made her almost pretty and a little different. Different? Maybe it was because she could read, the only woman in Aljustrel who could. Even now when she had to go out and do housework, nurse, work in the fields (Maria dos Anjos and Teresa were brides and couldn't help much), she still taught the Christian doctrine to other children besides her own; even women from other hamlets came to her for instruction. The Bible and lives of saints she read to all of them. Maybe if she wasn't so straight-laced, Manuel wouldn't be itching for the army, nor her husband for the bottle.

But Lucia knew a far more lovable side of her mother, one that could be tender and thoughtful for the needs of others and one which yearned for the deepening of their faith and knowledge of God. Sitting cross-legged on the bare rough boards next to the fire on winter evenings, she loved looking at her. Then, the dusk of the room, like the words in the big book her mother held in her hand, softened the strict lines in the heavy face and gave to the natural upturned curve of her mouth a grave tenderness. Her hair, thick and lightly streaked with white, shone in the arc of the lamp. The small gray eyes were sharp and happy with interest as she occasionally paused to explain a word or passage to her children gathered around her. (It was not enough to have answers at the point of the tongue but to have a proper understanding, as she insisted when teaching catechism.) For Lucia, the forcible words tingled with a warmth like that of the red embers in the hearth near her. Poor, poor Jesus. Crowned with thorns, scourged, dying cruelly on a cross; sacrificed for us, her mother explained. Ai! But there was joy too. His great love for all: little children, the sick and dying, the poor, the sinner. "Take up thy bed and walk." Her mother's low voice was sweet with compassion.

Not this afternoon. "As if I didn't have enough troubles already." In the narrow parlor with its two unvarnished chests facing a small table above which hung a crucifix surrounded by pictures of saints, Lucia stood backed to one of the low chests, her eyes dark and troubled, on her mother.

"So *this time* you've seen Our Lady!"

"Mama . . ."

"Don't lie; you know how I feel about that. This morning I heard the whole terrible story from your aunt. I'm so ashamed; I can already hear the neighbors, and as for Father Ferreira! Just wait until he hears . . ."

"But . . ."

"Never mind. What I can't understand is how you could make up such a story; you know very well, as Aunt Olimpia said, this is all your own doing. To make a lie about the Blessed . . ."

"It's true; it's not a lie. We did see . . ."

"Stop it!" Her mother took a step toward her. "I thought you had learned your lesson a long time ago when you and your friends bragged about seeing a . . . a . . ." Anger choked the rest; her face creased with it, she placed heavy hands on Lucia's shoulders. "You've trumped up this awful story — admit it! — and got Francisco and Jacinta to go along with it. Don't you realize these are holy things, that you will be terribly punished . . ."

"The Lady . . . she said she came from heaven."

"Lucia, I'm warning you!" The hands gripped her tightly.

"That's what she told me."

"Lord, help me! Don't think I'm going to fall for this tale, not for one minute. And to think that I let you make your first Holy Communion *when* I did." Her hands still on Lucia's shoulders, she shook her. "Unless you tell me you invented this wild story, I'm taking you to Father Ferreira. By now he's probably heard everything. You will kneel before him and confess — you hear me? — and next Sunday the *senhor prior* can announce to the whole parish that my daughter, Lucia dos Santos . . ." Here she burst into tears. Then she continued, ". . . has committed this terrible sacrilege . . . Lucia, why don't you answer me?"

Removing her hands, she waited, her own misery blinding her to the frightened, tearful face raised to hers. "You've always been stubborn, but this is just too much. You've nothing more to say? Well, then maybe the broom will change your mind."

Wiping her eyes with the hem of her skirt, Lucia waited for her mother's return.

Later she went up the road, her kerchief close to her face, eyes mist-covered and downcast, seeing neither her bare feet on the stones nor the small children across the street chasing a goat and happily shouting to her. She drew to her side of the stone wall as a donkey cart piled with brush approached, its youthful driver sporting a cap at a rakish angle. "Hey, Lucia," he called. "I just heard the great news. What did the white lady have to say? What did she tell you?"

Without raising her head she went up the road, crossed to the left, treading slowly over the uneven stones until she came to the great rock across the entrance to the Marto yard. Francisco was standing there.

"Where's Jacinta? What made her tell?"

"Did the Lady say we shouldn't?"

"No, but I knew what would happen if we did!"

He could see now that her eyes were puffed, her face swollen from crying. "Your mother hit you." Aunt Maria Rosa had a heavy hand, and sometimes she used the broom handle.

"Mama's going to take me to Father Ferreira . . ."

"Why?"

"Because she wants me to tell him it's all a lie."

"You can't do that!"

"I know, but, but what am I going to do?" She leaned against the big rock struggling with her tears. Francisco looked at her solemnly. Lucia was asking him what to do, not telling him, but asking! "I'm — I'm so sorry." That spanking must have been a hard one.

At the breaking note in the husky voice, Lucia looked directly into his eyes seeking an answer. After a brief moment he gave it to her. "You'll just have to tell him the truth."

"But, my mother . . ."

"Lucia . . ." It was Jacinta, peeking at them above the

stone fence. "Are you mad at me?" Mama, she knew, had already been down to see Aunt Maria Rosa, down and back and angry. She kept her toehold on the fence.

"I ought to be."

"Did your mother spank you?"

Francisco kicked the rock. "It's all your fault. Now she has to see Father Ferreira."

"Lucia, please, please forgive me. I was so happy, I couldn't hold it." Jacinta was running toward her. "I wanted everyone to be as happy as . . ."

"Look here. Stop it, don't cry. After all she didn't tell us to keep it a secret."

"But you told me."

"That's right, but there's something we've got to remember. I was thinking about it on the way up here."

"What's that?"

"My promise to the Lady yesterday. Remember? 'We will,' I said, meaning we would take all our sufferings for the sins which offend God . . ."

"And the Immaculate Heart of Mary," Francisco said slowly.

Jacinta nodded quickly. "And for the conversion of sinners." Wiping her eyes and nose with the back of her hand, she raised her head to one side and standing high on her toes, added, "After this we must always say every word of the rosary."

"*Sim*, and there's something else, too." Lucia was recalling the breezy words of the big boy in the cart, "What did the white lady tell you?" Including both Francisco and Jacinta in her glance, she said, "If anyone wants to know what the Lady wanted, don't say anything about sufferings, or the conversion of sinners, and so on. Just say that the Lady wants us to say the rosary."

Francisco listened closely, but he, too, had been thinking and remembering. A kind of sorrow that he had glimpsed in the Lady's eyes. That look had been with him, even at the supper table when the boys had laughed. Sure, he would pray for the conversion of sinners but there was something else, something he would much rather do. Just like Papa's arm had tightened around him last night, showing how much he loved him — comforting, consoling, making him happy. That's what he wanted to do, too, for her and for Him — for both of them. That wonderful light from the Lady's hands . . .

"You'd better go." Lucia turned homeward and nudged him as she heard her aunt's voice calling him.

"What do you have to smile about?" his mother said tartly as he approached. "After all that's happened around here! And what was Lucia doing out there, I'd like to know."

The next day the professor stood in front of his desk in an attitude of awesome dignity and with folded arms greeted Francisco. "We hear that you have seen a lady above a tree. Can you explain to the class how she got there?" The boys' laughter was enough of an answer for the teacher. During recess some of the big boys took turns pinning him to the wall until the bell rang. That ought to teach him to lie like that! Until school was out for the summer vacation, the boys, goaded by their teacher's scorn, kept up their harrassment. If everyone, they reasoned, knew that those three were lying, if the priest himself called him and the girls liars! Well! (Years later, a boy who had attended that school in Fatima and who later became a priest and the rector of the seminary at Leira, wrote a graphic and regretful account of the ill-treatment Francisco received at this time. He said that through this torment, even physical at times, Francisco remained humble, amiable, played if allowed, and always with a smile.)

After school that day, Francisco waited for João before crossing to the church where he intended making his usual visit to the Blessed Sacrament. "Don't say anything when you get home."

"About what?" João looked glum; he knew what Francisco meant.

"About the boys and the teacher."

"I've never said anything before, have I? But you should have told him."

"Told him what?"

"That it wasn't true, all that stuff."

Francisco turned away. If only Jacinta had kept her mouth shut.

But she hadn't, so Lucia bore the brunt of misunderstanding and contempt from both her family and neighbors, and in the coming days, even from strangers. One day, Jacinta saw an old woman, a stranger, lunge out at Lucia, and with a sudden thrust of her foot strike her on the leg. Running to her, Jacinta lifted Lucia's skirt and seeing the welt already red, burst into tears. "Why do they do this to you?" She stamped her feet. "Oh, Lucia, you have so much to offer up, but I don't have . . ."

"You have, too!"

"Like what?"

"Aren't you hurting for me right now?" She put her arm around the other's shoulder. "Offer that up, and . . . and, just think! Tomorrow is almost here!"

Lucia knew that everything was in readiness for Saint Anthony: flags for the carts, all kinds of sweet goodies, the music, and even Mama. For several days now Mama had been very, very quiet about the *Cova*, not even threatening — still just that — to take her to the *senhor prior*. She knew how hopeful Mama was that all these things in addition to the fireworks and the procession (for which a white dress and veil awaited her) would entice her to Fatima instead of the *Cova da Iria*. Poor Mama.

That afternoon near his cave on the *cabeço*, Francisco shouted against the same breeze that lazily turned the old windmill. "To-mor-row," he called, waiting for the echo to rebound. Mama had been baking white bread all day. Ai! No place had echoes like the *cabeço*. He cupped his hands around his mouth. Sometimes up here, he and Jacinta and Lucia sang out: "Ma-ri-a!" He did it now, listening as it trembled back, loud and clear. There was another name floating on the air; it was his own. His hands still at his mouth, he yelled back, "Ja-cin-ta," and before the word was back, she was running up the *cabeço*.

"Is Lucia up there?"

"No." He'd been praying in the cave only minutes ago. "Why?" He trotted down to meet her.

"I just heard Aunt Maria Rosa talking to Mama, and we — we can't go to the *Cova* tomorrow."

"We have to."

"She told Mama that it was crazy to let us go. 'They've got no business in the *Cova da Iria*,' she said, and lots of other things too. and Mama said, 'You're right. I'll see that they don't go tomorrow!' The way she said it!"

Francisco drew closer to her; why, was she trembling all over. "Look, Jacinta. The Lady told us to be there. She knew that tomorrow would be the feast of Saint Anthony, didn't she?"

"Yes."

"So she could have made it for another day."

Jacinta began to smile. "I told Mama I wanted her to come with us so that she could see the Lady, too. She got so mad that I told her that Saint Anthony isn't pretty like the Lady."

Francisco laughed. " Was Papa there?"

"No, why?"

Without answering and before Jacinta knew what he was about, Francisco was leaping over rocks and flying downhill, in his nose the sweet smell of green mint and the resin of pines. Papa, Papa, I know you can do it; he must still be sawing that dead tree.

"What, what did you say?" Wide awake, Olimpia shot upright in bed.

"You heard me." Her husband lit the candle beside him. "I know this comes as a shock to you, but I've been thinking and I've decided that the sensible thing for you and me is to get out of here today; skip Saint Anthony's Feast." His voice was blustery and his words fast as he thrust his feet into the dark trousers and reached for his boots.

"Skip Saint Anthony's Feast! Now you tell me! You mean — what do you mean, 'you and me'?" He was buttoning his shirt, his back toward her. "What's gotten into you, Manuel Marto? What will everybody say?"

"Nothing. Such a big crowd they'll never miss us."

"You mean you want to miss everything? The High Mass with all that beautiful singing — they've been practicing for weeks! — and, oh, yes! What about all that white bread I baked for the poor?"

"Florinda and Teresa can take it."

By now, Olimpia was at his side. "But why? It doesn't make sense; I don't get it."

He put his arms around her. In the long, unbleached muslin gown with its full-length sleeves, a long braid over one shoulder, she looked like a woe-be-gone *senhorita* who, ready for her first dance, had now been cruelly cheated of its joys.

"Look, Olimpia," he said softly. "There are lots of good reasons for us not to be here today. You know how Maria Rosa feels — teeth on edge, like the rest of the family, with all that wrangling. 'Let the *cachopos* go,' some of them say. 'What harm will it do?' 'Don't let them go,' the others answer; so if we're not here . . ."

"Listen to me, Manuel. Everybody will be at the *festa*. It's crazy to go off someplace. Where?" She didn't wait for an answer. Stepping back from his arms, she slumped on the edge of the bed, staring into the flickering candle on the small table. "I promised Maria Rosa yesterday that I wouldn't let Jacinta and Francisco go to the *Cova* today. She's right when she says that the Virgin Mary doesn't appear to children like ours, and that Bernadette was a very holy little girl before Our Lady of Lourdes appeared to her.''

"Now how does she know all that? If I remember right she didn't even know her catechism — doctrine — very well.'' He sat down beside her, put his arm around her shoulder. "If we're not here, the whole matter will take its course naturally, according to God's will, and not ours.'' Especially not Maria Rosa's, he thought.

"You're running away, and it's not like you, either,'' Olimpia answered, bending slightly toward the candle and blowing nervously at the wavering pyramid of flame.

He let that go. She didn't feel so stiff inside his arm now, although her chin was still sticking out a little. Well, he knew his Olimpia better than anyone else did. For all her *alegre de vivre* — joy of life — there wasn't a selfish bone in her body. Some women might be softened by a trinket, but not his woman. "You know how much we've needed a pair of young oxen. The ploughing has been hard — slow with these old ones.''

"I've seen that for myself.'' She was looking at him now through the corners of her eyes, but he could feel the sudden concern in the side glance. "What . . .''

"Jorge Alves was telling me that there are to be some very good oxen, good prices, too, at the market in Pedreira today. It would be a fine chance?''

"All right, all right. When do you want to leave?''

With a quick kiss on her cheek, he answered, "As soon as we can!''

Shortly after her mother and father had left, Jacinta ran into her parents' bedroom. "The bed's made,'' she called to Francisco. "Where are they?''

"They went to Pedreira, to the market.''

"How do you know that?''

"Papa told me. He came to my room before they left.''

"You mean they're not going to the *festa*? You mean

now we can go to the *Cova*!'' Seeing his knowing smile, her eyes widened. ''Francisco! You talked to Papa yesterday; that's why you ran so fast!''

———————

Chapter Seven

Summer, 1917

"The children should be getting here soon." Studying the sky, the frail, pretty woman lightly tapped the knee of the young man hunched on the rock beside her. He had a hump on his back; his head remained bent while some of the others (about thirty persons — men, women, a few children) also scanned the blueness overhead, alternately shifting their eyes to the crest of the hill as they had been doing for the last hour, hoping to see the trio. Uncertain of the exact location of the *azinheira*, they had settled midway on the hillside beside a shelving of heavy rock and a scantling of scrub oaks.

The first to arrive had been the crippled boy and his mother. On the way she had had trouble breathing, she told some of the other pilgrims: an old breathing problem, or maybe heart. "I'm only forty-four, but the doctor said, '*Senhora* Carreira, if you're not careful . . .' " She paused at the approach of a young couple: a lean, cheerful-looking man carrying a wicker basket and an earthen jar, his barefoot wife, black-kerchiefed and in a long dark gingham dress — a baby in her arms. Smiling at them, she said, "*Bem-vindos*! Welcome. I'm Maria Carreira and this is my son, John." After hearing their names, she nodded pleasantly. "I've been telling everyone that I live in Moito, only ten minutes away, but this is the first time I've ever been here." She moistened her pale lips as if the few words had tired her.

"It — it took us a lot longer than ten minutes, didn't it?" Lifting the baby to her shoulder, the young mother smiled shyly, looking toward her husband busy acknowledging the smiles and greetings of the others.

"It certainly did. We came all the way from Torres Novas."

There was a general nodding of heads. They all knew what a lot of tramping that must have been for the pretty young mother with eyes like midnight. And with such a precious baby, too.

"Well, I came from Boleiros." Holding a prayer book in her hand, the speaker was a girl about fifteen who earlier had come swinging down the trail, settling under a tree where she had been studiously reading until now. A long walk, too, many sympathetic eyes assured her. Regarding her thoughtfully, a squat man with salt-and-pepper hair below his cap, smiled widely from toothless gums. "You can read," he said admiringly, and then: "Lomba de Egua — that's where I live, and this lady and her husband;" his head and hands swung in unison toward a grim, middle-aged woman to his right, "are from the parish of Santa Caterena."

Cheerfully, they repeated their names, the names of their parishes; most of them bound together through their faith in a spirit of kinship and a rich poverty which they wore with simple dignity. No, this was not the first time Our Lady had ever come from heaven. Think of how many times she had come to see Bernadette! The sun was getting hotter; must be after eleven o'clock. No one had a watch, nor umbrella which would do a much better job than these skinny trees. But, look! Wasn't the rosemary here thick, so fragrant and pretty, too. The wheat and barley now in harvest looked good but everything was so costly. The war . . . And still nobody had yet come from Aljustrel. Perhaps with the children?

"Everbody's gone to the *festa*." The crippled boy, his head slightly raised, spoke for the first time. "My sisters thought it was crazy to come here instead of Saint Anthony's . . ."

"There they are!" a little girl shouted.

Grabbing their baskets and water jugs, everybody stood, craning their necks toward the top of the hill.

Francisco and his two companions were not alone, and to the group now watching, were indistinguishable from the flock of girls in fluttering white dresses. Like them, Lucia was also dressed in white, on her arm a white shawl and kerchief. To her mother's delight that morning, her wayward child had changed her clothes after returning early with the sheep, and dressing appropriately for the Solemn Holy Communion procession, had left for Fatima.

While at the pasture, Lucia had explained her plans to Francisco and Jacinta. After all, her mother had not actually forbidden her the *Cova*, so first she would go to the church. Thus, at Saint Anthony's, she had marched with her companions; then after Mass as the crowd milled around waiting for the customary blessing of their pastor at the top of his stairs, she had invited a large group of girls — thirteen — to accompany her. Stopping for Francisco and Jacinta, they had all walked briskly about two miles, Lucia's friends chatting nervously, uncertain about the wisdom of abandoning a celebration scarcely begun. But the parade and all the fun would last all day, while this exciting little jaunt couldn't take very long. Besides, Lucia was hard to resist, even if their parents no longer approved of her.

She now led them down the trail toward the little crowd expecting them, halting as a slight figure stepped out to meet her. Marie Carreira's eyes swept over her and Francisco and Jacinta on either side. "So you are the ones who saw Our Lady!" The breathless voice spoke with such certainty that Lucia regarded her curiously, unaccustomed to such deference. Without waiting for an answer, Maria Carreira introduced herself. "And this is my son John; he's only seventeen, but he's been a cripple since birth." The words came between quick breaths, her delicate nostrils flared with the effort. "Will you do the favor of asking Our Lady to cure him?''

Lucia barely nodded. Her eyes shifted to the *Cova* and then eastward in the general direction of Fatima. Without a word or backward glance, she resumed walking with everyone filing behind her. At the *Cova* she hurried toward the sprinkling of small oaks, with Francisco and Jacinta beside her, the small band of pilgrims still at her heels. About nine feet away from the trees she stood quietly. Behind her the light mingling of talk stopped. There was a hush, and after a few seconds of silence, Maria Carreira asked, ''Which tree is it?''

Taking a few steps forward, Lucia answered, ''This one.'' She raised one arm and touched the top branch. ''Here, right here. This is where she stood.''

''Will it be long now, before Our Lady comes?'' Maria Carreira asked. For a moment the landscape had reeled before her; she held tightly to her son's arm.

''No.'' But Lucia seemed uncertain as she made a halfway gesture to place the white kerchief on her head. Some of the women knelt; some kissed the ground. The men who wore their *bonés* no matter how hot the weather, removed them. A few girls pressed around Lucia. ''Are you sure?'' they asked doubtfully.

''Let's wait in the shade,'' she answered tersely. Everyone followed her to the big oak. As soon as they got there, the young mother handed the baby, now making waking noises, to her husband. She took three midget oranges from the basket and handed them to Lucia and her cousins, then took the baby back to nurse him. There was much chatting and laughing in low tones. Other baskets were opened and hunks of brown bread offered to those who had brought none. The little girl who had been the first to see the children, now gave Jacinta a push which brought other children into the game, including Francisco who quickly dropped beside Lucia. The kerchief and shawl in her lap, she sat very still, eyes turned toward the small oaks.

"Let's say the rosary," someone suggested. In fifteen minutes they were finished.

"We could say a litany; I brought my book." The girl from Boleiros had hardly begun when Lucia bounced to her feet. "There's no time now. Jacinta!" Hastily, Lucia arranged the shawl and kerchief (as if on her way to Mass, Maria Carreira commented later).

With Francisco and Jacinta at her side, she ran, followed by the others who suddenly were aware of a new coolness in the June air, a peculiar waning of light about them. Half circled around the tree, they saw only three children; Lucia's head tilted slightly, she clasped her hands. Those very close to her, like Maria Carreira, heard, "You asked us to come here today; please tell me what you want."

Francisco also heard Lucia's words, but they meant little because he was busily rubbing his eyes, trying to see through the blinding light, just as he had the month before. It seemed a long time before the little lady's figure began to emerge, but this time he saw her sooner and more clearly.

Again, she was bending toward him, so quietly, her eyes deep and lustrous, the sweetness of her look just for him. "You could see how much she loved us," Jacinta had said that first night in the kitchen. That love was all there again, but so was the same sadness as well. Against the beating of his heart he pressed his hands, hardly aware of the slender ones clasped in prayer and the small feet beneath the gossamer hem — the whole of her. Her dress with its frothy folds of light, the mantle's hood which again concealed her hair, making even more delicate the oval planes of her lovely face — these he sensed more than saw. It was the urgent meaning in the Lady's eyes that he understood best and that again held him captive.

"You asked me to come here today," Lucia had asked. "Please tell me what you want."

"I want you to come here on the thirteenth of next month at this same time and to say between the decades of the rosary this prayer:

O my Jesus, forgive us our sins, save us from the fire of hell, take all souls to heaven, especially those most in need.''

Lucia's lips moved quietly, repeating the prayer, as if she had heard it before. By now she had grown more accustomed to the light. Smiling, she clasped the white shawl, leaned forward, her eyes bright with the sheer loveliness of the lady.

"Will you take us to heaven?" After all, the Lady had promised heaven. Now, right now, she meant.

But there were other plans. "Yes, Francisco and Jacinta, soon. But you . . ."

"Not me?"

"My little daughter. Later . . . You are to remain longer."

"But what will I do without Jacinta and Francisco?"

"This makes you very sad, but Jesus wants to establish in the world devotion to my Immaculate Heart. He wants to make me known and loved."

"How can I do that?"

"Learn to read and write. Later I will tell you more. To those who practice devotion to my Immaculate Heart I promise salvation . . . Lucia, my heart will be your refuge and the way which will lead you to God."

Lucia again held the white shawl close; a tear trickled down the short blunt nose.

"Do not be sad. I will never, never leave you."

Lucia brushed away the tears. After all, the Lady had just said that she would never leave her. She would always be with her, at her side. Yes, yes, she would learn to read and write, she'd offer up everything, she'd give . . .

The Lady now extended her hands; she, too, had something to give — that same gift which the month before had swept them into the powerful presence of God, causing Lucia later to exclaim, "That light was God! I could feel it right here." Now streaming toward them, the encircling light this time broke into halves: one enclosing Francisco and Jacinta as it rose upward, the other spreading at Lucia's feet. The three saw a heart pierced by thorns at the right hand of the Lady.

The heart of Our Lady . . . that Immaculate Heart which had wept and shared in the agonies of her Divine Son's Sacred Heart — both wounded by the sins of the world. From the powerful light radiating from the Lady's hands, these things were intuitively understood. The heart was a symbol of the sorrow they saw shadowed in the eyes looking into theirs. And in their rapture they yearned to make up for those who loved not at all.

She was leaving them, rising slowly; then with her back turned, she moved in the direction from which the dawn spread each day.

"I can't see her any more!" Lucia faced the crowd.

"She's gone to heaven," Jacinta added simply.

Beside them Francisco said nothing. That heart! And the light in which he and Jacinta had stood . . . ?

The silence that had lasted about ten minutes was shattered. "What did she say?" "What did she want?" "Did you see how cool the air got, but now!" "And look at the top of the tree!"

It was immediately surrounded. The sturdy leaves were bent to the right. "Like someone had stepped over them."

"Please!" White-faced, Lucia tried to stop the plucking hands. "Not those up there! That's where she stood."

"Lucia, did you ask Our Lady to cure my son?" The weary lines were gone, the words flowed with ease.

For a moment, Lucia stared blankly at Maria Carreira. "I forgot. I'll ask her — next time."

"She is coming again!" In the sunlight, Marie Carreira's eyes were like sapphires.

"Yes, next month, on the thirteenth."

"I'll be right here; this time with my husband and my daughters."

Four o'clock. Most of the girls had returned to Fatima, not so much now to see the rest of the festivities as to share the news of their involvement at the *Cova da Iria* with those less favored. The young couple with the baby had also left, but fifteen or sixteen of the more reluctant now clambered uphill, unwilling to let the three out of their sight.

"You look tired," Maria Carreira told them, wondering at her new strength. She tested it with a deep breath (Jesus, how good it is to breathe like this!) and put a detaining hand on Lucia's arm. "Lucia, don't mind what some of the others said down there. They just don't understand."

Lucia knew that Maria Carreira was talking about the man who had angrily yelled, "You've told us over and over what a beautiful lady she was, but just what did she really want? You haven't told us anything about that."

"That's true," his wife had agreed. "All you say, you and your cousins, is that she said to say the rosary. It took all that time, just to say that!"

They were almost at the top of the hill; Lucia tightened Jacinta's hand in hers. It was true that she had told her and Francisco to answer that way (just say she told us to say the rosary) for fear that their prayers and sacrifices might become known. After today she was sure that warning was no longer necessary. The image of that bruised heart with its sweet overshadowing tenderness had been with her all afternoon, as it must have been with Jacinta and Francisco — its own reminder that this must be a secret, at least for now. They would talk about it later among themselves, and then only in whispers. The Heart of Mary — the Immaculate Heart of Mary. Everybody must know and love her, just as they did.

On the last rise of the trail after parting with the Carreiras, they heard, "Still on earth? How come the flying lady didn't take all three of you to heaven with her?" The derisive shouts from a few stragglers from Fatima were similar to those at the Martos' where visiting neighbors lingered in the front yard. "Was the white lady on the tree again?" "What news did she have this time?"

Hastening toward Papa whom he had seen at the lean-to, Francisco heard Jacinta's plaintive voice. "We can't tell you. It's a secret."

"So, you are back." It had been a long day since he had tip-toed into his son's room. Placing both hands on Francisco's shoulders, he said, "She, she was there again . . ." His voice was low, although no one was near.

"*Sim*! She was right there again!"

Good, good. He would ask no more questions. Did you hear her speak this time? Did she look the same? Did she have something special to say, to ask? Nobody had the right to ask anyone to give a secret away. Clearing his throat, he pulled at the big lobe of one ear. "By the way, tomorrow you must see the two new oxen; it's a little late now, maybe. They look very, very good."

Leaving Francisco, he walked toward the house, glimpsing his niece beyond the fence, headed home. Poor little thing. He hoped that by now Antonio had all the celebrating out of his system and was home, that Maria Rosa would be a little more understanding and gentle with her daughter, not that she didn't have enough to plague her. After all, Lucia had gone to Saint Anthony's, even been in the procession, he'd been told. And to think. Over fifty people, many of them strangers, had been at the *Cova*. Perhaps he and Olimpia should have been there, too. How great and glorious were the works of God, yet most people blindly refused to see them.

Chapter Eight

Lucia's homecoming that evening had been as cheerless as her uncle had feared. Her mother lost no time in venting her frustrations with an angry flush of words. "A little saint! Pretending to stay at Fatima, then sneaking away with all those girls!" There had been much more of the same, with her sisters also denouncing her for her sneaky, scheming ways.

Alone with her cousins for the first time since the late afternoon of June 13, Lucia began, "What do you think? Mama has finally . . ."

But Francisco, anxiously awaiting this opportunity because he had been unable to get some of his questions resolved by Jacinta (you'd better ask Lucia) now broke in, "How was it that you were in that part of the light that was on the ground, and Jacinta and I in the one going up?"

"Because I have to stay here, in the world."

"How long?"

"A long, long time, but you and Jacinta, you're going to heaven soon, without me. That's why you were both in that other light."

"Soon? Are you sure? Did the Lady say that?"

"Yes."

Suddenly, he wanted to laugh, jump up and down, play and sing for joy. He was oblivious of everything around him, even to the misery in the solemn glance Lucia threw him, but Jacinta was quick to see it.

"Don't be sad, Lucia. 'I'll be with you all the time,' Our Lady said. Remember?"

"Yes."

"You'll tell the whole world about her Immaculate Heart, how much Jesus wants everybody to love her, how much she loves them, too."

"And how sad she is because sinners offend God so much," Francisco added.

Francisco knew, Lucia thought. He understood; he didn't need ears to hear. "Francisco, the Lady taught us a prayer."

"What was it?"

"O my Jesus, forgive us our sins. Save us from the fire of hell. Take all souls to heaven, especially those most in need."

She repeated it slowly; the three said it together, and when they had finished, Jacinta said, "The Lady said to say it between the decades of the rosary."

Lucia nodded thoughtfully. They were on a narrow path edged with wild bushbeans. Picking some of the green pods (later these beans which grew everywhere would be shucked at the threshing shed), she looked at the other two now doing the same thing. "I had something to tell you . . ."

"About Aunt Maria Rosa," Jacinta prompted.

"She went to see Father Ferreira. Tomorrow morning, this time for sure, she's taking me to see him. 'You'll get down on your knees and tell him this is all a great big lie,' she keeps saying."

"Tomorrow!" Francisco and Jacinta exchanged glances. "Don't worry, Lucia." Jacinta hugged her. "We'll go with you, won't we, Francisco? I'm not afraid of Father Ferreira. We'll just tell him the truth — you know, like we really did see her, that she wants us to way the rosary . . ."

Francisco stared at her. Why only a few days ago — had she forgotten what had happened? — Aunt Maria Rosa had brought the news that the *senhor prior* wanted to see Papa. And so all by himself, Papa had climbed those stairs of Father Ferreira's.

"Where are your children?" Father Ferreira had asked

first thing in the slow draggy way that was so different, Papa said, from the fast clip of his parishoners. "I thought that you were bringing them with you. I hear, indirectly, of course, as I seem to be the last to be consulted — eh? — that the children plan to go back to the *Cova da Iria* . . ."

"Yes, they do."

"And you condone this! Don't you know that as a Christian father it is your duty to see that your children speak the truth, most especially on such exalted matters as these? You'd be well advised to stop this nonsense before it goes any further. What do you think all this does to the image of the Church? The government is only too happy to seize opportunities like these . . ."

And on and on, with Father Ferreira's face getting even redder when Papa finally said, "*Senhor Prior*, my children *are* telling the truth. I believe every word they say."

On hearing the story, Mama had gasped. "You told him that!"

"I certainly did, and do you know what else I told him?"

"I can't imagine."

"As I was coming down the stairs I turned around. He was still standing at the veranda door, so I said, 'For some time I've been thinking of asking you something.' "

" 'What is that?' he asked."

"I would like very much to have my Francisco and Jacinta make their first Holy Communions."

"You told him that when you know how he feels! So what did he say?"

" 'Confessions,' maybe! But not Holy Communion . . . . That's exactly what he said."

So! He had run out of the house, quick, without Papa seeing him. No Holy Communion, after all this time. No Hidden Jesus. And now Jacinta wanted to skip up those long steps of Father Ferreira's!

The next morning they did go up those stairs, but hardly skipping as they treaded behind Aunt Maria Rosa's heels.

The housekeeper, Father Ferriera's sister, opened the door, disappearing as her brother, wiping his spectacles called, "Come in, Maria Rosa. I'm glad to see you've brought the other two children with you." Perhaps, he thought, his well chosen words had given Manuel Marto some second thoughts. He hoped so. His manner was almost effusive as he led them throught the sunny veranda lined with geraniums in dark blue clay pots at the windows, into a somber room with a small desk topped by bookshelves and a large crucifix. As if recently arranged, two straight-backed chairs stood directly in front of the desk.

"Please sit down," Father Ferreira said, adjusting the glasses on his ample nose and still looking genial. Maria Rosa complied instantly drawing Lucia down beside her.

Standing behind them with his cap in his hand, Francisco felt almost happy. The *senhor padre*, sitting comfortably behind his desk, wasn't getting a bit red or angry like he had with Papa. Maybe today he would be different, maybe today he would be nice and friendly. But now he saw that Father Ferriera's eyes were pointed straight at him through the thick glasses while his head moved gently up and down at something Aunt Maria Rosa was trying to explain. Ai! How hard she had prayed and hoped and worked, just as she had told him before, that Lucia would stay away from the *Cova da Iria*, especially on Saint Anthony's Feast Day, or any other day, for that matter. If only he could get her to admit the truth that was all she asked. Certainly the broom hadn't done any good.

Father Ferreira had quit nodding; his probing eyes, Francisco saw, were still on him like a hawk's, as he suddenly murmured, "I've forgotten your name . . . "

"Un — uh, Francisco."

The *senhor padre* took a long time to clear his throat. Was the boy overshy? Or very slow? "I remember now; your name is Francisco Marto. Why did you go to the *Cova da Iria* instead of going to church on Saint Anthony's Feast

Day?''

As Francisco pondered the question (the Lady had asked them to go to the *Cova*, the day hadn't been a Sunday or a day when you had to go), Father Ferriera interjected, "Nothing to say, eh?'' The Portuguese benignity of his face was now sobered by deep wrinkles between his dark brows.

Francisco stared at the polished floor. Yes, he had something to say! Why won't you let me receive the Hidden Jesus? Of course, the words never came out. Looking up, he saw the *senhor prior's* thumb signaling him to the painted chest at the other end of the room.

The priest slowly tapped the enamelled copper clock on his desk. Not too bright, this boy. To think that his father thought he was ready for *comunhão*!

Her stout figure in its black cotton dress strained forward, Maria Rosa sat on the edge of her chair. Why bother with Francisco and Jacinta, she reasoned, as she saw the *senhor prior* considering Jacinta. Why didn't he work on Lucia, instead? The lines around her eyes and mouth tense, she tightened the black kerchief under her chin, watching him lean back in his chair, a shadow of a smile fetching back the benignant look.

"You are a very pretty little girl. How old are you, Jacinta?''

From his seat on the low chest, Francisco observed Jacinta's bowed head. Father Ferreira remembered her name, but he wasn't going to get an answer, anyway. Jacinta's head was getting lower and lower, until all he could see was the tail end of her red kerchief. And only yesterday she had been so brave! Francisco and I will go with you. I'm not afraid of Father Ferreira. We'll just tell him the truth.

"Look up,'' Father Ferreira was saying. "I only want you to tell me what has really taken place at the *Cova da Iria*. Were you playing make-believe, like children sometimes do, and grown-ups too? You have seen the little plays at Christmas time, eh?'' He paused, tapping the small enamelled

clock, waiting for an answer. "Can't you say something?"
He shook his head. "Short-tongued like your brother!" and
with the same thumb that had banished Francisco, he sent
her scuttling across the room to Francisco's side. Pulling
herself up beside him, she began swinging her feet; then,
reaching for her rosary, she blessed herself and began whispering, her feet still swinging.

At last! Maria Rosa's deep sigh filled the small study.
She closed her eyes, the thin mouth set tightly in its upward
curve. Please, Lord, please make Lucia tell the truth. Give
her a change of heart. Her hands working together, she heard
the pastor's voice.

"How old are you?"

"Ten."

Against the wooden slats of the narrow chair, Lucia sat
straight, her hands clasped loosely in her lap, her dark bangs,
recently cut by one of her sisters, a fringe under the kerchief.
Her mother nudged her. "Mind your manners. Stand when
the *senhor prior* speaks to you."

Lucia obeyed, but unlike her cousins looked directly at
the priest.

"You're not afraid of me?"

"I'm not afraid."

"Good! Then tell me the truth."

"We've seen a beautiful lady. She's all in white — very
white. She stands above a tree. We've seen her two times in
the *Cova da Iria*. She's brighter than the sun."

"Sounds like you've memorized your lines, eh? Is that
all?"

"She wants us to pray."

"What is this lady's name?"

"She hasn't told us yet."

"Lucia, I warned you!" Her mother's hand struck out,
then fell limply at her side. Lucia ought to be on her knees
begging forgiveness instead of sticking her jaw out like that.

Ignoring Maria Rosa, Father Ferreira asked, "What

does this lady want? There must be some reason for her appearance. Does she smile, gesture to you with her hands?"

"No, she doesn't smile; she's serious but sweet. She wants us to say the rosary."

"Do you mean to tell me this lady walks over a tree just to tell you to say the rosary?"

With a bounce, Jacinta came off the chest, slipping the rosary over her arm. "No, oh no, she doesn't walk at all! She comes from way up in the sky. I'll show you." Arms extended, head raised, Jacinta glided toward Father Ferreira, coming to a sudden halt as he arose abruptly.

"What kind of foolery is this? One moment you can't say a word and the next you are putting on a — a grand act. Of course! That is what I thought in the first place. Acting. You should all be ashamed of yourselves!" He turned to Maria Rosa who now seemed very pleased at the turn of events. He looked at her closely, his words slow and measured. "Yes, I think that is what is is — a great big lie that grew out of make-believe . . . unless . . ."

"*Ohla!*" Maria Rosa was on her feet. "I've always insisted on my children telling the truth, or else! Our old pastor, Father Pena, could tell you that. I had hoped you'd be able to shake the truth out of — What was that you just said? Unless, unless what?"

"Unless it is diabolical. You know it could be a trick of the devil. The Church has had countless cases in which people have been deluded by the devil, people who think they see visions. You've heard of exorcisms." His words, steady and unhurried, devastated Maria Rosa.

"My God, not that!" Rough hands gripped together, she stood motionless, her face a sickly white under its tan.

"No, now, I didn't say that it was the devil; I just said that it could be."

At the foot of the stairs, Jacinta snorted. "The devil! Why, he's an ugly old thing that lives down in the ground."

Close beside Lucia, Francisco saw tears streaming down her cheeks.

That morning Father Ferreira had unintentionally pricked a bees' nest. With the passing days, Lucia began to feel that the past had been a bad dream. The beauty that she had seen and felt, the loving entreating words she had heard, the beneficent power of the light from the Lady's hands, the visits of the Angel, which now seemed ages ago, had all been as Father Ferreira had said: "A trick of the devil." Otherwise, why would her mother, the whole family, and the neighbors treat her so badly? "Pretty soon she can eat what's left in the *Cova*," her sisters were saying every day as lines of people trampled over the potatoes, the peas, and corn. Maybe that was why Papa seemed to be drinking more and more. The devil was a mischief-maker, not Our Lady. And as for learning to read and write! How angry her mother had been when she had tried to tell her a little about that . . . So now she went through the mechanics of praying, moving in a loneliness of misgivings and doubts, wondering often at the increasing fervor of her two cousins.

One day both girls glimpsed Francisco, almost hidden from sight, lying motionless on the top of a steep rock. Seeing the tip of his cap, Jacinta called, "Francisco, what are you doing up there?" Getting no answer, she shouted, "Francisco! Can't you hear me? I know you can." He seemed part of the rock, just that piece of brownish cap sticking up in the air.

"He's praying," Lucia said, "leave him alone." She'd found him one day, just like that, behind a stone wall in a very far-off pasture. She and Jacinta had darted about, calling and looking everywhere until she'd found him bent over his knees, his face to the ground. When she had touched his shoulder, he'd looked as though half-asleep. "Were you praying?" she had asked him. "I started to say the Angel's prayer and . . ." She had known what he meant. Sometimes when you began using words with God, the words left, and only He was there. But not lately, not since Father Ferreira had mentioned the devil.

"It's time to eat!" Jacinta was still calling. "Come down, come down, Francisco."

Slowly he drew to his knees, peering over the high edge at them. A grin broke over his face. "Why don't you two come up here?" They could hear his laughter; with those long skirts they'd never make it, the laughter said.

"Let's go, Lucia. Come," Jacinta coaxed, ignoring the gloom on her cousin's face.

After many groans, scraping of knees and sliding which Francisco watched with steady interest, they reached him.

"Why didn't you answer me?" Jacinta asked indignantly.

"I didn't hear you, not at first."

"Why not? We weren't very far away."

"How come it took you so long to get up here, then? Well, I'll tell you. I was thinking about God, about Jesus, how great He is. I wish I could comfort Him . . ."

"I'm not going to dance anymore," Jacinta declared. "I've made up my mind about that. I'm going to offer it up as a sacrifice."

Never again! They both knew how much she loved to dance.

Her arms locked around her knees, Lucia looked down toward the *Cova* where a lively Maria Carreira was busy as she had been for days. I wish she wouldn't do that, Lucia thought. Hoeing, moving rocks, setting up a table with flowers. I just wish she wouldn't do it, that's all. I won't be down there, not on the thirteenth of July. There! She had finally decided on that. But she wouldn't tell Jacinta and Francisco, not yet. Misery welled up in her as she slid down the rock; it was still with her when she and the other two reached the *Cova*.

Hoe in hand, her soft brown hair loose around her face, Maria Carreira hummed softly, waiting for them. Never had she been so well, so happy, after seven years of sickness. On that wonderful afternoon of June 13, returning home with her son, she had resolved to return to the *Cova* daily. "Look at me," she told her family. "Sick for years, but now watch me breathe." She had felt a new strength surging through her body, an exaltation of spirit that had immediately communicated itself to her young daughters and to her husband. In fact, he had been the first to tell her about Our Lady's visit in May.

"I was working in a field with Antonio dos Santos today," he had said. "And what do you think he told me?"

"Antonio dos Santos?"

"Yes, he said that his youngest daughter, I think he called her Lucia, and two of *Ti* Marto's children, had seen the Virgin in the *Cova da Iria*. Kids! I couldn't help having a good laugh with him."

But she hadn't laughed. Leaning on her hoe she now called out to the three, "How do you like it?" one hand proudly raised to the high arch near the *azinheira*. With help, her husband had squared off a couple of tree trunks. Today she had hung a cross on the center beam. "We're going to put a lantern on each side of the cross, maybe tomorrow." With a quick smile at Francisco and the two girls, she settled the hoe, walked toward the little oak and rounding her arms to indicate an enclosure, said, "There should be a fence around this blessed tree . . . a little gate, too, on the side from which Our Lady comes." Others might call her the lady in white, but she would always say Our Lady . . . The children seemed unusually quiet today, even Jacinta. She glanced at her, sitting on a rock beside Francisco, then her eyes turned to Lucia, head lowered.

"Is something wrong?" Maybe it was the arch — something about it? "Lucia, about this arch. There are lots of people coming here to pray now. Sunday you couldn't count them on your fingers. Don't you think it's only right that we should make this place look as lovely as we can? Just think who it is that comes here!'' She smiled encouragingly, but Lucia said nothing, showed no expression. "Some day we must have a little chapel right here." Maria Carreira turned, contemplating the tree now shorn of many leaves. "A fence would keep people from completely stripping our little tree. But everyone wants a souvenir. By the way, Lucia, will you try to remember next time about John? Please ask Our Lady to cure him."

"What makes you think there is a lady?"

"What — what do you mean!"

"Nobody else believes me. Why should you?"

Her blue eyes looking troubled, Maria placed an arm around her. Her voice was gentle, but there was a note of chiding in it, too. "You know very well that I believe you, so does my husband, all my family, and lots of other people. Why do you think so many are coming here to pray?"

"That's the trouble! They shouldn't be. Do you know what Father Ferreira told me and my mother?"

"No."

"It's all a trick of the devil."

Maria withdrew her arm from Lucia's shoulder, considering. "No, it's not true," she said at last. She hadn't heard this story before; besides, Father Ferreira was a very good priest, zealous (maybe his sermons were a little too long) and dedicated. He must have had a reason. What could it have been? Poor, poor little thing. So that was what was bothering her all this time. She lifted her hoe, pushed it through weeds and fine rocks until she came to the bench her husband and a neighbor had hauled down with the table. Sitting, she said softly, "*Sim*, that must be the reason. The *senhor prior* has to be careful, very careful, especially in something as great as this."

"Why?" Jacinta jumped off the rock, landing close beside her.

"Because, my little one, the *senhor padre* represents the Church. That's why!" She bent over and gave her a quick kiss. "You see, if he said, '*Sim*, the Blessed Virgin is appearing in the *Cova da Iria* to three of my little parishoners,' what do you think the government — all the enemies of the Church — would say?"

"What would they say?"

With a broad smile, she caught Jacinta in her arms. " 'Aha! It's the priest who started this crazy business,' they would say. See?"

Francisco could see. Just like the professor. Even on the last day of school he had shouted, "Francisco Marto, you clout! It must have been the *senhor prior* who put you up to this nonsense." This time his head had struck a corner of the room when the professor had pushed him against it.

Maria Carriera was still trying to explain what she was sure must be the pastor's position. "Speaking about the enemies of the Church . . . just take Artur de Oliveira Santos, for instance." Her face, twisting on the name, as if she had bitten into a bitter olive, brought a giggle from Jacinta.

"Who is he?"

"A very wicked man. For one thing, he prints a newspaper that says bad things about the Church; many people read that paper . . ." Jacinta blessed herself as Maria added in an impressive tone, "He is the administrator . . ."

"What's that?"

"Well," Maria hunted for words. "He has his office in a big government building — City Hall — in Vila Nova de Ourém. Administrator means that he's a — a boss. He bosses Fatima, Aljustrel, Moito, all the hamlets in the *serra*." She knew a lot more about Artur de Oliveira Santos, but she'd said enough. Francisco didn't seem very interested, she noted, and Lucia not at all. Surely the *senhor prior* had not meant to frighten the poor child like this?

———

Chapter Nine

Summer, 1917

Dreading to tell Francisco and Jacinta, especially Jacinta, her final decision, Lucia put off the telling until Thursday, July 12. On that morning she took them to the well, hoping to evade the influx of visitors who might be finding their way to her house, for by now the news of the apparitions had spread beyond the parish boundaries. Cures for themselves or for others (please, please ask the Lady!), safety for soldier husbands and sons, conversions — these were the almost daily cries she heard. Perhaps she would have answered, "But I can't be there!" except for that fluttering in her stomach that just wouldn't let the words come out.

On the roof of the well, she now drooped beside Jacinta. Here it was that last summer on a day much hotter than this, they had almost fallen asleep after Francisco's trick with the lizard. Suddenly, for the second time, the Angel had then appeared before them, tall and flaming bright against these same trees smudged with dust, the cobwebs tight against their leaves.

"What are you doing?" he had asked that day. Clear and loud the words had sounded, even though Francisco had not heard them. "Pray, pray a great deal," he had said. So what? It had all been a bad dream — everything. Desolate, she stared blankly, the drone of bees on the other side of the stone wall pounding in her ears. Bad dreams — pictures that the devil had weaved to deceive her. "It's the devil's work," her mother said every day and she was right; but she wouldn't try to keep Francisco and Jacinta from going tomorrow.

Beside her, Jacinta rocked gently on her knees and with a little ripple of laughter chanted, "Tomorrow, tomorrow, dear Lady, I can hardly wait."

Neither can I, Francisco thought, spying a tiny red rose on a bush wound around some brown tussocks near the base of the well. This time he was sure nothing would keep them from the *Cova*. Nothing. But if Papa hadn't scooted Mama off to the market last time! Funny, how many people had been tramping down the *serra* into Fatima these last few days, most of them coming to their house, too. He leaned over and carefully plucked the little flower from its thorny vine, hearing his own thoughts jumping out of Jacinta.

"We won't have to worry about not going tomorrow, like last time, will we? And so many people! Lots of them camping . . ." She looked at Lucia, seeing the dull eyes fixed on the valley of the green fields below them. "Lucia?" Jacinta stopped rocking. Lucia had been so quiet, just a lot more, ever since early morning when they had taken the sheep to pasture.

Lucia turned toward her; numbly she watched Francisco hand Jacinta the wild rose after examining its dainty fine petals. "It was the only one," he was saying. She could wait no longer. Springing up, her light voice quivering high, she looked from one to the other. "I'm not going to the *Cova* tomorrow . . ."

There was dead silence: on seeing their blank faces change to disbelief, she added, "I mean it!"

Her words had fallen like the swift cracking of a huge branch on a still summer afternoon. "Why, but why?" Jacinta's words wept with her refusal to believe.

"Because — I have a good reason."

"A good reason! You know the Lady told us to be there. Besides, we can't go without you. You're the one she talks to, not me or Francisco."

"I can't, I just can't go."

Slapping her hands, Jacinta lashed out at Francisco. "Say something, don't just stand there . . ." She burst into tears. "The Lady will be so disappointed."

"You two can go without me. If the Lady asks for me — she'd talk to you if you would only say something to her — just tell her that I'm afraid of . . ."

"The devil," Francisco finished bluntly. That was Lucia's "good reason."

"Yes, the devil! Do you know what Father Ferreira told José Alves?"

"What did he tell him?" Jacinta's stormy eyes like her voice reflected deep distrust.

"He told him that sometimes the devil even goes to the table of the Eucharist." And with that she dashed off, leaving them to watch her running between two of the olive trees and over to the threshing shed where she disappeared.

There was something, Francisco decided later that day that he should have told Lucia — if only he had remembered it at the time! — something that ought to change her mind. He just had been too slow, but when she'd said that she wasn't going tomorrow it was as if a big rock had fallen on his head . . . Jacinta's crying hadn't done any good, either. Now he'd go back to Lucia's house and talk to her, now that he'd found the goat belonging to the widow. Running out of her yard, he saw Alberto, a boy from Fatima, crouched to the ground, a bird fluttering wildly in his hand, just as the elderly widow cried out her thanks to him from her gate. "Thank you and bless you, Francisco," she told him whenever he came to her house, which was often. He carried wood and water for her, even pastured her goat and four sheep, went off on errands to Fatima.

Grinning and tugging at the string he had just tied to the bird's leg, the boy stood waiting for Francisco. No stranger was Alberto; Francisco was only too familiar with him at school.

"Where is your *pifaro*?" he sneered. "You're so good at imitating birds; maybe if you'd play a little tune for this one, he might sing for us." He pulled the string sharply so that the bird thrashing at its leash flapped its wings helplessly.

"Don't do that!"

"Why not?"

"Because you're hurting him. Let him go!"

Alberto looked puzzled. "How come you're so brave, all of a sudden?" He came closer. "At school you never open your mouth, but now, just for a measly little bird . . ."

"I'll give you two pennies for him."

"Show me."

"Wait." Francisco ran back to the widow's house. "Please, I'll pay you back. Can you lend me two pennies?"

"Bless you, Francisco. I owe you a lot more than that!"

Francisco untied the knotted string, carefully examined the leg, then gently stroking the blue feathers, said, "Fly high, and don't you ever let yourself get caught again!"

He went to find Lucia. "She's out at the threshing shed," her sister Carolyn informed him.

The sun beat down on the piles of manure and short tufts of brown grass around the shed; inside, the scent of ripe grain was strong; new heads of pale blond barley covered the cement floor. Here the family took turns threshing with a flail — a wooden handle about two feet long at the end of which a short stick swung freely.

"What do you want?" Lucia dropped the flail. With her skirt she wiped her face, grimy with dirt and sweat; the bangs were like strings above her eyes.

"You've got to go tomorrow."

"I told you this morning. I can't."

"Look here. That light from the Lady's hands. You can't ever forget that!"

She gave him a glassy stare and turned her back on him.

"That light! Like being in God; you said so yourself. Remember?" He waited, hoping for an answer, but she wasn't moving a bit. "Can't you see the devil couldn't make us feel like that?" Her silence brought him hope. "Both times, the light . . ."

She turned back, her eyes still glazed. "Father Ferreira was right. You and Jacinta, go if you want to, but I am not going."

Early the next morning, July 13, Francisco and Jacinta, anxious but hopeful that Lucia might still change her mind, unlatched the corral gate. Out on the road, they looked to the south, hoping to see her as they so often did, coming up the road with her sheep. "Maybe she's already at the pond," Jacinta said, but she lingered behind, looking over her shoulder.

On their way they met a family group, a black-shawled woman, barefoot like her children, her husband wearing shabby hob-nailed boots. "Out pretty early, aren't you?" the man said amiably. "Will you tell us which one — there's a trail nearby, they say — to the *Cova da Iria*?"

As Francisco pointed with his staff to the road west of them, the woman looked at him vaguely in a tired sort of way. "Yesterday, we walked all day, almost, to be sure we would get here on time today. I'm so anxious to see the children — the three children. Do they live near here?"

"*Sim, senhora!*" Francisco answered, a twinkle in his eyes as he got very busy with the sheep.

"The *three* children!" Jacinta repeated, watching their departing backs. "I'm afraid we're not going to see Lucia."

She was right. Lucia wasn't at the Carreira pond, nor did they see her on their way home. Around Fatima they saw many different kinds of carts, an old bus, a couple of automobiles, and, in the square, family groups like the one they had met earlier.

Unaware that her two youngest children had returned and were kneeling beside Francisco's bed praying, troubled

and tearful (how could they go without Lucia?), Olimpia
hurried into her parlor after pocketing a few matches. How
still the house was. This morning everyone had rushed the
chores, eager to follow the crowds spilling into the *Cova da
Iria*. And she was just as bad. Never had she thought she
would be doing such a fool thing. But first she must run down
to Maria Rosa's. "She should go with me," she said aloud,
as if hearing the words would strengthen her resolve. From
the oblong table devoutly set with pictures of saints, Olimpia
took two wax candles. Blessed they were, to be used only on
rare occasions; today they might well come in handy. It was
really frightening to see so many strangers. Who could tell
what some of them might do to their *cachopos*; and what in
Saint Anthony's name were those people expecting to see?
She bit her lip, shook her head. Then now at the last minute
Lucia pretending that she wasn't going to the *Cova*! Never
mind, she'd be there . . . was probably there right now with
Francisco and Jacinta. Hastily, Olimpia wrapped the candles
in a white towel. If there should be some deviltry, she and
Maria Rosa would be ready with the candles.

Wiping her hands on her apron, Maria Rosa met Olimpia
in a kitchen smelling of milk and strong homemade soap.
"How come you haven't joined the rest of these imbeciles?"
Her words were vinegary as sour wine. "I suppose you know
that last night hundreds with their donkeys, and God knows
what else, slept all over the *Cova*. You should have heard
your brother this morning!"
"What's the matter with people? Can't they see all the
crops?" Olimpia watched her sister-in-law now straining
milk through a square of cheese cloth.
"You tell me. No more potatoes, nothing." Maria Rosa
dropped the cloth covered with small gobs of cream into a
bucket of rinse water. "Tell me, how do you think this is all
going to end?"
"I don't know, but I want you to come with me — now

— to the *Cova*."

"You want me . . ." Carefully, Maria Rosa set down the milk which she had been about to pour into a jug, brushed off some flies with one hand and glared at her sister-in-law. Little beads of sweat stood on her upper lip. "Olimpia, you must be crazy to think I'd go down there."

"No, I mean it. With strangers everywhere, there's no telling what may happen to the children. By the way, where is Lucia?"

"I don't know. 'I'm not going,' she said last night, but I'll be surprised if she isn't down there right now!" Olimpia nodded in agreement. "I'll tell you one thing, Olimpia, if it is Our Lady, strangers or no strangers, nothing will happen to them; if it is the devil, then . . ."

Olimpia broke in hastily, "You told us that Father Ferreira only said that it could be . . ."

"Speaking of the devil . . ." Maria Rosa's voice suddenly lost its saltiness. "The other night I heard Lucia scream in the middle of the night. When I went into her room she was sitting in bed sobbing. 'The devil, the devil! I saw him in a dream,' she said. 'He tried to grab me, laughing and yelling that he had fooled me.' "

Noting the sudden fear in her sister-in-law's eyes, Olimpia unwrapped the candles. "Look what I brought — blessed candles. Poor Lucia, but that was only a bad dream, Maria Rosa. Listen, we'll go down that short cut behind here and cross over; we'll find a place where no one can see us." Her eyes searched for some sign of yielding.

Maria Rosa wiped the sweat from her lip, slowly untied the dark apron. "If I go — I'd be a fool, but if I do, I don't want anyone to see me. I certainly don't want anyone thinking that my blessing is on this sacrilege, for that's what it really is!"

"So that's where you are!" It was Lucia. Dressed neatly, bangs smooth under a clean kerchief, her face dimpled and bright, she rushed toward the bed. "Yes, it's me!" seeing their eyes widening in incredulity. "Ai! You've been crying." She stretched her arms toward them. "I'm so sorry for all the worry I've caused you."

"What's happened?" Jacinta clung to her, half-crying, half-laughing.

"I don't know, not exactly, except when I awoke this morning that awful feeling in my stomach was gone. I felt like I used to feel, I knew it wasn't the devil . . ."

"We didn't see you this morning; where were you?" Francisco said.

"I was praying, thanking God." She laughed joyously. "Jacinta! Francisco! Let's go!"

In the depths of her being, delight at the coming visit which she had nearly missed gave wings to her feet, and like her, Francisco and Jacinta, now laughing, too, fled the house.

After being stopped repeatedly by hands begging for favors, they finally reached Maria Carreira's flower-trimmed arch, its two lanterns burning for the first time, their wicks pale and flickering in the glare of the July sun.

"Don't forget to ask Our Lady about John," Maria whispered loudly to Lucia, her eyes confident. Today at her side was not only John but her husband and daughters as she had predicted.

She now observed that *Ti* Marto, head bared to the sun, had managed to anchor himself behind his niece and two children. The usually humorous eyes looked serious today, she thought. Although he wore a brown suit and white shirt without tie like most of the men, his deeply tanned face showed little sign of the heat. Arms loosely folded, his moustache and hair shortly clipped, he stood erect like a soldier on guard, his large eyes shifting from the children directly in front of him to the crowd. Olimpia was right. With so many strangers about, you never could tell what might happen. His roving eyes calculated: at least three or four thousand, maybe more. They moved about in small clusters chatting quietly, some under the shade of the big oak to the far left, others in close circles throughout the *Cova* (poor Antonio), and the more fervent in kneeling rows behind him. Only a few stragglers on the wide slope above. Under a brilliant blue sky, here and there, the umbrellas of the cautious screened the hot yellow rays of the sun. No breeze moved through the trees, either. Was Olimpia under one of them or had she finally decided to stay home? How many of this crowd, he wondered, actually believed Our Lady would appear here today? Certainly not those two ruffians calling the children names as he'd tried to pass them on the upper trail. Did any of them really think they would see the mother of God above this little tree and hear her speak? Certainly not Manuel Marto. Such honor was not for him but for the innocent, the pure of heart. Aside from those piously kneeling behind him, most were just curious, maybe even hopeful. But many more were plain unbelieving, like his own Olimpia, the rest of his family, the neighbors, as well as the *senhor prior* who would rather sit up there in his glassed veranda than show his long face at the *Cova*.

Presently he heard Lucia, only an arm's length away, voice raised prayerfully, succeeded by a heightening of voices. Like a lilting lullaby the Ave Marias sang out — not only from the ardent and the lukewarm — but even half-grudgingly from some who had come to scoff. With bowed head, he also prayed. When they had finished the rosary, and the sun was hot at its zenith, Lucia cried out, "Close your umbrellas. The Lady is coming!"

As in the previous month, the sun again grew dim, as if a cloud lingered before it. A cool wind fanned the *Cova* and lightly stirred the trees. It seemed to *Ti* Marto that he heard a sound like the humming of bees or, maybe like what he imagined a telephone might sound like. But that was all. His eyes, like those of the crowd, were fixed on three children silhouetted against a small tree, hardly four feet high.

Chapter Ten

After the usual attempts at blinking and rubbing his eyes, Francisco began once again to gradually see the Lady as he had in the two previous months. How could he have forgotten? . . . It was almost like seeing her for the first time. Of course, sweetly familiar was her look of love just for him; wonderful, too, the shining elegance of her person for which he had not words. "The most beautiful person I've ever seen," would be the only description he would ever be able to give. Yet the beauty which filled him with joy and that held him motionless (his father, watching, likened him to a carving of stone) came not from her shimmering white mantle and tunic, made up as it was of so many hues of frost, sun, moonlight and snowy clouds but from the soft glowing eyes whose gaze now held his; a gaze which reflected the love of a heart he had plainly seen the month before, and that like her Son's cared deeply not only for him but for everyone — everywhere.

Beside him, Jacinta whispered fiercely, "Lucia, what's the matter? The Lady, can't you see? She wants to talk to you. Say something!"

But the splendor which she had so recently rejected and almost lost — now enraptured Lucia, and like Francisco, another figure of stone, she stood — unable to speak, stiff arms at her side. She knew that Our Lady had every right to feel and look reproachful; instead, here she was, graciously bent toward her, magnificent eyes regarding her with unchanged love and tenderness. How could this be? Moreover, today she sensed a deep sadness, one that, however, she saw — she knew! — was not in any way because of her. That she could tell. Head tilted to one side, she nodded a little with growing confidence. Her rigid arms loosened and she folded them tightly to her to guard her new peace and happiness. Ai! Our Lady understood everything. Her whole manner showed no displeasure; on the contrary, she seemed to be saying, "I know how much you have been hurting all these days. But do not be sad, my Little One. Remember what I said. My heart will always be your comfort, your refuge."

Lucia smiled. "What do you want me to do?"

"Come here again at the same time on the thirteenth of next month. Continue to say the rosary in honor of Our Lady of the Rosary — for peace and for an end to the war."

"Will you tell us your name?"

"In October . . . at that time I shall also tell you what I want."

"Hardly anyone believes we see you. Not Mama, not . . . Would you make a miracle so that they'll know we are not lying?"

"Yes, in October."

"I almost forgot. So many people want me to ask you for favors. There is João Carreira who is crippled . . ." She named all she could recall, and for each request received an answer.

When she had finished, the Lady said, "When you make a sacrifice, say, 'Jesus, it is for your love, for the conversion of sinners and in reparation for the sins committed against the Immaculate Heart of Mary.' "

Lucia repeated the words. "Jesus, it is for your love, for the conversion of sinners and in reparation for the sins committed against the Immaculate Heart of Mary." She said them with the same close attention that she had given to those the Lady had taught her in June with the request that they be said between the decades of the rosary.

The Lady now opened her hands. As in May and June, they saw the familiar position of her palms extended toward them; felt the same mystery and power in the powerful rays of light sweeping toward them; and immediately viewed with horror the ravages, the terrible effects of evil. Sin was an abomination in the sight of God; it was ugly and bad, a total rejection of His Love, His Goodness, His Divine Justice. The light from the Lady's hands which totally engulfed them, again opened for them a vision of knowledge, of understanding. In less than a second of time they understood with clarity and pity the meaning of what they saw in the flames of fire at the Lady's feet where demons and souls like red-hot coals appeared shrieking and groaning.

It was at this moment that *Ti* Marto and those nearest heard Lucia's cry, "Our Lady, Our Lady!" and Jacinta's, "Ai! *que morre*! — I shall die!" Breaking into a sweat, arms out, he sprang forward, hearing the cries of alarm around him; but before he could touch them, their stance had become one of utter calm. The deathly pallor of seconds ago was gone, replaced by a luminous quality that shone in their eyes and in the slightly flushed tones of their skins. "How beautiful they look!" he heard Maria Carreira exclaim.

"You have just seen hell where the souls of poor sinners go," Lucia and Jacinta had heard. **"To save sinners God wants to establish in the world devotion to my Immaculate Heart."**

Lucia watched the Lady quietly. She had seen on the first day of her appearance that she had a certain way of speaking, not like the Angel's whose words had struck her ears and mind with the exactness of a good preacher, enunciating each word of his sermon with fine care. With the Lady there was a great difference. Her words were words but for the most part they were not words. They were few and as frugal as fruitless trees in winter; nevertheless, their sense had an amazing simplicity that cut into her mind and opened a world utterly new — yet one which she could understand and totally remember. She would never be able years later to explain this phenomenon to others, especially to those without this experience, but it was now in this way that she heard the Lady's warning.

"If people do what I tell you, many souls will be saved and there will be peace.

The war will end, but if offences against God do not cease, another worse one will begin.

When you see a night illuminated by an unknown light (on the night of January 25, 1938, Lucia judged that the extraordinary aurora borealis she saw was that light) you will know that it is the sign that God will punish the world for its crimes, by war, famine, persecutions against the Church and the Holy Father.

To prevent this I shall come to ask for the consecration of Russia to my Immaculate Heart and for Communions of Reparation.

If attention is paid to my requests Russia will be converted and there will be peace. If not she will spread her errors throughout the world causing wars and persecutions against the Church. Many of the good will be martyred. The Holy Father will have much to suffer; several nations will be destroyed.

In the end my Immaculate Heart will triumph. The Holy Father will consecrate Russia to me. Russia will be converted and there will be some time of peace in the world." (The formula for this consecration was later given to Lucia by Our Lady. It was to be made with the Pope and all the Catholic bishops of the world.)

This third visit was the longest but the Lady still had more to say. At no time had she requested secrecy, not even at her first visit when Lucia had begged Jacinta for silence. The visits of the Angel, the reception of Holy Communion on the heights of the *cabeço*, the sight of the Heart of Our Lady struck by thorns — all these by their nature had held them silent.

Now ready to leave, the Lady said, "These things which you have seen and heard today, and a secret which I am about to tell you, tell no one yet, except Francisco."

Well hidden behind a fort of granite and a few olive trees close to the *Cova*, Olimpia had earlier seen her husband move swiftly toward the children. Raising her candle high, she had come to her feet, crying, "Maria Rosa! Something's happening to the children. Look at Manuel, at the Carreiras — all of them standing as if . . ."

"Wait." Under a tree partly buried by rocks, the back of her wide skirt over her head, Maria Rosa had laid a strong hand on her sister-in-law's skirt. "Your Manuel's right there, ready to march. What in heaven are those three? — what kind of tricks are they trying to pull? This is the worst yet."

Now, twenty minutes later, the shoddy spectacle of her daughter Lucia — standing before thousands of people, nodding and gesturing, was thankfully at an end, for the present, at least. She sat on the ground, her head bowed in her hands, a bitter taste on her tongue.

"Maria Rosa! Look over there. I guess everything's over. The sun is hot again. Did you notice how cloudy-like it was at first, and now everybody's opening their umbrellas again?"

"Olimpia! What do you expect this time of day?"

"And that cool wind; it's gone now!"

"I never felt hotter in my life." Wiping her face, Maria Rosa finally raised her head. "Don't worry; your Manuel's on the job. I see he's got Jacinta on his shoulder, and Lucia is busy — busy talking."

But it was those around Lucia who were spinning the words. "What made you look so scared?" "Was it something the Lady said to you?"

"I can't tell you; it's a secret." A lot more than one

secret. These things . . . secret I shall tell you . . . to Francisco, but no one else . . .

Lucia became silent, letting the questions fly by. She was pale and shivery in spite of a sun sheering its white heat at the *Cova da Iria*. Her young face resembled a carving of wood, features drawn darkly together. She seemed anchored to the ground, hemmed in by relatives, neighbors, and friends, begging for her attention.

"Lucia —" It was Maria Carreira, at last close enough to put her hand on the small thin shoulder. "My João . . . I thought I heard you ask. What did she say?"

Lucia nodded uneasily, silently regarding the hopeful, wistful face as if considering. Maria met the look; her blue eyes filled quickly, then she nodded back. "It *is* God's will," she said, smiling through her tears.

———

Chapter Eleven

"Here they come!" Hair flying behind her, Jacinta darted out of the kitchen as Francisco reached for a stool. Throwing it on the table, he gingerly stepped on it and disappeared through the trap door above.

This was not the first time that he and Jacinta had hidden from inquisitive strangers streaming into Aljustrel since July. The story of the mysterious lady's appearance had spread throughout Portugal, aided by those who had been there on the thirteenth and by the Portuguese secular press, intensely anti-clerical.

Sweating under the hot tiles but secure and flat on his stomach (spiders were no way as bad as some people), Francisco listened to the voices below.

"Are your children here?"

That was the first thing they always asked.

"We've come a long way to see them, to talk with them."

The voice was youngish, high but slow. Like some of the other ladies he had seen lately she would be wearing a gold watch at the bosom of her long lacy dress, a big straw hat on her head, maybe a feather in it, too.

"That is true." A man's voice had taken over. "We have come a long ways — from Oporto — and my wife would be very disappointed, *Senhora* Marto, if we had to leave without seeing your children, your niece, too. So, will you do us the favor . . ."

"We have some gold coins," the young wife's voice interrupted eagerly. "I hope you will take them as a little gift? Lucia's mother wasn't very nice about it when we were at her house. She absolutely refused to take them."

On his back now — it sure was stuffy hot — Francisco continued to listen, his eyes on broken bits of blue sky in the tiles above. Better to be melting up here, Francisco, he told himself, than have someone catch you like that lady from Lisbon. "Does your lady eat potatoes and kale?" she'd asked, laughing and winking at the others. No wonder Mama gets upset, her voice full of mustard now.

"I don't want any of your gold or anything else! The children could be anywhere; the *serra* is pretty big, you know. They might even be down at my brother's well playing. There are fruit trees there and — and —" Her voice was ending a little more friendly as she added: "It's shady down there and not so hot."

It was there that he found the girls. He was sure they would be talking about hell as they had for days now, and not playing as Mama had said. He flopped down on the well beside them.

"Some day you'll get caught," Lucia said.

"What do you mean?"

"Jacinta told me about the trap door." She laughed then turned serious. "We've had so many visitors, now even Carolyn has to take the sheep out sometimes. That's why I haven't had time to tell you all the Lady said . . ."

"You told me about Russia . . ."

"Some, but I haven't told you *everything*." She glanced questioniogly at Jacinta to see her shaking her head, tears in eyes deeply troubled. No, it was as she had thought. Jacinta had not told him the secret. These days it *was* the terrors of hell that loosened her tongue and her tears.

"Lucia, Lucia, why is it that Our Lady didn't show hell to all those people, too? Why didn't you ask her?"

"I forgot," she would tell her over and over.

"If they could see it they would never, never sin again. Hell, Hell . . . all that fire and all those poor souls. How sorry I feel for them. I thought I would die when I saw it."

"So did I; if it had lasted any longer . . ."

And then sometimes Jacinta would fall to her knees. "O my Jesus," she would pray aloud, "forgive us our sins, save us from the fire of hell, take all souls to heaven, especially those most in need."

Francisco's reaction to hell had not been quite the same. Although for a split second he, too, had viewed with horror and pity demons and souls buffeted by flames of fire, it had been the Lady's expression of sadness that had brought a lump to his throat and a flood of tenderness through his whole being. "Through the merits of His Most Sacred Heart and through the intercession of the Immaculate Heart for the conversion of sinners," the Angel had said that last time before giving him Holy Communion. Those two hearts would always come first — to love and to comfort . . . then sinners . . .

He got off the well, looking down at the two girls. "Did you see how sad Our Lady looked?"

"Yes," Jacinta answered quickly. "Lucia, will hell ever end?"

"No."

"Like heaven, forever and ever?"

"Yes, forever and ever."

"Lucia, what sins, what are the sins that send people to hell?"

"Missing Mass on Sundays, stealing, lying, swearing . . ."

"And for one word you can go to hell!"

"If you're not sorry."

Pale, Jacinta said gravely (later, dying in a Lisbon hospital she would declare that the sins of impurity would send more souls to hell than any other), "Our Lord wants everyone to know, to love Our Lady. Right?"

"Yes. He wants devotion to her Immaculate Heart."

"Then you'll have to learn to read and write, just like the Lady said."

At Jacinta's words, the dark brows drew together, but Jacinta continued, "You must tell the whole world about Our Lady, about her Immaculate Heart, and don't forget, don't ever forget to tell about hell!" Arms locked around Lucia, eyes looking deeply into hers, Jacinta waited. "Lucia?"

"*Sim, sim,* I won't forget, Jacinta. Did you tell Francisco? I guess you didn't, about the secret the Lady said I could tell him?"

Straddling a rock, Francisco said, "A secret? The Lady told you to tell me?"

Lucia nodded.

He jumped to her side. "She told you to tell *me* a secret?"

"Yes, when she had finished speaking about Russia, about how there would be another war, much worse even than this one if people didn't stop . . ." Distracted by the smile she saw beginning to sparkle in his eyes, Lucia paused abruptly, "Why are you smiling?"

Why the Lady must have said his name — "Francisco" — just like that!

"Look here!" She tapped him on the arm. "Are you listening? The Lady told me a secret. She said I could tell you but not anyone else."

The smile was all over his face. "You can tell Francisco," she must have said. Those lips had said his name. "Go ahead, tell me the secret!"

"I will," but glimpsing the tight look in Jacinta watching her, Lucia stopped.

"Was the secret about hell?" he asked.

"No, but that's a secret, too, and what she said about another war coming if . . . so is her heart with the thorns. All those things . . ."

"Well, what is it then?" At last her hesitation made him curious.

Catching sight of Carolyn through the trees, jug on her head, Lucia bent quickly toward him, mouth at his ear. Now, unsmiling, he stood mutely, hardly aware of Carolyn's noisy approach. He would die first before ever telling it . . . die . . .

"Hiding again!" Setting her jug on the ground, Carolyn pushed back a rock on the well, reached for the big bucket near it; then, unwinding the long rope, eyed each one disdainfully from a round scolding face. "A fine sight you are," she said, looking directly at Jacinta's dirty tear-stained face. "You ought to wash your face once in a while." She turned from Jacinta to Lucia. "While you're having a great time out here, what do you think is happening back there? Falling to pieces with strangers, that's what the house is doing. I've a good mind to tell them where you're hiding."

In the days preceding August 13, the flow of people into Fatima and Aljustrel increased. The rich, with the exception of the clergy, were the most hostile. "It's the priests I dread most," Jacinta often said. "They ask mixed-up questions, trying to trap us."

Not all priests were insensitive. One day, the three saw a donkey coming down the road with a lanky driver in a black suit and white Roman collar, his feet trailing the ground. Lucia had not seen him in four years, but the old intimate smile, the high wave of his hand, sent her bounding toward him in recognition. "Father Cruz!" The priest who had heard her First Confession and had gotten Father Pena to allow her to receive Holy Communion!

Beaming, his thin face marked by smiling lines that ran from small sharp brown eyes down his cheeks, the priest dismounted. "God bless you, God bless you my child." She was in his arms, then turning to Jacinta hanging back shyly beside Francisco, he exclaimed, "This must be Jacinta!" Four years ago this small child must have been hardly a toddler, he thought, as he embraced her and her brother.

"Were you on your way to the *Cova da Iria*?"

"No," Lucia answered frankly. "There are so many people there now, so sometimes we go to the *cabeço* — it's way up high and nobody goes there. We can be alone to . . ."

"Pray," Father Cruz finished for her. His shrewd eyes studied each one closely; placing his hand affectionately on Lucia's shoulder, he said with a gentle smile that included the three: "Today, my little ones, instead of going to your *cabeço*, how about taking me to the spot where Our Lady comes to see you?"

Turning the donkey in the opposite direction, Father Cruz again mounted him. Through the mid-afternoon they moved leisurely up and down the trail toward the *Cova,* seeing the purple star thistle and dried bushbeans amid trees and rocks in bright yellow rings of sunlight and shadow.

After a few inquiries about their brothers and sisters, the health of their parents (he had been on his way to visit them), Father Cruz ventured, "Lucia, I hear you have seen her three times?"

"Yes, Father."

"I have also heard that she has promised you a miracle!"

"Yes, because, well, you see, hardly anyone here believes us."

"You know something? The *senhor prior* thinks we're lying." At Jacinta's sudden outburst, the priest's narrow shoulders lifted almost imperceptibly. Indeed, he well knew how the good pastor felt. His conversation with him that morning had left no doubt. "You were saying, Lucia?"

"Because I want people to believe us, I asked her for a miracle."

"Just like that!"

"She said she would!"

Chuckling, Father Cruz removed a large white handkerchief from his breast pocket and wiped his forehead.

"When?"

"The last time — in October."

They continued on until the donkey, barely moving, came to a dead stop, his nose in the weeds beside the trail. "We're almost there," Francisco said as Father Cruz dismounted. He had been thinking as they moved along like a snail with lots of stops that if Father Ferreira was anything like Father Cruz, he and Jacinta would by now be receiving the "Hidden Jesus." Only yesterday, Papa had taken him and Jacinta to Father Ferreira, right into the sacristy. "I've brought my Francisco and Jacinta; they are ready for their first confessions." Although he had added, "Ask them anything you want," Papa had not meant what Father Ferreira thought.

Tightening his lips, the *senhor prior* had answered, "The matters which I think you refer to are not matters for the confessional. I shall hear them right now, but as for Holy Communion, no! Next year, perhaps."

"Francisco," Father Cruz was looking at him now. "What is it Our Lady wants?"

"I don't hear what she says . . ."

"Oh . . ."

"But I tell him," Lucia said quickly.

"And that is?" He didn't really want to probe, to ask more than he should.

"She wants everybody to love God, to change their lives . . ."

"To be good and say the rosary!" Jacinta added.

With a big laugh, the priest swung her high in his arms. Watching him, Lucia thought how easy it was to be free and happy with Father Cruz; but not even to him could she say more. She would have liked telling him that they loved going to the *cabeço,* not only because they could be alone to pray but because there they had seen in great majesty an angel of the Lord two times. Some things could be told, some could not, and those were the most. Father Cruz, she saw, was watching her with smiling eyes that understood.

When they reached the last stretch of the trail that would take them over the bosom of the hill down into the *Cova*, Father Cruz stopped the donkey.

A learned missionary Jesuit in his middle fifties, with much experience in the ways of human beings, he was also known and respected for his high degree of asceticism. Yet this encounter with the children had heightened his consciousness of the awesome power of God. "Let the little children come to me," He had said. Here was living proof of that loving request. Free from artificiality, these three little ones appeared but little different from their peers in the *serra* who also had a charming maturity beyond their years. Perspicaciously he sensed, no, he knew without doubt that spiritually Lucia and her two cousins had received extraordinary graces.

"My little children," he said with strong feeling, "my dear little children." His voice faltered. "With so much love, the good God has chosen the three of you. You must never forget to thank Him for the special favors He has given you."

Again he reached for his hankerchief, this time not to wipe the sweat from his brow.

For the short period he remained at Fatima, he continued to counsel them. To Lucia, especially, his words brought comfort and inspiration. They were like the ones he had given her in the confessional at the age of six and which she had never forgotten. "Keep your heart pure for God . . . your soul is the temple of the Holy Spirit."

About the eighth of August, Francisco heard the loud talk even before he came into his yard. At the kitchen door, Aunt Maria Rosa was waving an envelope like the one in Papa's hand. "I think Artur Santos is doing us a favor. *Sim,* a favor. Maybe now, at last! he's the one who can untangle this sack of riddles."

"Artur de Oliveira Santos never untangled anything!" There was a grim look on Papa's face. "Tell me, sister-in-law, what kind of favor is that which orders little children to court? Well, I can tell you this much. I've no intention of sitting my two on a horse or a burro and taking off with them down that rough road; it's at least six miles from here to Vila Nova de Ourém.''

"But it's a court order! August 11, 12:00 P.M. Now listen to me, brother-in-law. You'd better be careful. Artur . . ."

"Artur Santos! *A-ha!*"

Papa fixed his face just like Maria Carreira had twisted hers that day in the *Cova* when she had said the same name. Now, why — why would he want to see them?

Like a great Amen, Papa intoned, "Court order or no court order, I refuse to take my Francisco and Jacinta.''

Chapter Twelve

Ti Marto looked up from his breakfast to see the dejected figure of his brother-in-law at the door, an unsmiling Lucia beside him, her face almost hidden by a shoulder-length kerchief of dark blue. It was Saturday, August 11. In a clean white shirt, his cap at an angle that belied the gloom on his somewhat handsome face, Antonio dropped on a stool as Lucia hurried to Jacinta's bedroom. "Well, are Francisco and Jacinta going?"

"Antonio, I told your wife already. I've no intention of taking them to Ourém. That road calls for a good rig which I don't have."

"I'm taking Lucia on the burro."

"Poor thing. Ups and downs — rough going all the way. You shouldn't take her."

Antonio flinched and, standing, waved his hands defensively. "Fooling all these people. Like my Maria says, it's time somebody took her in hand, someone like Santos. Francisco and Jacinta, too. Look here, you don't seem to be in any hurry."

"I've some work to do first, but I'll be along later."

"Later! If we're going to be there by mid-day . . ."
You'd think Manuel Marto hadn't a care in the world, as if the reins of the Republic were in his hands instead of Artur Santo's. "Lucia!" His voice shot through the house.

"I've got to go now," Lucia told Jacinta, "and I'm scared. I remember the day when Maria Carreira told you about the administrator."

"Don't be scared. We'll pray for you, and you can tell him that I'm just like you. Francisco, too!"

"Lucia!"

"I'm coming, Papa."

He was already in the yard beside the burro, but at the kitchen door her uncle put a detaining hand on her arm. "Lucia, Lucia, don't look so worried. A little later *Ti* Manuel will be along. He'll be there!"

It was nearing noon when he rode into the sprawling old Moorish town of Vila Nova de Ourém with its crumbling medieval castle high on the terraced hill. The main square was almost deserted; its cobblestones, like the spread of red roofs, reflected the glare of the blazing sun. Hitching his horse to one of the posts in a long wooden rack, he saw Antonio and Lucia walking toward him. She was limping. "The place is shut down," Antonio shouted. His face was flushed, the white shirt now soiled and wet with sweat. As they drew closer, *Ti* Marto noted the scratches on one of Lucia's cheeks, smudges of tears and dirt on her face. Her kerchief sat back on her disheveled hair; there was a long rip in her skirt. She must have fallen off that burro more than once. Taking her by the hand, he struck a cheerful note. "So the powers that be are taking their siestas! Antonio, what say we have a little something to eat and drink." He found a small cafe wedged between an even smaller pharmaceutical store and another one which featured in its window mantillas from Madrid — fine embroideries, the sign read, from Madeira.

Antonio and Lucia had gone to the wrong building. According to the stocky, talkative cafe keeper, the *Senhor* Artur de Oliveira Santos had moved to another street. Ah, yes, he'd be there right now. No siesta for him nor for anyone else who worked for him. How else could a tinsmith accomplish so much in so short a time, he wanted to know, as he set down a tray with bread, cheese, a bottle of wine. Black brows high, he counted off on each stubby finger: "President of the Municipal Chamber, Deputy Judge of Commerce, founder and president of the local lodge of Masons,   and only the good saints knew what else. Ah, yes, editor of the *Ouriense* in which he loved to blast the Church. With a stealthy glance at the front door, he lowered his voice. "And did you know that not long ago, Santos arrested a half dozen priests and kept them in jail eight days! Without anything against them, either!" Somehow, the conspiratorial whispering was respectful and admiring, and on the same note he finished, "Artur is no man to be fooled with."

Within the hour, again holding Lucia's hand, *Ti* Marto entered Ourém's City Hall with Antonio muttering at his heels. For a moment he hesitated at an open door to his left.

"Come in. It's about time!" From a desk, a sallow-faced young man in a light-colored suit beckoned. Beside him a notebook in hand stood a man wearing a green visor; a few feet away, two men looked up from a table stacked with papers. But *Ti* Marto was quite aware of who the boss was here. He needed no introduction to the thin Administrator strutting toward them.

"I told you, you were to be here at mid-day." He worked a huge gold ring on his finger. "What the devil took you so long, anyway?"

Dropping Lucia's hand, *Ti* Marto ignored the question. "I'm Manuel Marto and this is my brother-in-law Antonio dos Santos and . . ."

"I knew who you were as soon as I saw you." Santos was glaring at Lucia. "Where are the others? Don't tell me you didn't bring them!"

"The road is steep and rough; on it even a *burrito* cannot hold a child, especially if she is not used to riding." *Ti* Marto placed his hand gently on Lucia's head.

"Now, who is she?"

A revolving fan suspended from the ceiling did nothing to dry the sweat that dropped from Antonio's forehead. "Lucia. She's mine . . . she's only ten years old." Mopping his brow he floundered on, "The other two belong to him."

"Sit down," Santos said brusquely, indicating two chairs. Antonio immediately fell into one; *Ti* Marto remained standing. "Lucia, over here." She followed Santos. The green-visored clerk had joined the other two men at the table now curiously watching.

Studying the stolid child facing him across the desk, Santos took in the stringy wet bangs, the tear-streaked face, red and swollen, the torn skirt at the knee. Scared? Perhaps, although she was looking him straight in the eye . . . dour and cool, he'd say. "Who is this strange lady you've seen on a hill?"

"In the *Cova da Iria*."

"Don't be impudent. What is her name?"

"She hasn't told us yet."

"You don't say! And you see her coming from heaven, I'm sure."

"That's where she comes from."

Deaf to the snickering from the table, Santos cupped one hand over his acquiline nose and considered Lucia with dark speculative eyes. "What is the name of your pastor?"

"Father Ferreira."

"You see him often? Not just in church?"

Lucia looked puzzled.

"What I mean is: Doesn't he go to this place, this *Cova da Iria* with you? Isn't this so? At first, wasn't it he who took you?"

"I've never seen him there."

"The *senhor padre* has nothing to do with your story. Now, now. Is that what you're trying to tell me?"

Lucia put a quick hand to her cheek, winced; but there was a sudden gleam at the back of her eyes. Father Ferreira at the *Cova*!

"Drop that smirk and tell me this: What is this great secret everybody is talking about?"

A sudden stillness came over Lucia's face; the slight flash of humor had faded as quickly as it had appeared. Her eyes left his and her words came softly. "The Lady has come to see us three times. She always comes from the east, then she stops above an *anzinheira*. She asks us to pray, to say the rosary . . ."

"Look at me!"

She complied.

"I didn't ask you from what direction she came. I asked you about this — this so-called — secret . . ."

Lucia was looking away again. "I can't tell you about that," she replied, her eyes turned in the direction of the clock on the dark yellowish wall just above him.

"Do you know, do you have any idea who I am?"

She looked back at him, this time with that same amusive flicker in her eyes. "Oh, yes, *Senhor* Administrator."

Pounding his desk, Santos fumed, "*Senhor* Administrator is right. Do you know," with a side glance at *Ti* Marto and Antonio, "that there is a law forbidding religious gatherings outside of a church — like what is happening down there? I'm now, listen carefully to this, young lady, ordering you to stay away from that place." His face had taken on a peculiar shade of crimson. "If you don't, so help me, I'll have you killed!"

Hands clenched at his sides, *Ti* Marto stepped forward. There was a white line around his mouth. "You don't know, you absolutely don't know what you're saying," he said in measured tones. "Believe me, *senhor,* it was not easy for me to come here today with all the work that needs to be done. But before I leave here, I must tell you this much: My children, my little niece here, are not lying. On matters as sacred as these? Never! I know them too well for that."

The burst of laughter from Green Visor and his two companions altered Santos's mood. With a wide grin, he pointed to Antonio who had risen to his feet and was grinding his cap between his hands. "And you, do you believe this story?"

"Me? Oh, no, *Senhor* Administrator. These are just

women's tales.''

"Good! Now, Lucia — remember — you are not to go to the . . .''

"But I have to! She told us to be there day after tomorrow.''

"You, you . . . when I just told you not to . . .'' Then with that same speculative look that had accompanied his accusation of the priest's involvement, he said, ''Day after tomorrow? Humph! I see you're not very good at taking orders. Let's see . . . day after tomorrow is — is Monday.''

Ti Marto didn't like the words nor the tone of the voice. Like bad fish they smelled. And that wild threat of having Lucia killed! What kind of man was this, anyway?

Early that evening after getting a full account of Papa's story, Francisco and Jacinta waited at the well, mindful of Lucia's words that she would meet them there on her return. It was too early for Angel lamps, not so high above, to be lit. Because of the heat, the children of Aljustrel now played happily in their yards and out on the road. They would still be playing there when moonlight like the nimbus of a saint, lay over the hills. And now, just before the stars began to flicker, one by one, Lucia appeared, running with outstretched arms toward Francisco and Jacinta. "I knew you'd come back,'' Jacinta cried tearfully. "I knew it! Carolyn said you'd been killed, but we prayed all day.''

Teeming with people, Fatima, on Sunday, August 12, was no longer a microplace of the few. Vehicles of every description — bicycles, carts, carriages, automobiles — stood everywhere. While crowds lingered around the dusty square, many visited the church and even the cemetery beyond where a sign read: "Our bones await yours.'' The majority were pilgrims on foot, large families, carrying baskets of food and blankets, ready for a night under the stars of the *Cova da Iria*.

In the kitchen of Manuel Marto that evening most of his family, heavy-eyed with weariness, slouched on their stools and benches. From early morning, people had come in long lines of procession just as they had at the Santos's house, with the usual curiosity, the usual litany of requests for the children. It had been difficult to accomplish the most simple domestic duties as well as the outside chores.

On the floor, Francisco idly observed João, mouth wide open, sleeping in his favorite place — under the kitchen table. Today he had been thinking all day of seeing her tomorrow, way before Mass this morning when visitors had begun arriving. One very strange lady had knelt at his feet. "Please bless these beads for me; make a sign of the cross over them."

"I can't do that," he'd told her and some of the others that wanted him to do the same for them. "Take your rosaries to a priest." People ought to know better than that.

Sitting up, he saw that João was still asleep, mouth still open, as Papa announced: "It's time for bed!"

Mama reached for the lamp as some of the family began stirring, then stopped, her hand in mid-air. "Ai! I forgot to tell you, Manuel, with all this commotion today. Maria Carreira was here; she is terribly worried . . ."

"Why?" Papa unbuttoned his shirt at the neck.

"She says people are leaving money, lots of it, on that table she put by the tree."

"So?"

"She doesn't know what to do with it. When she asked Maria Rosa if she would keep the money, Maria Rosa told her that's the last thing she'd ever do, and I told her the same."

"Nothing wrong with that."

"Then who do you think should take care of the money? What should it be used for?"

Listening, Francisco reached for a small faggot beside the hearth. Funny, no one seemed to know what to do about the money. Why not give it to the poor? he thought. Teresa and Florinda were asking Papa for his blessing; big feet were shuffling around him; then suddenly he was holding the twig by one end and the other was almost in João's big wide mouth.

"*Ora!*" The tight hand on his wrist was Papa's. "Francisco Marto, what are you doing? Don't ever let me see you do such a thing again!"

"The very one who expects to see the Virgin tomorrow!" Mama cried. Immediately everybody was wide awake and indignant on hearing what might have happened. Why, he could have choked poor João. Some saint! Where was Jacinta? In bed. Well, that's where *Senhor* Francisco should have been. The hot water those two could get into and soaking everybody else with it.

"To bed," Papa said. "Tomorrow is another day."

Tomorrow came too early. Not only had people to be fed and dressed in clean clothing, the house tidied, but animals also needed care and food. There was a cow to be milked, hay to be forked into mangers and water carried.

Hastily returning from a field, *Ti* Marto caught sight of a buggy—a kind of glorified surrey with four seats, two in front and two in back. It stood directly in front of the parlor door. A couple of other buggies stood close by. These visitors lost no time. Entering the kitchen, he heard voices coming from the parlor and saw Olimpia's stiff figure, her eyes full of warning signals. Wordlessly, one finger at her lips, the other hand pointed impressively toward the parlor, only a few feet away.

Why all the secrecy? he wondered. By now, they should be used to all kinds — the high and the mighty as well as the poor and the not so mighty. Pouring water into the basin, he began washing his hands when he felt Olimpia pulling his sleeve.

"What is it?"

"Sh!"

He took the towel off its nail. "Don't tell me there is a king in there," he teased, wiping his hands.

"King!" she whispered witheringly. "It's Artur Santos; that's who it is!"

With the towel still in his hand, *Ti* Marto walked into his parlor, blind to all his visitors but one. "What are you doing here?"

"Ah, *Senhor* Marto!" Straw hat in hand, Santos rose hurriedly from his chair beside a young man wearing a Roman collar. "Surprised? I don't blame you." He smiled widely and bowed, undaunted by his host's cold regard. "You may not believe this, but I have come to see the miracle, too!"

Ti Marto gripped the towel in both hands. So this was the same man who only two days before had forbidden Lucia the *Cova*, who even threatened death and had treated them all like red dirt beneath his fancy shoes.

"I know what you are thinking, and I don't blame you. Let's just say I've had a change of heart. A doubting Thomas who also wants to go to the *Cova da Iria*, hoping to believe." Santos exuded charm, smiling expansively at the priest and two couples crowded together on a chest.

Mutely, *Ti* Marto regarded Santos. He was up to something, and it was not good, whatever it was. Those sly smiles and bows didn't fool him any. Seeing a miracle . . . doubting Thomas. No wonder that on Saturday he had felt deep in his bones that Santos wasn't finished.

"I'm afraid, *Senhor* Marto, that you still do not believe me. To show you my good faith, let me take the children to the *Cova da Iria*."

"They don't need anyone to show them the way."

"But they could show me. By the way, where are they?"

As if in answer to his question they appeared in the doorway, Lucia at her father's side. Without a glance at Antonio, Santos exclaimed, "Lucia!" He had recognized her, although she hardly looked like the same girl he had seen on Saturday. Except for the scratches on one side of her face, the olive cheeks were shiny with color, the dark eyes bright. There was an air of high expectancy about her that even the sight of the administrator did not immediately assault. Nodding, Santos gave approval to the clean pinafore and spotless blouse, the smooth brown hair in its tight braids. He laughed lightly, all earnestness and sincerity. "I see you are not as surprised to see me as your uncle was, or your father," he added, his attention now including Antonio. "You see, I've had a change of heart as I've just informed my good friends here. How about riding with me to the place, Lucia? I've never been there. Are these your cousins? What say that the three of you show me the way?" He was the picture of easy camaraderie as his glance embraced everyone in the parlor.

"No." Some of the glow had left Lucia's face. "We always walk."

"Isn't it getting near that time? I saw hundreds of people — hundreds! — on their way." Santos glanced quickly at his gold watch, quickly returned it to his vest pocket. "It's already after eleven o'clock."

"We know when to go." Lucia's voice was adamant.

For the first time Santos appeared nervous. Fussing with the gold ring on his finger, he looked from Lucia's set face to *Ti* Marto, then back at Lucia.

"Ah, I almost forget!" He tapped his forehead, closed his eyes. "Before coming here I had a little talk with your good pastor. He told me to be sure to tell you he wants to speak to you before you go to the *Cova da Iria*. It's very important that he see you, he said. I don't see how I forgot . . ."

Lucia's troubled eyes sought her uncle. Clearly, they said: If Father Ferreira wants to see us we should go, but not with the administrator.

Ti Marto flung the towel over one shoulder. "Very well,

Senhor Santos. I have to change my clothes. Afterwards, Antonio and I will take the children to the pastor's house . . ."

"But I could take them so quickly . . ."

"No, no, it's just a few minutes walk from here."

"Have it your way; I'll meet you there."

———————

Chapter Thirteen

It was nearing eleven-thirty when *Ti* Marto and Antonio, almost trotting behind their children, came within sight of the tall parish house. There was Santos's buggy, all right, close to the low brick wall, the horse's reins loosely wound around the buggy whip. *Ti* Marto gave a quick wave to the old, black-clothed woman crossing herself in the shadow of the church door as she curiously eyed their haste. Across the hard-baked surface of the rambling square, two men lounging in front of a cafe also watched. The heart of the village was silent in the white heat of the August day, deserted for a field two miles away where thousands now awaited the children's arrival.

"There they are, the *senhor padre* and Santos." *Ti* Marto pointed to them angrily facing each other at the threshold of the veranda. His face red and angled at Santos, the *senhor padre* was thumping the air with an opened hand at Santos, who now seeing them, shouted, "Lucia! Get up here! The rest of you stay down there."

Lucia again stood in the same study where two months before, Father Ferreira had terrified her with his talk of Satan. "You wanted to see me?" she asked him now.

"See you? What gave you that idea?"

Santos cleared his throat noisily. "It's as good a time as any for you to see this young lady," he said insolently.

Father Ferreira gave him a long look. For some reason, Santos had tricked Lucia and the others waiting downstairs, into coming here. Why? To delay their noon outing at the

119

Cova? Moreover, Santos on his arrival had immediately accused him of instigating this "beautiful hoax" with the endorsement of the Church.

"Lucia, suppose you tell *Senhor* Santos who put you up to this mockery — who taught you to say all these things you have been telling everyone. The truth, remember!"

"The Lady in the *Cova da Iria*." She glanced down at the small enamelled clock on the desk, looked across at the seated, scowling priest.

"Don't worry about the time. People who spread lies like yours go to hell. You are old enough to know that, eh? Deceiving thousands and thousands!" Eyes fixed on Lucia, his ill-humor shifted from Santos to her. "Look at this crowd today!" The whole of the *Serra de Aire* was in the wide spread of his accusing arms. "I repeat: People who tell lies like yours go to hell. You'd better think about that if you haven't before, eh?"

"I won't go to hell because I tell only what I've seen. People go to the *Cova* because they want to; we never ask them."

"And what about the secret?" Santos broke in.

At this intrusion, Father Ferreira stood. How Santos had ever become an administrator, an editor, or anything else! Yet to his own discomfiture, he found himself asking the same question. "Is is true that this lady confided a secret to you?"

To Lucia, the voice seemed less harsh. "Yes, she has, but I can't tell you." Then, almost roguishly, leaning toward him, she said in words much faster than his, "If you like, I can ask the Lady for permission to tell you!"

"Enough! I've had enough. Let's go!" Without a word to the *senhor prior*, Santos caught Lucia by the arm. "We'd better hurry," he told her, forcibly pulling her through the veranda. "It's getting very late; *now* I will have to drive you to the *Cova*."

With the same urgency, his hand still gripping her arm,

he came to the foot of the stairs where *Ti* Marto and Antonio waited with Francisco and Jacinta. Waving his hand to them, he lifted Lucia into the back seat. "Sorry the *senhor prior* took so long," he shouted; "but don't worry, I'll get them down there on time." Briskly, he swung Jacinta into the back beside Lucia and elbowed Francisco into the front seat. "I'll see you at the *Cova da Iria*!" Even as he spoke, he unwound the reins and with a crack of the whip was off.

The thing happened so swiftly that *Ti* Marto stood staring beside the gaping Antonio until he saw that Santos had taken the wrong road. By then it was too late.

Very early that morning, streaks of crimson across the eastern sky headlined a glorious new day for Maria Carreira. Wearing a black kerchief, her slim figure in a simple, black cotton dress, she left her small house in Moito, pins and ribbons in a pocket, a heavy bag on one arm. A muteness of early morning sounds and smells greeted her: the scent of dry grasses, the scurry of small furry creatures through dry leaves, a fluttering of wings in the trees, the lumbering passage of an owl. With the scarlet pearl of daybreak, all nature for Maria now blended into a syncreticism of praise to the Lord for all His creation. Breathing deeply — still an incredible, incredible joy! — she prayed. Our Lady would be here today! Not too much later, when the sun was up, her family would begin joining her and those who had been on the march for over two days — most of them families whom she now saw asleep on their blankets among rocks and under trees.

Humming, she tied bows of ribbon on the arch and arranged flowers she had gathered on the way, placing them on the table where already lay a few scattered coins. Shaking her head, she gathered them into the big cotton bag. Nobody wanted this money, not even the *senhor prior* whom she had approached before talking to Maria Rosa and Olimpia. She knew what she would like to do with it. Build a little chapel in honor of Our Lady — right here. It had been her dream right from the beginning. She had said that so many times, people were beginning to call her Maria de Capelinha — Maria of the little chapel. She liked that. Perhaps today she would get an answer; she had talked to Lucia about the problem.

"Will you ask Our Lady what I should do with the money?" Lucia had promised.

There was not too much longer to wait, she thought, as the first rays of the sun began stirring those who had camped during the night. Gradually, their voices drifted toward her, gentle voices that belonged to gentle people, she mused, who with their few belongings tied in bundles beside them had slept in their clothes. Many of them were beginning to open stringed bags or wicker baskets with the usual tough brown bread, cheese, and fresh fruits. They opened water jugs from which each one in the family drank. The morning air was blessedly cool, and little children, seemingly as low-keyed as their parents, ran and jumped over rocks, hiding from one another behind trees, happy in this new experience which for them was a holiday. And so the morning wore on. Reaching out for a wistful-looking little girl shyly approaching her, Maria Carreira heard, "Good day, Maria de Capelinha."

She swirled toward the sturdy figure behind her holding a square cardboard box. "Why Maria dos Anjos!" she exclaimed, holding back the words: "Whatever are you doing here?"

Lucia's oldest sister regarded her with amused, fine brown eyes. She had thick-growing hair, good features, more regular than Lucia's, and no olive in the healthy pink cheeks.

"I see you're surprised to see me."

"Well, yes, I am."

"I don't blame you." After all, she could hardly blame Maria for being startled at one of Lucia's family inching her feet so close to the *anzinheira*. By now, everybody must know how they all felt at her father's property being ruined, taken over by every João, Jorge, and Pedro, including Maria Carreira. It probably would shock her to see what she had in the box. Opening it (she had only come here on the spur of the moment with the pretty candles when her husband had offered to keep the baby), she leaned over and, smiling faintly, placed the candles with their glass holders on the table, missing the quick look of pleasure on Maria Carreira's face. Still bent over, her hands went up to the bright kerchief that effectively set off her small ear pendants of gold; then her body stiffened, the slight smile tightened as she viewed the bulky bag. Shaking her head, she straightened, looked pointedly at the other, one hand flipping the bag.

"I wish I could find someone who would keep this money," Maria said quickly. "I asked your mother if she would. Did she tell you?" She was troubled at the expression she saw breaking in the pretty eyes.

Maria dos Anjos didn't answer. It would take lots and lots of sewing and weaving, she reasoned, to earn a sackful like that. She began feeling a renewed sense of discomfort remembering innuendoes she had heard. What's that woman from Moito doing with all that money? What can you expect when people see all those flowers on the table? If there was no table, there would be no money. People just don't leave money on the ground. Maybe her mother was right. This whole thing was crazy. "My mother would never keep it for you," she blurted, her candor reminding Maria Carreira of Lucia.

"That's what she told me." Maria made her voice quiet. "Is she coming today?"

"I don't think so."

Maria Carreira was tempted to ask the other why she had come, but the matter of the coins, however, still clung unpleasantly to her — as if she were guilty of some law-breaking. Still keeping her voice quiet she said, "Lucia promised me she would ask Our Lady today about the money, what should be done with it." And seeing the disbelief in Maria dos Anjos's narrowed eyes, she added: "You still don't believe Lucia, do you?" Her glance went to the tree now encircled by a low new fence. She had done some of the work herself. "But you will when you see the miracle in October. By the way, where is Lucia? The three are usually here by this time."

"They've probably been detained at Father Ferreira's. You see, Artur Santos, the administrator . . ."

"Artur Santos! What . . ."

"Aunt Olimpia told me he wanted to take the children to see . . ." She never finished. From the hill above there were shouts and cries. "The children are gone! They've been stolen. The administrator ran off with them!"

Maria Carreira had heard enough. Artur de Oliveira Santos. Trembling, she placed both hands on the table. The crowd which had been so quiet now yammered shrilly and indignantly. She closed her eyes tightly and tried to pray . . .

"Maria, Maria!" It was her husband's voice, his hand on her arm. "Look!" Without moving her head or glancing up she knew something had happened; she also knew that this was the time for the Lady to appear. The strident voices were hushed now, replaced by soft exclamations of wonder and broken words of amazement. Slowly, Maria raised her head.

Shortly after her husband and brother-in-law had left with the children for the priest's house and the rest of the family had gone to the *Cova*, Olimpia began to feel a sharp anxiety that had begun when the administrator had knocked at her door that morning. She now attempted to set the house straight, swept around the hearth needlessly, checked the milk pans in the pantry, went through the bedrooms shaking clothes and putting them into chests. She had not yet made up her mind about going to the *Cova* this month. Maria Rosa had assured her that she had no intention of finding another hiding place, peeking at doings that could only nail her down with stomach cramps as it had in July. The memory of Maria

Rosa's lively description and gestures of their awkward maneuvers behind the rocks, candles in hand, brought a fleeting smile to Olimpia's eyes. There were times when Maria Rosa could break out of that hard shell; if only Antonio didn't drink so much. Well, she had worried herself stiff last month, afraid of what strangers might do to the children, and what had happened? Nothing. So now why this queasy feeling? By now she ought to be used to outsiders; she'd seen plenty of them, God knew. Finally, no longer able to restrain her fears, she tore off her apron, smoothed her hair and picked up a square kerchief. Running out to the road, she stopped suddenly, stood very still, her head cocked in the direction of the *Cova da Iria*. It was only about a mile and a half northwest of her house, yet she could hear voices from that general area. She took a few steps further as she saw two small boys of a neighbor followed by their father, speeding toward her and shrieking, "Francisco and Jacinta are gone! The man with the straw hat stole them."

"It's true," their father agreed. "I just heard *Ti* Marto myself telling that crowd at the *Cova*. He said that it happened right there at the *senhor prior*'s house. Santos threw the *cachopos* into his *carro* and with a crack of the whip was gone. They never got to the *Cova* at all. I guess he must have taken them to jail."

Hands clenched together, Olimpia stood stricken, unable to speak, her worst feelings now confirmed. Jail! Unmindful of her neighbors, she started in the direction of the *Cova*, faltered for a moment, then turning in the opposite direction began running, uttering broken bits of prayer. Jesus, Jesus . . . Mother of God . . . Could the government arrest children, like those priests Manuel had told her about who had done *nothing* — really put them in jail? I'll have you killed, Santos had told Lucia.

A few minutes later, she burst into Maria Rosa's kitchen, the kerchief still in her hand, her wide eyes black with fear. "Santos! He's taken our children. Stolen them right from under Manuel's and Antonio's noses. Yes, João Alves and his boys just told me." Her hair was half down and a long hairpin dropped to the floor.

"Calm yourself." Maria Rosa's voice was low. "Sit down!"

But Olimpia moved closer to her. "Calm yourself!" she echoed. "What's the matter with you? Don't you understand? Santos has run off with our children, we may never see them again! And you tell me . . ."

"That's going pretty far — never see them again. He's probably gone off to some place nearby, just to keep them from the *Cova*. He'll bring them back later." The upward curve of Maria Rosa's mouth was set, the small eyes suddenly grave and thoughtful. "You know — yes! — let me tell you something . . ."

"Don't tell me anything! Jacinta, my poor, poor little baby. She must be so scared. Never before has she been away from me. Francisco won't be so afraid, but . . ."

Maria Rosa interrupted her. "I can't understand, I never will! Your Manuel falling for that stunt by the tree last month — all that groaning and carrying on. And when people asked what had happened? A secret! I'm sick of the whole thing."

"João Alves said Santos took them to jail!"

"Look, Olimpia, let the great administrator straighten Lucia out, if he can! When I see these busy nitwits stomping over the vegetables, snooping around our houses, their burros chewing the pastures, all wanting to know secrets. I could . . ." For different reasons, Maria Rosa was now as aroused as Olimpia. "And now this wild talk about a great miracle! I tell you this is the best thing that could happen!"

"Are you crazy? That villain steals our children and you tell me this is the best thing that could happen — exactly what you thought the other day after getting that summons." Mimicking her sister-in-law's gestures and voice, she quoted her. 'Maybe now Santos can untangle this barrel of riddles!'

That's exactly what you said. Ai! If only I could get my hands on that scoundrel!''

"Oh, my!",Maria Rosa said dryly. She sat down heavily on the wooden bench beside the table, unaffected by Olimpia's outrage. "I know it's no secret that we've lost everything in the *Cova* — the pastures, too, so now the sheep must be sold; we need the money. It's true we'd lost other fields before this, but things have gotten so much worse, and so has your brother. Would this be true if Our Lady was really appearing to our children?'' She sighed heavily. "That's why I'm glad, really hopeful that Santos will — that's right — untangle this riddle.''

She wiped the sweat from her face, laid both elbows on the table and with hands on either cheek watched Olimpia pick up the hairpin from the floor, coil her hair into place above the small, shell-like ears. Hair up or down, angry or laughing, Olimpia was a very pretty woman, she thought dispassionately, at the same time saying, "You know, Olimpia, there is hardly a day — *sim!* — hardly a day that I don't give my Lucia a spanking — hard, too. May God forgive me, but . . .''

Not too distraught to hear the anguish in Maria Rosa's voice, Olimpia dropped down beside her. Gently, she placed her hand on her arm and patted her. "I'm sorry . . . so sorry.''

After discussing more sanely the events that had taken place that morning and speculating on what might have happened at the parish house — what part the *senhor prior* might have had — Maria Rosa washed her face and without disturbing the tight knot at the back of her head, tied on her kerchief. "I'm going back with you, to your house . . . where is everyone, I wonder. No visitors!''

However, they did meet some neighbors returning from the *Cova* who repeated what they already knew. By the time they reached the Marto house, the sun was already far into the west; and there in the yard, arms upraised, *Ti* Marto stood surrounded by other members of his family, several neighbors, and a few residents from Fatima and Moito.

"No, no," he was disagreeing. "Father Ferreira, I've decided, had no hand in this. Santos, I'm sure now, hatched the whole scheme before he ever showed his face here this morning. He had it all planned."

"Then why did Santos go to the parish house if Father Ferreira had nothing to do with it? He must have been in cahoots with the administrator!" The voices belonged to a group of youths who now stopped at the sight of Maria Rosa and Olimpia entering the yard.

"Manuel, Manuel!" Weeping openly, Olimpia threw herself into her husband's arms. "How did it happen? You don't think? — Maria Rosa is sure that he'll bring them back tonight."

"No, I don't think so, Mama." Olimpia's oldest son, Antonio, was running into the yard followed by two other young men about his age. "We just got back from Ourém. We saw Francisco and the two girls on the administrator's balcony; there were other children there, too, and when we shook our sticks — we wanted Santos to know how we all felt — a lady rushed out and took them all into the house."

"See, Mama? The children will be all right!" Her husband's voice rode high, but she heard a word break. "You'll see! Our Lady will keep them under her mantle. Some day we'll have the answers, but for now we must leave all in God's hands."

During this time Maria Carreira had been standing beside Maria dos Anjos who early that morning had regarded her with such crisp doubt. Now laying her hand lightly on Maria Carreira's arm, she declared, "*Ti* Manuel is right! Our Lady will take care of them. Look, just look, at what she did for us today!"

Immediately voices melded together. "When the children were supposed to come, the sun grew dim, a little cloud came and stood above the tree. There was a light, a flash of light — just like the children must see it!''

Maria Carreira closed her eyes, just as she had done when the sun had been in the middle of the heavens and she had leaned on the table, hearing the irate shouts turn into cries of wonder. At her husband's bidding she had opened her eyes and seen the delicate cloud, like fine lace, above the little tree, the beautiful petals of flowers falling and disappearing, even as others were crying, ''Look, the flowers.'' She opened her eyes now to see Maria dos Anjos waving to her mother who stood, face immobile and expressionless, on the periphery of the group. ''Mama, you should have been there,'' she called. ''When it was all over I saw an old man, a stranger. His hat was in his hand and he was bowing and bowing. He'd seen the flash of light, too, and all the colors everywhere — red, pink, blue — just like the rest of us. Why, even the lanterns on the arch were gold. 'It's a miracle,' the old man kept saying, 'a miracle!' ''

''To think that Our Lady would have done that, just for us!'' Ruefully shaking her head, Maria Carreira directed her words to Maria Rosa.

''You're all out of your heads, all of you crazy!'' The deep tones of Lucia's mother cut the air edged with miserable unbelief.

Chapter Fourteen

On Tuesday morning — around eleven o'clock — Santos brought the three children from his house to a room near his office, where a white-haired woman sat knitting at a table. Almost as wide as she was short, she bounced off the bench, a half-finished sweater in one hand, her light blue, red-rimmed eyes searching each one of the three.

"This one is Lucia, the one I was telling you about, and these two are the cousins." Santos pointed to each in turn. "You say you have such a way with little ones, so now let's see what you can do with these!" At the door he swung around, his forefinger pointed at Lucia. "Don't forget, young lady, what I've been telling you. You're not only going to jail, all three of you, *but* . . ." He emphasized the last word with a knowing look at the *senhora*, which was not lost on Francisco; he knew exactly what the administrator meant.

Last night and this morning he had repeatedly wheedled, coaxed, and shouted: "If you don't tell me everything, if you don't tell me that secret, you're going to be boiled in hot oil until you die."

"I've told you all I can," Lucia had answered tearfully, but it was Jacinta who cried most of the time calling over and over for Mama; yet the more she cried, the wilder Santos got. At one time he'd seen tears in his wife's eyes as she slipped her three children out of the room. She was pretty with soft black hair and creamy skin, and had been kind, urging them to eat, offering them her children's picture books with big

130

letters on them. When it was time for bed she had taken them
into the prettiest bedroom he'd ever seen — pale pink walls
trimmed in blue. Two shiny brass beds stood side by side but
there was no crucifix on the wall, no pictures of Jesus or
Mary or any saints, not anywhere. After they had knelt and
prayed, Jacinta had said, "How disappointed the Lady must
have been when she didn't see us today!" As if God didn't
tell His mother everything. And now who could this fat, fat
senhora with the round red lips be? Unlike the administrator,
she was speaking with a polite voice.

"Please sit down." With a plump hand she indicated the
bench on the opposite side of the table. She also sat, smiling
brightly from one to the other, clearing her throat with funny
little noises while opening a drawer where she replaced her
knitting with a narrow white box.

Jacinta began crying against Lucia's shoulder.

"You're not going to be afraid of me! I have little grandchildren just like you. All I want is to be your friend."

"But I want to see my mother," Jacinta sobbed.

"You will. Nothing is going to happen to you, not if you
tell me the truth. That's why I'm here, just to help you. All
you have to say is: 'We made it all up.' Just as easy as that,
and back to your Mama you go. Now, isn't that better than
going to a jail full of bad men?" Her voice had risen; she left
it in the air. She had no intention of adding any threats about
burning oil. Whatever had possessed His Highness to think
up a thing like that? She fussed with the satin covered box.
These children looked like they had been torn apart,
especially the little one.

"I know none of you wants to go to jail, but I'm afraid
the administrator really means it when he says that if you
don't confess . . . ? Come, be good children, and tell me.
Wasn't it all just a game, a lovely, lovely game? You thought:
'We'll pretend that there is lightning, then suddenly a beautiful lady all in white comes down from the sky. She stands
above a tree and tells us secrets!' I used to play like that when

I was a little girl. So do my grandchildren, all the time." The senhora's voice was sweet as jelly, but she was wheezing a little now and clearing her throat with those gravelly sounds as she waited. Her only answer came from the long swinging pendulum of the clock above. Her eyes narrowed. Not a word, not one word.

She was not a religious woman, but her instincts told her that what she saw in these impassive faces was something beyond her experience. A widowed mother of six, once a teacher and now a part-time secretary and matron of sorts, she had prided herself on having a good insight into the inner workings of human beings. "Let me try talking to them," she had urged Santos, full of self-confidence after hearing him out.

"She'll tell you about the lightning the first time they saw this lady, and — oh! — how beautiful she is, and that the rosary must be prayed. But damn it!" he had said bitterly, "through it all you can see she is lying, holding something back."

Holding something back. Right. These were poor children, unused to rings and trinkets. Right! Well, she was ready. Standing suddenly, the box in her hand, she opened it with an air of grandmotherly gusto. "Isn't it lovely?" she asked holding high a golden chain with a small heart-shaped locket. "Here, let me show you something." In her white cotton shoes she sped toward the window with that lightness of limb peculiar to many of the corpulent. "See how it shines in the sun! I wish I had it myself. You can have it if you just tell me . . ." She stood looking at the chain and openly admiring it; turning slightly she saw Jacinta, head up, now watching her with wide eyes. The little one *was* interested. This time walking slowly, she came toward her smiling, both hands spreading the chain. "Isn't it beautiful?"

"The Lady has a gold light around her mantle that's lots prettier than that!"

The *senhora* bit her rounded lip. A gold light, a gold light around the Lady. This was just too much. "Do you know there are guards here, right in this building — right now! — ready to take you to jail?" One hand indicated its proximity while the other dropped the chain into the box, snapped it shut and placed it in the drawer with the unfinished sweater.

"I'm not going to wait any longer. Lucia, are you going to say something or just sit there like a mummy, that sullen look on your face?" The words were angry ones, but the *senhora's* voice, like her face, had assumed a weary pathos that touched the heights of melancholy and brought a reluctant response from Lucia.

"We have seen a Lady." O Jesus, how many more times would she have to say that? "She does come from heaven, but we never played any kind of game, like you said."

"Perhaps it's not something this lady said to you, just something else that's holding you back? Some kind of secret?"

"I can't tell you." With that little furl of brow, the words came with a finality that sent the white-haired *senhora* to her quick feet. Stubborn, stubborn — like mules. Santos was right. The words "Will you still feel this way when you see that big tank of oil?" rushed to her lips, but shaking her head firmly she said, instead, "I suppose you would rather die than . . . ?" She was looking at Lucia, but it was the boy's voice she heard first.

"Yes!"

So he had finally opened his mouth. Considering him, she recalled Santos's earlier comment. "That boy is a clam; you won't get a word out of him." Well, she had — one; and it told her plenty. The natural redness of her face and neck deepened as she looked at the clock on the wall. All this time and nothing accomplished except that she knew for certain now that nothing *Senhor Santos* might dream up would do any good.

Folding her arms over her broad bosom she stared at

each one in turn. "Lucia, Francisco, Jacinta." Her red mouth formed each name deliberately. Her color began to subside, and with a chortle that seemed to rise from infinite depths, she whispered loudly, "Republic, Democracy, Liberty," names Artur de Oliveira Santos had given three of his children. That tinsmith! In spite of such high-falutin' names, she doubted those kids of Santos could ever stand up to this trio. But then who could? Shrugging her shoulders, she said, "Follow me."

They were on their way to jail. The jail, which was on the ground floor of the same building, seldom housed more than a dozen inmates — usually drunks and petty thieves. A few wooden benches stood against the walls. Here and there, time-worn blankets, like gray shrouds, hung from long nails. There were three windows with iron gratings; near one of these the three now sat on a bench, Lucia's arms tightly around Jacinta.

It was not their plight, nor the musty room, nor the stench of urine, the nauseous smell of unwashed bodies that most distressed Lucia. It was Jacinta. "You're going to be sick if you keep crying like this. I've told you over and over: Our Lady will take care of us."

"But we're going to die, and I want to see Mama and Papa first."

Edging past Lucia, Francisco whispered, "Look, Jacinta, all this we can offer up for sinners." He knew how she felt, really felt about that. She moved closer toward him, now nodding her head and wiping her nose with the back of her hand. Francisco's words weren't new, but he said them like he wasn't afraid, not of anything. He repeated them for her, his eyes encouraging her. "For poor sinners, Jacinta." She kept nodding, her eyes never leaving his. Our Lady, she knew, would take care of them just like Lucia said, but before she took her to heaven she did so much want to say goodbye to Mama and Papa. Dabbing at her face, now with the edge of her skirt, she said, "In reparation for sinners, and for the poor little Holy Father."

Recently, two priests had spoken to her about the Pope — his sorrow and concern for the Church, his deep compassion for all the people in the world, especially for those now in the agonies of a terrible war. Since then, filled with a new tenderness and regard for the Holy Father, she often spoke about him to the other two, reminding them that they should pray for him. "Why doesn't he come to see us?" she had asked Lucia one day. "Everybody else does."

The prisoners now watched her and her two companions with dull but inquisitive eyes. Most of them had slept off their wine. What was the world coming to when little kids could be locked up like this? Bearded and grimy, their dirty caps pushed down over their ears, they were for the most part vagrants — a ragged lot — with the exception of a handsome, black-haired young man. Nattily dressed, his narrow shoulders carried an arrogant head. Long before the key had rattled in the lock and the jailer had appeared with the three children, he had paced the cell, a lithe tiger, fuming at the squalor, the stinking smells, the sight of the slovenly figures sprawled on the floor. That he should be incarcerated with such *canaille* simply for getting caught at a jewelry store. In Oporto or Lisbon, but here in this second-hand town! If he ever got out of this mess, he'd clean his feet of this place but fast.

With a jaundiced eye he now observed the children. What tomfoolery could have brought in these three little idiots, but more to the point was: What kind of a damned fool had dragged them in?

"Whoever brought you here . . . ." He halted as he came closer.

Facing the window, the three stood close together. "Jesus, it is for your love, for the conversion of sinners, and in reparation for the sins committed against the Immaculate Heart of Mary."

"Hey! What kind of prayer is that? I never heard it

before." In fact, he had to admit that it was a long time since he had heard any prayer, or even said one.

They turned to him, eyes on guard. He lowered his head slightly, his blue-black eyes never wavering from them. "Come on, don't look at me like that! Can't you see we're all friends here," he said mockingly as two of the other prisoners padded toward them.

"How come?" one of them asked.

"What he wants to know," the tall young man said, his brows raised high at Lucia, is: Who put you into this stinking jail, and why?"

She hesitated, "Well, it's because . . ." She looked at the dark blue eyes still staring so hard at her. "It's because the administrator thinks we're lying."

"About what?" These poor kids looked half-dead on their feet, praying, frightened out of their wits, especially the one with such tiny hands and big eyes. He bent toward her. "What could a little thing like you be lying about?"

"It's about the Lady — the Lady in white . . ."

"The lady? In white? Oh, no! I'll be the son of a monkey with six fingers! I'll bet you're those three children down there at, at . . ."

"Fatima," one of the prisoners said. Most of the men had shuffled toward them, now fully witted. They were all acquainted with the story in one form or another.

"And you mean to tell me," the young man looked incredulous, "that you're in here because . . ."

"We won't tell the secret," Jacinta finished. "And he says if we don't, he's going to boil us in oil."

The men began to mutter and to swear, but with his long hands at his waist, the young man reared his head and gradually the big room filled with his laughter. This was the most preposterous thing he'd ever heard of.

"Listen, come over here beside me." He motioned to the three and gently sat Jacinta beside him. "Why don't you be smart and make up a secret — something to make that fox let you go. For instance, let me see — *sim!* — you could say that . . ." Three shaking heads stopped him.

"That would be a lie," Francisco told him.

For a long moment the young man studied the fine, sensitive face. He looked down, remembering. This boy reminded him of a picture of a Boy with a halo which had hung in his room when he was a child. The artist had almost caught this wide-eyed look of artless simplicity, but not quite. Ah, the word was innocence . . . untainted innocence. He looked up to find Francisco watching him.

"Did you really see a lady?"

"Yes."

"And was she Our Lady?"

"Yes."

Repressing a sigh, the young man stood. A rosary in her hand, Lucia was saying, "We're going to say the rosary now."

"Wait." Jacinta removed a silver chain with a medal from her neck and handed it to the handsome figure beside her. "On that nail, please." He took it from her, first examining the medal which on one side had a figure of Christ — the Sacred Heart — and on the other, one of the Virgin holding a scapular. He found himself on his knees as Lucia began: "In the name of the Father and of the Son and of the Holy Spirit."

They were all kneeling now on the rough floor, the men with their caps in their hands. Noticing that one of them had not removed his, Francisco rose from his knees, walked over to him and whispered, "*Senhor*, when you pray you should take off your hat."

"*Sim, sim!*" Sheepishly, the man dropped the old *carapuça* on the floor. Still standing beside him, Francisco lifted it and set it on a bench.

Heads bowed, they prayed, each decade of the rosary, each mystery recalling something they had forgotten: the tender love of the Christ and that of His Mother who had shared his joys and sorrows — from Bethlehem to Calvary. For most of the men the words brought a comforting meliorism and a nostalgic sweetness. For the young thief a trumpet had sounded.

At the last "Amen" he stood and with a harmonica at his mouth took Jacinta by the hand. "Let's dance!" He began whirling her around and as the music gathered speed, the prisoners clapped their hands and sang, their miseries for the moment forgotten. In the midst of a *fandango*, the key in the lock rattled and a serious-looking man with heavy brows the color of his brownish suit appeared at the door.

They had been in jail two hours.

An outraged Santos received them in his office. "You think this is a big, big joke! One moment you are dancing, the next you're dead cuckoos that can't hear, see, or sing. Well, you had better open your beaks because the time is here — right now!" Stuttering, he pounded his desk, nostrils distended, eyes wild and accusing at the pale exhausted faces before him. There was hardly a hair's breadth between the three. "I've given you, each one of you, every chance to speak up. And you, Lucia Santos," his hands slapped the desk noisily, "have admitted over and over that there is a secret, but, oh no! You can't tell it!" He turned to the guard at the door. "Is the oil ready?"

"Sim, senhor."

"You hear that, Lucia?"

She made no sound as her arm tightened around Jacinta.

"I'm warning you; this is your last chance."

In the silence that followed, Santos stood slowly, his sallow face tight. Pointing at Jacinta, he said softly, "Take her first."

The guard took her out of Lucia's arms.

Arms folded tightly, Santos walked to the table piled with copies of his *Ouriense*. Now that these two had seen the other one dragged off, it was just possible that they might finally talk. That stupid boy — hardly one word out of him in two days. What kind of children were these, anyway? No fear. Damn, anyway, he never thought the thing would go so far. Now, what? Whispering . . . perhaps . . . He waited.

"Don't cry," Francisco was whispering. Lucia's tears were heavy. "Francisco, Francisco — poor little Jacinta."

"Let's pray that she won't be scared, not too scared."

Santos turned on his heel to see Francisco getting to his knees.

"What are you doing?"

"I'm going to pray for Jacinta . . ."

"What kind of boy are you, anyway? Don't you have any feelings? Do you realize what's happening to your sister right now? Are you ready to die for some foolish secret?"

"I am."

"Take him out, right now!" Santos cried to the guard who had returned.

As Francisco left the room, Lucia took a step toward him, then half-fell into a chair, sobbing.

Santos came and stood over her. How was he ever going to explain this stubbornness, this steel in the spines of these unbelievable children, to his Republican compatriots, to his Masonic brothers? This girl was bright (although he doubted she could read the simplest words in his children's books) as both her speech and conduct at his house last night had convinced him. Education — that was what the country needed. He wished he had more — all that he had he had gotten himself. It was the young who must be taught to see that the Church was a tyrant, holding the peasants in slavery and ignorance, and always for its own glory. Always the Church, always the priests. If the "secret" would surface, the problem, he felt, would somehow resolve itself. At this point he wasn't sure he was going to resolve anything, but he'd give it another try. "Lucia . . ."

The guard turned a key and shoved Francisco into the same room where earlier the white-haired *senhora* had dangled the chain in front of Jacinta. Jacinta was clinging to him, and now for the first time he let the tears fall, too, as she kept saying over and over, "Francisco, Francisco." Finally stepping away, her back against the door, she looked pointedly at him. "You know something? There's no kettle of oil in here!"

"You, you mean . . ." His eyes shifted from hers to the wall clock now chiming the half hour. He felt a little sick, kind of, all over. Slowly, he walked over to the empty table, turned toward her and slumped on the bench. "Maybe, Francisco, he's just trying to fool us!"

He nodded cautiously. "Maybe." But he'd been sure the administrator had meant every word. Last night at his house he had even told them that the caldron was much bigger than a wash tub.

Jacinta broke into his misgivings. "Is Lucia? . . ."

"She was there with him when I left."

Crumpling to the floor, Jacinta burst into tears. "Maybe we won't see her again. You and me, soon, Our Lady said, but not Lucia!"

He had thought of that, too. He got up and walked toward her when she jumped up, a hand to the door. "Someone is coming!" They both stood frozen as heavy steps and low voices approached, tarried at the door, then gradually receded.

In a quivering voice barely above a whisper, Jacinta asked, "Did you hear *that*?"

"*Sim!*"

"There is no oil! 'The trick isn't working.' That's what they said!"

They still didn't move, but now Jacinta no longer looked like his sick little sister who had wept wells of tears to see Mama. A boundless relief colored her wet cheeks; and she was smiling at him from shadowed eyes, the first time she had smiled since the horse had galloped away from the parish house, leaving Papa out in the road, his arms empty in the air.

Kneeling beside her, he asked, "Were you terribly afraid? I mean when the guard took you out."

"I was so afraid I couldn't even pray, but I would die before telling the secret."

"I prayed for you."

"Francisco! Well, now let's pray for Lucia."

They had hardly begun when the lock turned, the door opened, and there she stood with that little worry frown on her face and tears on her cheeks.

———————

Chapter Fifteen

It was now Wednesday, August 15. The Mass of Our Lady's Assumption was over, but the sweet scent of incense still lingered in Saint Anthony's Church as white-vested acolytes extinguished candles that sent soft white smoke through the sanctuary and around the altars on both sides of the darkened church. Sober-clad women and children, the usual occupants of the rough unsteady benches at the front, filed out under the vigilant eyes of their patron saint, Anthony of Padua, preeminently encased in glass at the right of the main altar. His brown habit was simple, in marked contrast to the other Franciscan nearby — the poor little Saint Francis of Assisi whose habit was gold-trimmed, suggesting that his earthly poverty had been rewarded in heaven. At the rear of the church, departing men and boys, who had stood for most of the Mass, made hasty signs of the cross and kissed their thumbs.

One man alone remained on his knees. No matter how hard he had tried to unite himself to the Sacrifice taking place on the altar, his thoughts had splintered wildly. Two days, an eternity, since the children had been snatched right before his eyes. A hundred times he'd blamed himself for that. But today on Our Lady's Feast she would bring them back safely, despite the rumor that they had been whisked off to Santarém, a small city to the south. A rumor it had to be. Had not their Antonio seen them at play on the administrator's balcony? But then that had been shortly after their abduction. And Santos? How would he treat the children? The way he had lashed out at a mere child. But these were not mere ordinary children. Only a few days before he and his brother-in-law had been summoned to Ourém, he recalled being awakened about one o'clock in the morning by a faint muffled crying. Stealing away from Olimpia's side, he had cautiously lighted a candle and on the tips of his feet, followed the stifled sounds into Francisco's room where he had found him sobbing under the coverlet.

"Francisco, tell me, what's wrong?" Through the light quilt his hand had felt the long shudder as the weeping had ceased, and by candlelight he had seen the face wet with tears.

"I didn't want anyone to hear me."

Hearing the pain which the words could not hide, he had sat on the bed. "What is it? Can you tell me?"

"I was thinking . . ."

"Yes?"

"About Jesus . . ."

"You were dreaming?"

"No . . . I feel so sorry for Him . . . so many, many sins."

"That is true," he had whispered, not knowing what to say, how to comfort his son. Back in bed again his eyes had not closed. That a boy only nine years old . . .

He saw now that Father Ferreira was already kneeling at the prie-dieu in the sanctuary, making his thanksgiving. A few women knelt before the big altar of the Sacred Heart, others before a statue of Mary clad in crimson and blue-mantled, a serious-looking Child in one arm. Noting that most of the worshippers had left as well as his own Olimpia whose tears hardly ever stopped, he made a deep genuflection to the Blessed Sacrament. He stood quietly gazing at the gold tabernacle door. Moments passed. He was smiling as he stepped into the church yard to be greeted by cries from a large crowd. Most of them were from hamlets throughout the parish who during the summer months made a social event of

Mass days, visiting and eating their lunches around their carts.

"*Ti* Marto," some of them called now. "*Ohla* — up there on the *senhor prior's* stairs. The children are back!"

Mounting the steps swiftly, he caught Jacinta in his arms and "kissed her with his tears," as he said later. "When did the three of you get back?"

"Just now," Francisco answered. "Your blessing, Papa."

"Your blessing, *Ti* Manuel."

His arms had room for them all. "You're all right?" They nodded. "Thank God. Who brought you back?"

"The administrator," Jacinta answered. Pointing beyond the threshold to a slight man hovering in the shadows beside Father Ferreria's sister, she added, "He did, too." The small man came to the door. "They're fine, as you can see," he said nervously, his eyes fluttering from *Ti* Marto toward the crowd below.

Suddenly, as if all the winds from the *serra's* perimeter had converged on the area fronting the garden below, words snapped and crackled. A group of youths, some of whom had been present in *Ti* Marto's yard on late Monday afternoon, were swinging sticks and yelling. "The *senhor prior* is in this thing as much as Santos. Both of them. The government has no right to steal children from their parents." The crowd which only a moment before had been tearfully waving and endearingly throwing kisses at the heartwarming reunion of *Ti* Marto and the children was now spleenful with angry words. "The boys are right. The *senhor prior* must have had something to do with it!"

His thanksgiving interrupted by the shouting and loud talk, Father Ferreira pushed his way through his parishoners and at the head of the stairs confronted *Ti* Marto with stony eyes. "You are a scandal, *Senhor* Marto, exciting the people against me like this. You surprise me."

"You surprise me, too, *senhor prior*. You're mistaken.

I've had nothing to do with what is going on down there, not that I blame those boys much, especially when they see that the children are back to the same spot from which they were carried off. You can't argue with that!" Stepping down two treads, he called at the top of his voice, "Boys, boys! Listen to me. Stop raving against the *senhor prior*, against the government, the administrator. Whose fault it may be, the fault has been permitted from on high. The children are back and well — thank God for that! So do the favor of saying no more!" In the silence that followed he looked up to see Father Ferreira now at an open window.

"*Senhor* Marto speaks well." He waved a hand toward his congregation as a man wearing a hard straw hat ascended the stairs.

"Ah, *Senhor* Marto!" Santos spread out his hands in good will. "I'm afraid I am always surprising you, but you can see for yourself how well the children are. No hard feelings, right? How about a glass of wine to celebrate this happy homecoming?"

"That isn't necessary."

Now recognizing Santos, the crowd began murmuring; and again the boys brandished their clubs.

"Look. I've changed my mind. I'll have that glass of wine, after all." Stepping closer to the administrator, *Ti* Marto motioned to the three children. "You'd better go home; I'll be along very soon." Walking beside Santos, he followed the children down the stairs, gave a friendly wave to the boys uncertainly watching. With an occasional nod to everyone, he proceeded with his gesturing companion to the tavern at the edge of the square close to the cemetery.

Inside, they went into a dark, partly enclosed room, set with a square table and four chairs. Santos laid his hat on the chair beside him. "Bread and cheese with the wine," he told the bald man cheerlessly regarding him. As soon as they were alone, he moved his chair closer. "I hope you weren't worried. We took very good care of the children. Sometimes the Republic has to take things into its own hands, for the good of the people."

"For the good of the people!" *Ti* Marto's face stiffened. "That was a terrible thing to do, a terrible thing."

Santos looked pained. "Now, *Senhor* Marto . . ."

"That's right, and the only reason I sit here with you is that it's hard to say what those boys might have done . . ."

"Those boys? Forget them! I have something far more interesting to talk about, to tell you." Waving off the straight-faced but curious man lingeringly setting a tray between him and *Ti* Marto, he filled their two glasses. Drinking thirstily, he shuddered. "Awful!" but he continued to drink. *Ti* Marto looked on, his own glass untouched.

"*Senhor* Marto, I was about to tell you how open the children were with me." He smiled, running the heavy ring around his finger. "Of course, I'm sure my good wife helped the cause; she was very good to them. But — now hold your chair! They told me their whole story, even the secret!" Mistaking the sudden gleam in the other's eyes, Santos threw back his head. "I'm glad you are as pleased as I was. Now you and I, without any rancor, can discuss the whole matter openly." There were more ways than one to pluck a goose.

Ti Marto shook his head in disbelief. "You never give up, do you? Why, those children would die first before ever telling their secrets — to you, to anybody, even to their own parents."

Santos leaned back in his chair and except for the hardening line around his mouth there was no change in the feline face. Die first . . . he ought to know that better than anyone else. He poured himself another glass of wine.

Walking out of the tavern — the crowd had thinned out by now — they saw Santo's buggy waiting, the little man in the driver's seat.

"I'll take you home," Santos said stiffly.

"*Obrigado*, but I've got to make a stop at the post-office.''

Although it was within easy walking distance, Santos began to argue. His face was puffed, his speech bitter. "You're afraid to ride with your own administrator, even to the post-office."

"Very well, but just do me the favor of leaving me right there; my feet can take me the rest of the way." Getting into the back seat, he heard a passer-by cry out, "Now the administrator is running away with *Ti* Marto!"

That day at *Ti* Marto's house the mood was one of ebullience at having Francisco and Jacinta home again. However, as the story unfolded about their confinement in the Ourém jail, the threats of death by hot oil, the reaction became one of resentment, horror, and incredulity at the knowledge that even in pretense Santos could have tortured the children so cruelly.

"To think that he had the bloody gall to sit at that table, gabbing about how well he had treated them, even wanting to take me home," *Ti* Marto declared, pulling hard at the lobe of his ear. It occurred to him as he saw a new respect in the eyes of Florinda and Teresa and the boys that this ugly kidnapping business might be bearing fruitful seeds. They had learned that their brother, sister, and cousin had been ready to die for their "secret." Nobody was ever willing to die for nothing. He was not so sure of his Olimpia, not yet. Right now she was like a mother hen — overwrought and overjoyed at the return of her two little chicks.

At Lucia's house the reaction was different. It was not that the family was not glad to have her back. It was the disappointment, vigorously expressed by her mother and echoed by her father, that the administrator had failed to solve the mystery. In this climate of little sympathy, Lucia's account, unlike Jacinta's vivid one, came haltingly, unconvincingly. There were, however, two exceptions: her married sisters, Maria dos Anjos and Teresa, both of whom had been witnesses of the marvels at the *Cova da Iria* on the day of the children's abduction.

On Sunday afternoon, August 19, four days after they had returned from Ourém, Lucia stopped at the Martos' with her sheep. That morning after Mass, she and Francisco and Jacinta had been invited to lunch with her sister Teresa and her husband, thus postponing the pasturing to the unusual hours of afternoon. Now, instead of Jacinta, it was João who appeared in the driveway with Francisco and their small band of sheep. "Jacinta can't go," he sang out. "Mama wants her to go somewhere, but here I am! Where are you going?"

"*Valinhos.*"

"Good." He knew that *Valinhos* was a fun place where you could play "hide-out" games and everything. It was riddled with rocks and full of crumbling stone walls, some higher than a man. It belonged to one of Lucia's uncles and was near Aljustrel. From it you could go down, down, wall after wall, to the foot of the *cabeço*.

The day was one of those rare pleasant ones in August, a short interlude between much hotter days. The air felt almost cool, and the brooding quiet of the *serra* reflected the serenity of the distant mountains, the pure blue cloudless sky above. They strolled along, sometimes sitting on rocks while the sheep browsed, for now the grass was stubby and brown. At one time, João had been happy to waive his responsibility of sheep-tending; today he was equally happy to go along with Francisco and Lucia. Silent, for the most part, they listened to his chatter. Had João been Jacinta, the talk would have been very different, as it always was when they were alone.

"Did you know," João asked Lucia now as Francisco lingered behind, "that your father and Maria de Capelina had a big rumpus in the churchyard this morning?"

Lucia shook her head at him. There had been no rumpus. She had been right there beside Papa, singing high inside because Papa had gone to Mass. He had looked so good and so handsome, his speech low as he had talked with Maria Carreira. Papa . . . She loved him dearly and always prayed for him. Sometimes he got very red and talked angrily, but he never spanked her.

"Maria de Capelina told your father she'd heard that he didn't like her in the *Cova* . . ."

"Listen . . ."

"And then Uncle Antonio said, 'You can pick all the flowers you like there, but just don't go building any chapels!' " João's white teeth flashed in a big smile. That was just the way the neighbor had said it.

Lucia shook her head again. It was true that Papa had said that, but she'd heard the teasing behind the words, even when he had added, "I hear that you are finding much money on my property."

"I don't know what to do with it," Maria had answered. "Nobody wants it!"

"Neither do I."

It was then that Maria Carreira had turned to her. "Don't forget to ask the Lady next month about the money?"

This morning she had promised her again. Next month.

It was about four o'clock when they reached *Valinhos*. They turned into the narrow wagon road shadowed by a row of old olive trees beside a stone wall with a wide gap. A few feet away, growing in a narrow fissure of stone stood an *azinheira* with dark green leaves, a little taller and fuller than the stripped one in the *Cova*. One behind another, the sheep went passed it on to the rocky pasture, when abruptly, the turquoise blue sky and the gentle quietness of the day altered and became dead silent. The air grew cooler, the sunlight less bright — as if time had suddenly stopped. Beside the *azinheira*, Francisco exchanged a quick glance with Lucia. "The Lady!"

She nodded vigorously.

"What's happening?" João's black eyes were wide with excitement.

Lucia was at his side. "Quick, João, run fast as you can. Get Jacinta; the Lady is coming."

"Are you sure?"

"*Sim* — the signs!" Lucia thrust her hand into her pocket. "I'll give you two pennies, one now and one when you get back. Hurry!"

"No, no, I won't go. I might miss her."

"João, you run so fast; get Jacinta. Please!" She pressed the penny into his hand and pushed him.

He sped, never stopping. "Mama," he yelled at the back door. "Lucia wants Jacinta right now!"

"What for?"

"Where is she? Lucia gave me a penny to get her."

"What's this all about?"

"The Lady is coming — to *Valinhos*. We saw the signs . . ."

"Now you tell me. She's at her godmother's."

As soon as João and Jacinta reached the break in the rocks where the *azinheira* grew and where Francisco and Lucia waited, the three immediately saw the flash followed by the light which always preceded the Lady.

In a moment she was there, beautiful and very real in brilliant whites above the green branches. She hadn't waited for next month! Her arms were out to them, eyes so soft and tender, telling them how pleased she was with their love and courage which had not once faltered, even when they were faced with death.

In less time than would take to say twenty or twenty-five Hail Marys, the Lady answered Lucia's questions and gave her own message.

PRAY MUCH AND MAKE SACRIFICES FOR SINNERS. MANY GO TO HELL BECAUSE THERE ARE

NONE TO PRAY FOR THEM OR TO MAKE SACRIFICES.

Yes, as she had promised before, she would make a miracle in October so that those present would believe. Some of the sick would be cured within the year. The money should be used for the Feast of Our Lady of the Rosary, for processions in which the three would take part. The rest could go toward the building of a chapel. In October, Our Lord would be present — blessing the world. Saint Joseph and the Child Jesus would also appear.

She was moving away. The fading afternoon sun now bleached silver the olive trees and scattered its shadows over a thousand variegated rocks. Seeing the enraptured faces of the others, João wailed. "I never saw anything. I looked and looked — like this." He stretched his eyes wide. "But I never saw her."

"You know something, João," Jacinta said. "The Lady knew I couldn't go to the *Cova* last time, so here she comes to *Valinhos*," she pointed to herself, "and even waited for me to get here. If *you* hadn't come after me . . ." Her finger was now pointing at him.

"You wouldn't have seen her!"

Jacinta nodded and turned to the tree, arms raised. "Help me. I want to take this branch home — the top one — where she stood."

Neither Francisco nor Lucia tried to stop her.

Moments later, Jacinta and Francisco left the other two. Nearing home, Jacinta said, "Let's go to Aunt Maria's first." They found her in the parlor with visitors, including Maria dos Anjos and her baby.

"Aunt Maria! We saw Our Lady again; this time at *Valinhos*."

"So! Our Lady appears to you wherever you go."

"See this branch? Her feet were right above it."

"Come here, let me see." Maria Rosa reached for it, touched the leaves to her nose. "Um . . . What kind of fragrance is this? It's not perfume, not violets, not roses." She

took a deep breath. "No, but it's a beautiful smell. Try it."
She passed the branch around. The others also commented
on the unusual fragrance and like Maria Rosa were unable to
identify it. "No *azinheira* ever smelled like that!" Maria dos
Anjos exclaimed, putting the baby on the floor.

"Jacinta?" Chin in hand, Maria Rosa regarded her
young niece thoughtfully. "You say . . ."

"*Sim*! It's the very one she stood on. Wasn't it, Francisco?"

He nodded.

"Why don't you leave it here?" Aunt Maria Rosa
asked. "Maybe someone will come along who can tell us
what this smell is." She laid the branch on the table; and as
soon as her back was turned, Jacinta snatched it and ran,
Francisco close behind her.

Scooting uphill, Jacinta laughed over her shoulder.
"You know something, Francisco? Aunt Maria Rosa is beginning to believe us."

"I don't know about that. Tell me, what did the Lady
say today?"

They had come to the great big rock across the road
from home. Looking at the small green branch in her hand,
Jacinta said quietly, "She wants us to pray very much, to
make sacrifices for sinners. Lots of them go to hell, she said,
because no one prays for them, nobody sacrifices for them."

Chapter Sixteen

Toward the last of August, Lucia set out early one morning with her sheep. Tomorrow they were to be sold — they had to be! There was a lump in her throat, not only for their loss—each one was so special!—but for the parting words which had become a daily reminder of her transgressions. "Too bad you didn't choose *Valinhos* for your tricks instead of the *Cova*," her mother had scolded. "At least there's not much the devil could hurt there."

"I'm sorry, Mama," she had answered, as usual.

"Does that bring our bread back, the sheep that have to go tomorrow? You've turned this world upside down. No wonder Father Ferreira wants to leave."

After giving directions for a pasture which was far off and one which a neighbor had offered for the day, her mother had cautioned, "Stay under the trees when you get there. Today is going to be a scorcher; better not come back until sundown." Then at the door: "You don't have to worry about visitors today, which is a lot more than I can say for myself. Here, don't forget your *merenda*—what there is of it."

The snack, what there was of it, would go to the poor children from Moito who probably would already be waiting for her at the pond. There were three of them, sometimes four. They were the ones who had given them the answer to Jacinta's questions: "What can we do? What can we offer up? What sacrifices can we make?"

"How about our lunches?" Francisco had asked. "We could give them to the sheep."

Instead, they had given them to the raggedy children with begging hands; and when their own hunger got too bad, they ate seeds and roots—things like that. As for Father Ferreira wanting to leave: it wasn't only Mama who blamed her for that but most of the parish. This *senhor padre* worked hard, they said, visited the sick regularly, helped the poor, gave good sermons. Even though he called her a liar, she was sorry that he wanted to leave because of her. She was sorry, too, that she just couldn't like him. Maybe if she could tell him more than she had, but what?

There was too much that couldn't be told. Russia, for one thing. In the war was it on the side of England and France where Portuguese boys were fighting to keep out the Germans? That's why her brother Manuel said he wanted to go even though he said it was the biggest war the world had ever seen. So many countries. Yet the Lady had told her that unless people prayed and did penance there would be another war, even bigger and much worse. Russia would spread her teachings so that many nations would be destroyed. She remembered everything the Lady had told her about that—and everything else!—on the day when they had seen hell at her feet. Some of those things she had talked over with Jacinta and Francisco. Not that he asked any questions about it. He was waiting for just one thing—waiting in that light that had gone straight up to heaven. Jacinta had been in it too, but then Jacinta always wanted to know everything. As for herself—she was tied to the earth, but waiting, too . . . for many things. "When you see a light . . . I shall come to ask for the consecration of Russia to my Immaculate Heart . . ."

She was now almost to the Carreira pond. "Lucia, Lucia . . . " It was the poor children from Moito; today there were four of them.

At this same hour, Olimpia was breaking bread and slicing cheese for a bigger *merenda* than usual. "That pasture is a long long ways off," she told Francisco and Jacinta. "Keep out of the sun as much as you can today. I hope the girls and I can get the washing done without someone dropping in. Do you know," her thumb pointed in the direction of the out-house, "that sometimes there's not even time to get out there and . . ." Her voice rose but glancing up and seeing the two pair of eyes quietly watching her, she stopped, her words suddenly soft.

"I know you're both sorry, like Lucia, that this is your last day with the sheep, but it's just too much trouble forever sending someone out to find you."

"Then why do you?" Francisco's eyes regarded his mother warmly. "We don't have to come home."

"You mean when all these priests keep saying. 'Do the favor,' I should say no?" She stared at him, then began to laugh. Her eyes rolled upward as she glanced at the trap door above. "Sometime when you're up there, I might just let one of those fancy visitors take a peek at you! Ah, you thought I didn't know." She pinched his cheek lightly.

When Francisco and Jacinta arrived at the big pond, they found Lucia with the four children, their eager hands out as usual. As soon as the sheep had finished drinking, the trio led them across country mounded with outcrops of rock and scatterings of trees which grew a little fuller as they finally turned into a narrow road. In its crook stood a small stone house. They went past it into a field spotted with oaks and sparsely covered with short yellowing grasses.

"Crickets and, and frogs!" Jacinta wiped the sweat from her face with the back of her arm as the sheep breathing fast hurried toward a shallow pool. It was covered with brown algae, but the sheep lapped the water thirstily.

"That water doesn't look too bad." Jacinta moistened her lips.

"My mother says that we should never drink from the Carreira pond," Lucia told her, "and this one looks worse."

Silently, they watched as if they had never seen sheep drink. Sometimes, little children without their clothes played in the Carreira pond, Francisco thought, and even drank from it. He'd seen them do it lots of times . . . He swung away. "Look." He pointed to a tallish tree. "Let's go over there." Without another glance at the water, they ran toward the oak as if it might suddenly disappear. "It's shady here," Francisco said, even though the hot sun spilled down through the branches thick with acorns. Listless, they sat close to the trunk of the tree. Finally, Lucia brought out her rosary.

They prayed slowly, even slower between the decades: "O my Jesus, forgive us our sins, save us from the fire of hell, take all souls to heaven, especially those most in need."

On finishing they sat mesmerized by the sheets of heat waving before them, the monotonous chirping of the crickets and the occasional outrage of frogs.

"Water . . ." Jacinta said suddenly. "My mouth . . ."

It was so unlike her that Lucia jumped up, noting for the first time the flushed face and strange glassy look. "That little house—I'll go there and get some water." She was looking at Francisco now; his face was deeply flushed, too, the eyes glazed like Jacinta's. The heat must have . . . "Wait, I'll be right back."

A slight, stooped old woman with snow-white hair met her at the door. "Good, good!" She rubbed her arthritic gnarled hands together. "Come in," she said with a toothless smile that lit a mask of wrinkles. "What is your name?"

"Lucia."

"Lucia? I saw the three of you go by with the sheep. You're not, are you? . . ." The trembling old voice stopped, uncertain and hesitant, as if its owner had forgotten what to say. She shook her head sadly. "Sometimes I just can't remember. Ah, yes, don't drink that water out there; it's bad. Wait, I'll get you some." From a low shelf she took a cup and small jug half filled with water.

Lucia reached out for the jug. "I'd like this for my cousins. I'll be right back."

"You're not leaving already? Wouldn't you like something to eat? A piece of bread . . ."

"No, thank you. I've got to go."

The old woman came close, looked at the wet bangs and rubbed her hand lightly on Lucia's arm. "Why, you're sweating all over. I wish . . ." She smiled apologetically trying to recall that wish.

"Drink this, Francisco." He had left the tree to meet her.

"I can't."

"Why not?"

He countered: "What did the Lady tell you to say before making a sacrifice?"

"O Jesus, it is for your love, for the conversion of sinners, and in reparation for the sins committed against the Immaculate Heart of Mary."

He nodded.

"You've already offered it up! But it's not right if you're going to be sick . . ."

"I'm all right now—Jacinta, too. It was just sitting there like sticks hearing those crickets and frogs."

Lucia tried to hand Jacinta the jug. "No." She turned her head. "If only sinners could see hell . . . if only they could see it like we did!"

Lucia swallowed, wetting her lips. Her mouth was dry and every bit of her thirsted for that water. With the jug still half full, she retraced her steps to the house. When she returned she saw Jacinta doubled on her heels, her hands clasped tightly over her ears and Francisco sitting nearby with his head in his hands.

"What? . . ." She had stayed too long with the lonely old one. Laying her hand on Jacinta's shoulder, she asked, "What's the matter?"

"My head, oh, my head — it's bursting! Can't you tell those crickets and frogs to stop?"

"Now how can she do that?" Francisco was eyeing the girls through his fingers. Inside, his head was flip-flopping. With a crooked smile he came to his feet and went to Jacinta. He took her hands in his. "Get up. Come on. Don't . . . don't you want to . . ."

"Suffer for sinners? You know I do. Let the old crickets and frogs sing!"

Several days later, already into September, they came by *Valinhos* on their way to the *cabeço*. There on the wagon road, Lucia found a rope which she began winding around her arm. "Ouch!" She looked at it thoughtfully. Here was something extra. "You know," she said half to herself, "what this would be good for?"

"What?" Jacinta asked.

"We could tie it around our waists under our shirts. Wouldn't that make a good . . ."

"It would!" Immediately, Jacinta's hand was on the rope.

"Make what?" Only half listening, Francisco had been studying the braided hemp. A lot of things he could do with it.

"Make a good sacrifice." The rope, about two yards long, was now in Jacinta's hands. "We'll tie it around our waists—underneath—like this."

He watched as she took one end to demonstrate. "It will have to be cut three ways." He was squatting on the ground hunting for a sharp stone.

As soon as they had tied on their cords, Jacinta declared, "I'm going to wear mine all the time, even when I go to bed, but I won't let anybody see it."

"That's right! If they knew," Lucia said with a grimace, "they'd be sure to want to know what else . . ."

Francisco gave a long shudder.

"Is the rope hurting you, Francisco?" Jacinta had both hands at her waist. Hers felt pretty scratchy.

"No." But he could already hear some of those grand

senhoras if they got wind of some of the things they did. He shook his head.

"Tell Lucia about those ladies yesterday," Jacinta said.

"I was just thinking about them."

"Tell about the one with the beaded purse."

"Oh, I thought she had a chicken feather in her hat!"

They laughed, and Francisco walked on.

"I'll tell Lucia, if you don't," Jacinta called.

"Well . . ." Jacinta would be able to tell the story a lot better than he ever could. Throwing a rock in a straight line toward the *cabeço,* he turned toward them. "Little boy, would you like to be a carpenter when you grow up?" His voice wasn't sounding a bit like the *senhora's.*

"A carpenter?" Lucia was frowning, both hands at her waist. Maybe she'd tightened the rope too much.

"That's what she asked him," Jacinta cut in. "And holding his head very straight, like this," Jacinta's nose tilted upwards, "Francisco said, 'No, *senhora,* I don't want to be a carpenter.'" She dragged the "no," trying to make her voice rough and trembly like Francisco's.

Loosening the cord a little, Lucia laughed merrily as Francisco now took up the story. "Do you want to be a soldier, a doctor?"

Again Jacinta interrupted. One arm high, the fingers daintily curved, as if holding the senhora's black beaded purse, she raised her eyebrows. "Ah, I know, I know, little boy. You want to be a priest!"

Suddenly the light mood changed. Wordless, they sauntered up a sharp incline, past a stoop of stone; and as the two girls followed Francisco up the hill, Lucia said in a low voice, "What did Francisco say when the *senhora* asked him if he wanted to be a priest?"

There was no mimicry as Jacinta said simply, "I don't want to be anything," he said, "I just want to go to heaven."

A beautiful quietness hung over the *cabeço*; a panorama of hills and valleys had turned overnight into autumnal

shades of red, orange, and bright yellows. September 13 was
not far off.

———————

Chapter Seventeen

"Do you know it's way after midnight?" Olimpia moaned, turning her back to her husband as he got into bed beside her.

Nobody knew better than he. Throughout the day, from the time the sun was up and long after it was down, their house had never been empty; sometimes with a few of the rich but most of the time with the poor who at this very moment were settling themselves for the rest of the night in the *Cova da Iria*—just as they had done back in August. "But thousands more this time," he said aloud. "This afternoon Fatima was packed with every kind of rig . . ."

"I know! bicycles, automobiles, and even mules!" Olimpia's voice was icy.

"Plenty are walking; shoes, blankets, and the good Lord knows what else on their heads and backs. They've come from the coast, from everywhere. I met a young newspaper fellow from Lisbon who told me . . ."

"I'm dead tired," Olimpia said over her shoulder. It wasn't like him to be so wordy at bedtime. "I'm sure, Manuel, that all these 'thousands' including your newspaper fellow were in this house today! I can tell you I'm not looking forward to tomorrow. How did this ever happen to us?"

"I've wondered the same thing myself lots of times," her husband answered quietly. He laid his arm lightly over her and kissed her cheek. "Good night, Olimpia."

Her hand tightened on his. Good night? Why, it was already Thursday. Wide awake and weary no longer, her eyelids fluttered. She must get some sleep. She had hardly dozed off when she heard her husband's feet on the floor. Well, she hadn't slept a wink and now it was time to get everyone up. Like a race of some kind—trying to get everything done before the callers began knocking.

Many came, but the prime concern of thousands was to find a location that would give them a view of the phenomenon they had traveled so far to see. The September weather was perfect, mild and pleasant; the hills and valleys muted with a mellow fruitfulness and a quiescence presaging winter. In another month or so, heavy rains would strike, but now the grapes were sweet and ready for harvest; olives, rich and ripening; fields of gourds, squash, and yellow-red pumpkins lay beside their crisp prickly vines.

In the Marto kitchen, the big hand of the clock moved swiftly toward eleven o'clock. At the door, Francisco and Jacinta poised for flight and dressed in their best clothes, waited. Unlike other occasions they were to be escorted to the *Cova da Iria* today by their families; even Lucia would be accompanied by her mother and father. Why not? If the whole of Portugal was descending into their fields, Maria Rosa asserted bluntly, it mattered little if she and her family were now to do the same. She certainly had no intention of hiding under her skirt as she had in July.

Impatiently tugging at her braids as she saw Teresa rush past with an armful of wet clothes, Jacinta exclaimed, "Francisco! We ought to go right now. I wish . . ."

"What?"

"That Mama could see the Lady today!"

And Papa, too, Francisco thought, hearing him call: "Come on—everybody! If we don't leave now, we may not make it with all these crowds."

It was a wonder that they ever got to the *Cova* on time. From every knoll, from stone walls, and even from tree tops the cries came: "*Por favor*. Please, please ask Our Lady to bring back my son from the war . . . my daughter cured of blindness . . ." Beseeching hands caught their clothes. Sometimes in an attempt to cleave a passage, *Ti* Marto carried Jacinta in his arms, finally aided by three men who forcibly pushed back the supplicants on the trail not only with their arms but with their sharp tongues.

On the wide slope, with a commanding view of the *Cova* stood four men. One of them was Monsignor João Quaresma, Vicar General of the diocese of Leira. Another was his close friend, Monsignor Manuel Gois. Both priests, accompanied by Father Manuel Silva from Leira and the pastor from Santa Catalina had left Leira at dawn. More in a spirit of adventure than one of faith they had set off in a rusty buggy driven by a gaunt old horse.

"Did you ever see so many people?" Monsignor Quaresma reddened with the effort to make himself heard. "Where have they all come from?" On a knoll below him a little girl dressed in a pink dress and wearing a bonnet to match, smiled shyly at him from her father's shoulder.

"They've come from everywhere!" Monsignor Gois shouted back. "Lucky to get this spot. Look, João, down there, near that arch. Something is going on!"

It was more a nervous flurry than a melee, caused by the arrival of the children and their families. Amid tense cries: "Move back, move back," Lucia had managed to get close to the tree. Drawing Francisco and Jacinta to her side, she knelt and with her head turned slightly to the right, began to say the rosary. Those around her took on the words. Many tried to kneel as a crescendo of voices — thousands — arose with Ave Marias resounding under a tranquilly blue sky and a sun bright but only pleasurably warm.

At the last "Amen," Monsignor Quaresma, rosary still between his fingers, eyes closed, felt a quick pull at his sleeve. "João — up there!" Monsignor Gois pointed toward the east.

Raising his head — a vast silence had fallen over the throng — Monsignor Quaresma saw under the cloudless, incredibly blue sky a lighted globe, very large, gliding slowly. His eyes followed the gleaming sphere until it reached the area directly above the *azinheira* where it suddenly disappeared. Quickly, he turned to his fellow priests, unable to voice the tumult within him. Everywhere cries broke the deadly quiet of a moment ago. "What was that?" he finally managed.

"Our Lady!' Monsignor Gois shouted.

"You saw! . . ."

"No, just the big globe — shining, luminous . . ."

Words stilled, and over the crowd a silence again fell, intensified by the fading light and cooling breeze which occurred at each appearance of the Lady. Every neck was craned toward one spot. Minutes went by, but not many, for this visit would be the shortest. Monsignor Quaresma felt it had ended when he heard the little girl in pink cry out from her father's shoulder, "Papa — the shining ball! See? It's going up, up. Now it's gone!" No matter how hard they tried, neither Papa, nor the priests, nor those around them were able to see the globe this time.

At the tree, Lucia was on her toes, a finger pointed high. "If you want to see her, look up there!"

Although only those who were near heard her words, a multitude that had been voiceless for the brief time the children had knelt and stood, now came alive. I know I saw it! What could it have been! A huge ball like that — full of light. Did you see it disappear above the tree? But how?

Some seminarians home for vacation went through the crowds. "Did you *see* the globe? How did it look to you?" They found one woman weeping; she had seen nothing. They came to a tall, distinguished-looking man speaking with Monsignor Quaresma and his friends. He was the Reverend Doctor Manuel Nunes Formigão, canon of the cathedral in

Lisbon and also a teacher at the Seminary of Santarém. He definitely had seen no globe of any kind, shape, or form.

"I was about two hundred yards from the children," he declared, thoughtfully stroking his short beard, "and the only thing I did notice as people called out and pointed to the sky was a peculiar dimming of light which I attributed to natural phenomenon." He lifted heavy brows. "You say you saw this globe — you were all standing together?" His sober eyes questioned each priest in turn. They all nodded affirmatively.

"I . . . I can't help thinking . . ." He didn't finish the sentence. Mass suggestion . . . hypnosis . . . not uncommon.

Reading the expression on the Reverend Formigão's face and hearing the doubt, Monsignor Quaresma raised his voice. "I'm sure it was a genuine, supernatural manifestation. I saw the huge globe coming, full of light, very clearly. Yet later I couldn't see it at all when a little girl in front of me pointed toward the tree. You should have seen her face — no doubt about her sincerity. 'See the shining ball! It's going up . . . now it's gone!' But now none of us could see it."

Many were dispersing and making their way uphill to a number of lightweight busses, carriages, carts, and automobiles. Silently, Father Formigão walked along with the others. He had been asked by the patriacharate in Lisbon to interrogate the three children, to submit a detailed report of his findings. But not today. Emotions, for one thing, were too high. Besides, right now, he felt a downright distaste for the whole business. "It didn't last long — this visit," he commented dryly to his companions who were too deeply into their own thoughts to answer.

Francisco and the two girls agreed that the Lady's visit had been her shortest; they were all too brief. They had not seen the great globe. As usual, the Lady had given an answer to each one of Lucia's requests on behalf of her supplicants. She had repeated her requests for praying the rosary and her promise made at *Valinhos* that in October Our Lord and Saint Joseph with the Child Jesus would appear blessing the world.

"There are many who say I am a trickster," Lucia had told the Lady; "they say I should be hanged or burned. Oh, please do make a miracle so that people will believe me." It was the third time Lucia had asked and the third time the Lady had given her an affirmative answer.

"Why did you ask her again?" Francisco asked.

"Because more and more people are saying that I should be hanged or burned!"

"They can't mean it!" He felt as if someone had slapped his face hard.

"Lucia!" Jacinta's arms were around her cousin's waist, then feeling the cord under the thin blouse, she said, "Francisco, Our Lady said she doesn't want us to wear the ropes at night, only in the daytime."

"She said that?"

"*Sim,* but you know something? She also said Our Lord is pleased with our sacrifices." Seeing the brightness in his eyes, Jacinta dimpled. "And next time — she said it again — the Child Jesus and Saint Joseph are coming . . ."

"To give their blessing to the world," Lucia finished, showing dimples, too, a deep smile in her eyes.

On September 29, Father Formigão returned to Aljustrel. He questioned each one of the children alone. Their forthrightness of manner, the simple candor of their words, dispelled some of his skepticism. Two days before the last apparition, he again interrogated them separately in the presence of three witnesses. By now he was convinced of their veracity and determined to be present at the *Cova da Iria* on October 13.

Coming into her parlor after he and his companions had left, Olimpia found the three huddled together on a chest whispering, their sudden silence bringing to mind words she often said these day: "What do they talk and talk about? But just try to get near them . . ."

"I see you weren't expecting me," she said guardedly, straightening the holy pictures on the table where the priest had recently left his papers. "Did Father Formigão get all his answers?"

Before they could think of an answer, a knock came at the parlor door. Quick-stepping through the kitchen and circling the back of the house, they took off for the cave hidden on the hill opposite Lucia's house. It was late afternoon, and the browning leaf stalks and light undergrowth of brush on the hillside shimmered in golden dust. Because of its proximity, the cave had increasingly become a haven — a retreat for prayer, especially for Francisco and Jacinta who were not so much in demand as was Lucia. There was little privacy at the *Cova da Iria* now, and although the favorite solitude of the *cabeço* was not as far away, this spot was even closer and often more conveniently accessible in times of emergency.

Running most of the way, they had scarsely spoken a word until they halted by an oak that grew beside a scree of mashed rocks near the cave. Then, as if they had been corked in a bottle, words burst from Jacinta.

"He kept writing and asking questions and questions and questions! 'What direction does she come from? How is she dressed? What color is her hair? Does she wear earrings? Can you see her face clearly?' " Breathless, Jacinta rushed on. "Why do people keep asking us the same questions over and over? And then the secret! 'Did you hear the Lady tell it to Lucia? Is the secret to make you happy, to go to heaven, to make you rich?' "

Watching the pebbles dribbling through his fingers, Francisco said, "Did he ask you? — he did me — if the people would be sad if they knew the secret?"

"I told him they would," Jacinta answered. "What else did he ask you?"

Francisco dropped the small stones and rubbing his hands

across his trousers drew out his rosary and held it so that the crucifix, caught in a beam of light filtering through the tree above stood sharply outlined. Contemplating it, he answered slowly, "What most people ask. 'Did she laugh or cry' . . . did I hear what she said and did she look at me, and . . . and . . ."

"And what?" Jacinta asked curiously.

"Was she beautiful?"

Lucia drew a deep breath. "And you said?"

"She is the most beautiful person I've ever seen!"

Splendor. That was the word Father Formigão had used with her. "Lucia," he had asked, "does the splendor which covers her — is it beautiful?"

"More beautiful than the light of the sun and . . . and *much much* brighter!" she had answered him.

His pen had moved lightly over the paper making words — her words. Why, she wondered, had he asked her if the Lady had appeared to her last year. "No, Father Formigão," she had told him, "I never saw her before. May was the first time."

The writing had stopped, then continued after she had added, "I never told that to anyone because it's not true."

"How long does the Lady stay?"

Not long, she'd told him, not saying that it was never never long enough.

"Is it long enough to say one Our Father and one Hail Mary?"

More than that, her answer had been, but maybe never as long as it might take to say the *terco* — five decades of the rosary.

"The Lady asks for your prayers?"

"Yes."

She had also told him about the prayer the Lady had taught them to say between the decades of the rosary. He had written that down, too, asking her to repeat it slowly. "O my Jesus, forgive us our sins," slowly as he had asked.

"Is the secret (here Father had laid down his pen and removed his glasses) just for you?"

"No, for the three of us."

"If the Lady is going to take you to heaven soon, what good will it do for you to learn to read and write?"

To heaven soon? "No, the Lady never said that."

"About how old would you say the Lady is?"

"About fifteen."

Father had raised his head suddenly. "Fifteen?" Then after a moment: "How does she look? Describe her."

She had done the best she could, but as usual, there were no words, no paint brush, that could paint the lovely magnificent eyes, the sweet dignity, the shining lovableness of her.

There had been other questions. The *senhor padre* had finally gotten up from his chair, smiling a little at her. Capping his pen, he had asked, "Aren't you at all afraid that people might try to harm you on the thirteenth if there is no miracle?"

"I'm not afraid."

Again Father had sat down and uncapped his pen. She was sitting so close to him that had she been able to read she could easily have made out the words. But she thought she knew — *not afraid*. It was the same answer she had given over and over to Mama, to Papa, to her sisters, and to all the neighbors who for days now talked of little else but what might happen to her and to them if no miracle appeared.

———————

Chapter Eighteen

On Friday evening, October 12, the dos Santos's kitchen was filled with nervous, long-tongued neighbors who after a hasty, last-minute conference had decided Maria Rosa and Antonio should whisk Lucia off to some relative — still time! — or at least, lock her up in a room on the morrow. Moreover, if no miracle happened, they might all be killed. Soldiers had been seen on the approaches to the *Cova da Iria;* it was also being said that the administrator planned not only to bomb the *Cova* but their houses as well.

When everyone, including Antonio dos Santos, red-faced and ill-tempered, was still shouting, Maria Rosa motioned her youngest daughter to the small weaving room between the kitchen and the parlor. In the half-darkness,where the spinning wheel and looms were barely discernible, Lucia was concious of her mother's disapproving eyes.

"You hear what they're saying out there? Artur Santos doesn't always make noises like he did last summer. If he bombs our houses and the *Cova,* if all these people, after seeing they've been fooled and there is no miracle . . ."

"Mama, please don't worry."

"Don't worry! When there's no miracle tomorrow, what do you think all those miserable souls out there — you could hear their voices, even down here, all day long! — what do you think they're going to do! Just take up their wet blankets — hear that rain! — and politely go home. Lots of them don't even believe in God; they'll kill us all."

170

"There *will* be a miracle."

"So you keep saying; how can you be so sure?"

"The Lady promised me."

"Listen, Lucia, people sometimes think they see and hear all kinds of strange things when they don't see or hear anything. I never saw a great ball with lights last month, only some petals falling, and that, like everything else, could be exactly what Father Ferreira once said. The devil has many different ways of working and . . ." Now accustomed to the darkness, she was struck by the dark-circled eyes looking wistfully at her, and a sudden compassionate feeling of protective tenderness welled up within her. Mother of God! All day long . . . one knock after another. We'd like to speak to Lucia, to ask her . . . ask, ask. Ai! Her poor, poor child.

"Listen, my daughter. Let's go to confession now — it's not too late. We'll be ready then for whatever happens — for death itself." Getting no response, she cried out, "If there's no miracle tomorrow that crowd could kill us! Can't you see that? May the Lord assist us for I'm terribly, terribly afraid — for all of us!"

Lucia's arms went out to instantly feel her mother's clamped tightly around her. "Oh, Mama, Mama!" How long had it been since Mama had held her like this? Looking up into the tired, tormented face bent to her, she whispered, "Don't be afraid. Our Lady won't let anything happen to us tomorrow, but if you really want me to, I'll go to confession with you."

"You're not the least bit afraid? . . ."

"No, I'm not. The Lady will do everything she promised."

Maria Rosa loosened her tight hold of Lucia. "I see they've stopped yelling in the kitchen, but — mind you! — no matter what happens tomorrow, I'll be at your side."

Nine or ten miles away at about the same time of evening but in a large village — Alburitel — a young boy about

Francisco's age sat on the tiled floor beside the hearth with some of his younger brothers and sisters. His name was Inácio Lourenço. He was darker than Francisco, with jet black hair and quick eyes that missed nothing, according to his teacher, the Dona Delfina Pereira Lopes. Tonight those eyes were fixed on a handsome blond relative from the North who had stopped for the night on his way to Fatima. He was a vigorous, lively young man breathing zest, vim, and good spirits.

"At the very last minute," he had explained on his arrival, doffing a black felt hat, "my friend was unable to come. As you know, the two of us had planned this weekend as a holiday to see the fireworks at Fatima. However, he had some last-minute revisions to make on a thesis, so . . ." With an expressive shrug of his broad shoulders he had dismissed his friend from the University of Coimbra where both were students.

Now with Inácio's parents, the *Senhor* and *Senhora* Lourenço, he sat talking at a round table covered with a cloth finely embroidered and where the light from a candlelabrum brightened his forelock and heightened the healthy color of his ruddy face. Facing him, a thin old man, long of limb and wrapped in a black moth-eaten cape, regarded him with the same fierce attention as the boy Inácio motionless by the fire. The elderly *Senhor* Fernandes lived alone and often dropped in to visit with the Lourenços. Like the boy he kept his silence except for an occasional mutter from sunken lips — whenever there was a slight pause between the words tumbling from the spirited student.

What crowds! A reporter from the *Diario* had told him that that morning he had counted 240 carts, over a hundred automobiles, hundreds of everything heading for Fatima, and that believe it or not, just out of Vila Nova de Ourém alone. "I wager there will be over 100,000 people there tomorrow." Eagerly, he turned to his host. "Did you see Avelino de Almeida's editorial this week? It was really something. But, then, the newspapers — nearly all of them are free thinking and anti-clerical — have been blowing up this Fatima thing sky high . . . the alleged miracle, especially since last month when there was all that talk of a flying object appearing and disappearing suddenly. You heard about that? No wonder I had trouble catching a bus today. The trains were full, too, and whole families afoot on awful roads. You've never seen anything like it and moreover . . ."

"Roberto! Just a minute." Laughing, his host held up a halting hand. A man with thinning hair in his forties, he had a strong tanned face. "What did Almeida say in the *Seculo*?" While he didn't subscribe to the popular Lisbon newspaper, he esteemed the *Seculo*. Biggest circulation in Portugal.

"He wasn't at Fatima himself last month, but nothing, he says, will keep him away tomorrow. All mass suggestion, he writes — so powerful that people cry, faces become pale as corpses. Naturally, he blames the Church, a tremendous hoax perpetrated by the Church."

Here the old man made a series of assenting nods. "Almeida is right," he mumbled, his toothless gums setting firmly on the words.

Inácio's mother cleared her throat and leaned across the table toward Roberto. Except for the dark eyes now self-assertive and angry, she resembled an old painting of a Madonna — straight black hair parted in the middle above a lovely oval forehead. "Roberto, do the favor of telling me," she said sharply, "just exactly what does Almeida think the Church can gain from what's happening now at Fatima?"

"Money!" Roberto shouted, amused at what he felt was her naiveté.

"That is exactly what I thought you would say!" The *Senhora* Lourenço's thin nostrils flared distastefully.

"Of course!" Roberto answered unruffled, emphasizing the words with a pull at the blond forelock. "Capitalizing on this enormous trickery — the Church plans to build a mammoth, world-wide shrine, like at Lourdes, enriching its already rich coffers. What better . . ." He stopped abruptly, catching for the first time the flare in his cousin's eyes, the flush on the smooth cheeks. "Mind you," he said lamely, "this is what is spouting out of all the journals."

But the *Senhora* Lourenço had already sought her children with vigilant eyes, lastly seeing the dark ones so much like her own. Unblinking, Inácio sat spellbound, black eyes riveted on their guest. Dismayed, she turned back to the table.

"None of what you say is true. The Church is our stronghold; it is all of us united to Christ. It is wrong to make a separation between priests and people . . ."

Her husband stood hurriedly, reached for a pipe and a can of tobacco on a shelf next to some books. "Of course, Roberto, you know there are no lodging places at Fatima, so, many people stay here overnight, rent carts . . ." He filled his pipe slowly, glanced at Roberto with a half-grin, carefully avoiding his wife's eyes. "It's good for business." He was about to say that naturally Cousin Roberto was a welcome exception, when his wife with a caustic "good for business!" hurried to the hearth. A moan of wind sounded in the chimney. "It's time for bed," she said loudly; "you children should have been there long ago."

Leaping to his feet, Inácio confronted her and his father. "May I — please!" His eyes implored them both. "Can't I go with Roberto tomorrow — to Fatima? Roberto, you would take me, wouldn't you?"

"Inácio!" His mother's voice quivered. "What's gotten into you?"

"Listen to that wind," Roberto said hastily, with a little whistle of his own. "I bet there's an ocean full of water in it . . ."

"And school tomorrow," Inácio's father said, smiling at his son. "But . . ."

Afraid of what that "but" might lead to, his wife placed

a firm hand on Inácio's head. "No! To bed." This young man had already heard too much from Roberto. But, Inácio stood stuck to the floor, his gaze glued to the ruddiness of the pleasant face beaming toward him.

"Wake up, boy." The *Senhor* Fernandes, who up to now had been almost inaudible except for the occasional muttering, struggled to his feet. Still wrapped in the black woolen cape, his *carapuça* pushed down to his white bristling brows, he shook a bony finger at Inácio. "Forget this crazy business about lighted balloons, ladies appearing above trees. Tomorrow you belong in that school house with your teacher, Dona Delphina. I'm certain you won't see her giving credit to such foolishness, nor the whole of Alburitel, for that matter." Drawing the cape closer, he took a springy step toward the door, then turned suddenly. "What's the matter with you, Roberto?" he growled, catching an odd grin on the young man's face.

Roberto's face took on a deeper tone of red, as if the old man had heard the words at the tip of his tongue. "You crazy, salty old cod. With all that mumbo jumbo I didn't think you had it in you!"

This time shaking his finger at Roberto, the old man boasted, "We have two chapels in this village, and except for a few old ignorant women, they're always empty. I can assure you," a proud tone creeping into the crusty voice, "that very few from here will, like you, go on such a fly-by-night journey tomorrow. Good night!" Opening the door he let in a great gust of wet wind.

At the departure of Inácio's mother with the other children, Roberto saw that Inácio still hadn't moved. Noticing the solemn lines of disappointment on his face, he laid his hands on the narrow shoulders and playfully shook him. "Listen, Inácio. That boy and those two girls are just play-acting. There won't be anything resembling a miracle tomorrow. You go on to school, like our old friend said. Young people like you (and me, he almost added) belong to the educated future of Portugal. Education, that's the thing. Ignorance breeds superstition."

"I still wish I could go with you."

"On my way back, I'll tell you everything, but it won't be about any big miracle, I can assure you." Throwing back his handsome head, Roberto gave a great laugh. "It will be only about thousands of bedraggled, disappointed souls crying harder than the clouds are doing right this minute. Now go upstairs with your brothers . . ."

"A good idea," Inácio's father said, quietly adding, "I'll see you later, Inácio."

Early the next morning, Roberto was surprised to find Inácio waiting for him at the head of the stairs. "Do you know how old that boy is?"

"What boy?"

"You know, that boy from Fatima — the one who sees the Lady. How old is he?"

"Oh, that boy! I don't even know his name, but he's probably five or six." Something demanding in the coal black eyes made him say, "Today I'll find out. I might even get a chance to ask him." Hmmm. With half the citizenry pouring into God only knew what kind of an ant-hill!

"And his name, too," Inácio said.

Driving off in his rent-free cart (favor of *Senhor* Lourenço) and still in a celebrative mood, Roberto held the reins lightly as he peeked at the sky from under the brim of his black hat. The blackening clouds looked like great birds with long necks and tails and spreading wings, he mused, flying straight from the Atlantic. Sprays of light rain touched his face. Soon reaching heavier traffic, he tried to avoid the sloppy red ruts in the narrow road. "What a mess," he laughed; "what a mess it's going to be!"

Far from laughter and on the verge of tears, Olimpia could see only the "mess" around her. "Get out, all of you!" she cried. "You're trailing mud all over the house." Unheard, she stood in the middle of her kitchen, eyes screwed to shut out the sight of the red gobs of mud on her floors and the people who so carelessly scurried about sitting on her beds, stools, and chests, each one bent on dumping sacks of troubles on Francisco and Jacinta — as if they could remember all those messages! Even saints wouldn't be able to keep all that in their heads. My daughter has consumption . . . my son is deaf . . . Ai! The world had gone mad; nothing made sense anymore. She put her hands to her head, squeezed her eyes hard and let out a piercing cry that brought her husband to her side.

"Patience, woman, patience."

"Patience! Don't talk to me about that. We could hardly get to bed last night, and now here's another batch. Nothing stops them, not even rain. Just look at these floors!"

"Now, now . . ."

"You know what's going on in there?" Olimpia motioned her head toward their bedroom. "The Baroness de Almeirim, no less! She's brought fancy dresses for the girls, flower wreaths for their heads. And Maria Rosa is in there, too, with Lucia."

"Eia! So what! Fancy dresses and pretty flowers!" Reluctantly, Olimpia began to smile faintly as her husband expanded, "Why, they'll look like little angels with those flowers on their heads, but I'm afraid . . ." He shook his head regretfully, eyes full of laughter. "With all this rain they'll also be wearing their shawls and kerchiefs, and Francisco his *carapuça* without flowers! But now we'd better be getting ready to leave. This is a steady rain . . ."

At the *Cova da Iria,* thousands trying to keep dry were of the same mind. Under his umbrella, Monsignor Quaresma contrasted the day with that of a month ago when under the warm sun of a perfect autumn day, he and his friends and myriads of others had witnessed the graceful gliding globe. Today he was certain there would be another manifestation, perhaps even greater.

In a different frame of mind, Dr. Formigão was also

present. Although now convinced of the children's honesty, his experience of the previous month — when he had seen no prodigy of any kind — still made him skeptical. It was one thing to believe in the sincerity of these children, quite another to blindly swallow their extraordinary testimony as concrete fact. After all, he reasoned, the Church never demanded credence in private revelations, even when it gave its blessing.

Next to him was a friend, scarfed and wearing an overcoat and rubbers — Almeida Garrett, a prominent professor at the University of Coimbra, the only university in Portugal and one of the oldest in Europe. It had originally been established in Lisbon in 1291, then transferred to the city of Coimbra in 1306. Five faculties included law, theology, medicine, mathematics, and philosophy. Its library, museums and laboratories were on an extensive scale. Other educational establishments were a military college, a royal college of art, a scientific and literary institute and an episcopal seminary. A busy man at the university, Dr. Garrett had opted today for a place unknown to him until recently.

With a good view of the lanterned arch below, where a tight little band of men and women seemed to be in command, Dr. Garrett judged with satisfaction that he couldn't be much more than a hundred yards away from the hub of action. Truly, the wide bosom of this hill, from crest down including the big hollow below, must be holding at least seventy thousand people, perhaps more. Nearly a tenth of the population of the country. His wandering eye now noted a familiar figure, not only a friend but a student jockeying in beside him.

"Roberto!"

"Good day, *senhor!* What a roar!" His voice was barely audible. "If I haven't had a time getting down this far. Umbrellas!" His own was closed, but he seemed oblivious of the light falling rain. "Is that the tree down there?" He was on his toes, peering with squinting blue eyes under the brim of the damp hat. "Look! It's nothing but a bare trunk — but that must be it! — with flowers and . . ." His words were lost in the cross-current of sound. "Sorry, but I've got to get down there. *Adeus,*" and now Roberto was jostling his way down through the crowd, always turning to his left with a "faz favor" until he finally reached the floor of the *Cova.* Here it was just as crowded, but stepping high on a rock, he saw the lanky figure of a man — a priest — pacing close to the arch, a breviary in both hands. From his hat down he looked wet, his clothes rumpled, as if, Roberto surmised, he had slept in them during the night. He watched him come to a sudden halt, consult the watch in his vest pocket, then with a prolonged shaking of his head, resume his measured tread, unmindful of those around him. But now where were those three mysterious seers, Roberto asked himself. Only after a dozen inquires had he learned the boy's name for Inácio. It was Francisco — Francisco Marto. Other than that, nobody seemed to know anything about him. In a tavern someone had told him, sarcastically, "They say he doesn't hear this lady. Oh, no, he's not deaf. Probably some dumb little kid the priests have thrown into the act."

Chapter Nineteen

"Papa, Papa!" Jacinta screamed. "Papa!" A tall stranger had just lifted her from the crowd packed around the arch. Gently, his big hands set her down. "Don't cry. Your Papa is right here."

After a fearful hour, the children and their families had finally reached the *Cova* under a steady, cold rain. They had been stopped every foot of the way by pilgrims soaked to the skin, many standing in ankle-deep mud. Under her sodden black shawl, Maria Rosa stood close to Lucia as she had promised the night before. In the name of all the saints, she shivered, why had Maria Carreira covered the naked tree with all those ribbons and flowers! Dripping wet like me . . . A feeling of nausea tingled through her. The nightmare of sliding through slush and fighting off countless hands had unnerved her, like the shooting pains of a bad tooth. She steadied herself against Antonio. He was still holding Lucia's hand. Over mud puddles and through a sea of umbrellas he had never let go of her. A miracle in itself. A miracle! O Jesus, don't let the devil deceive so many souls. Lord, come to my assistance. Mother of God . . . She pressed her lips tightly and continued to pray. She was soaked to the bone, but the sickness in her stomach and that dull pain that had gnawed at her for days was better. Beads laced in her fingers, the deafening din in her ears, Maria Rosa waited.

Half under the umbrella which his father tried to steady over him and Jacinta, Francisco also regarded the tree, but unlike his aunt, the battered flowers and ribbons didn't bother him. He felt neither wet nor cold. The buzz of countless voices, topped by the booming voice of the man who had rescued Jacinta, was a million bees he scarcely heard. Nor did he see Aunt Maria Rosa settling on a bench with his mother and Maria Carreira as the priest, doggedly reading his breviary, forged a circle around some women huddled under one umbrella. He was alone, just as alone as he sometimes was, hidden behind a stone wall where he could listen to God. In a few moments she would be here — for the last time. Already, he felt a *saudades* — a feeling of loving homesickness for her, quickly banished by the remembrance of words that always made him want to sing and make music. Heaven . . . soon: That thought was a gust of wind that blew everything else away. Maybe, maybe, he would see the Child Jesus and St. Joseph today. St. Joseph had been a good, good father — like his own. His eyes must have lighted up like Papa's, smiling deep down as he had swung the little Child high in his arms. And the Child . . . merry and laughing back. And now, Francisco's thoughts winged into prayer so that he hardly heard the wrathful, upraised voice.

"It's past midday! Where is your Lady now?" Tucking the black book under his arm the thin priest turned angrily on Lucia. "Do you know what time it is?" He replaced the watch in his vest pocket which he had consulted a dozen times. "It is way past the hour."

Lucia stepped from her father's side, looked up at the gray curtain drawn across the sky. Frowning, she shook her head at the glowering eyes fixed on her.

Patience, Olimpia thought, seeing the tempest on the priest's long face. Patience, like her Manuel had reminded her that morning. In sheer weariness, she lowered her head, vainly trying to follow the beads in her hands the way Maria Carreira was doing beside her: head uplifted, lips moving softly with Ave Marias, so joyfully, so full of faith. How could she pray like that? With all this noise! Olimpia looked up seeing her brother in profile: sad-faced, cap hard on his brows, a hand in one pocket, boots muddy. Poor Antonio. What good could he ever get out of the *Cova* after this? And suppose there was no miracle? Would the crowd? What would Maria Rosa do to Lucia? The rain had lightened, but — now! — whatever had come over the skinny priest again, waving his prayer book around like that?

"It's all an illusion," he was barking at Lucia, who now stood between Jacinta and Francisco. "All night! I have been here all night — soaking wet. You'd better go home, right now, where you belong. You hear me? Go!" The cords stood out on his thin neck. "Our Lady doesn't lie!"

Lucia put both hands over her mouth, shook her head. "Anybody can go home if they want to, but I . . ." Her eyes filled with tears.

Menacingly, the priest gestured wildly, then stepped toward her, the hand with the book, out, as if to push her. "Go on, go home!"

"I'm standing where I belong!" She was crying now. "Our Lady said that she would come today; she's always come before, and she will today, too." She looked sideways, paused; then seizing Jacinta's hand, exclaimed, "*Ohla!* Here comes the Lady; I just saw the flash."

A hush gradually spread over the great amphitheatre. The Lady had arrived, went the word. Heated discussions and opinions, rosaries, litanies, hymns — all ceased until the merged breathing of the throng became almost inaudible.

On the edge of the bench, Maria Rosa clutched the wet shawl tightly around her throat. "Make no mistake, Lucia," she called above a whisper. Eyes steadfastly on her child, she became aware of a strong, familiar fragrance. She took a deep breath. Of course, of course! She remembered immediately: that afternoon when Jacinta had rushed into her *sala* with the small branch, green and prickly, from *Val-*

inhos! Taking it into her hands, a sudden, new and delightful scent had filled the room. "Not perfume, not violets, not roses," she had said, smelling the branch. "What is it?" Nobody in the room had known, but now she knew. Perfume, yes, but not of this world. She needed no other miracle. Her tears fell freely, and she knew that she wept for many reasons. My poor, poor Lucia.

From her line of sight, she could see her piquant face with its snub nose and full lips that she had never considered pretty (beauty demanded a tiny mouth) grow delicately beautiful, the skin translucent, the dark eyes sparkling. The same aspect of beauty enhanced the other two motionless figures beside her. Maria Rosa listened to the light high notes of her daughter relating requests and messages she had received from so many.

In the month of May, contemplating for the first time the Lady in the blinding light (her mantle and tunic were always defined by various shades of white), Lucia had cried in wonder, "Where did you come from?" Before the end of that visit, she had little doubt, if any, about the Lady's identity. It wasn't so hard to know that this was the *Nossa Senhora* — Our Lady, the Mother of God. In June, like her two cousins, she had seen the thorn-covered heart, a symbol of love and deep compassion for all human beings and had learned that God wanted His mother loved and honored, and reparation made through devotion to her Immaculate Heart.

Lucia also knew the Lady by many titles, including Our Lady of Sorrows, Our Lady of Carmel, Our Lady of Lourdes. Her question: "Will you tell us who you are?" meant precisely: By what name shall we know you? And the Lady's answer on that July day — the day of the vision of hell — had been: "In October, I will tell you who I am and what I desire."

According to that promise, Lucia now heard in the Lady's unusual way of speaking: "I am the Lady of the

Rosary . . . continue to say the rosary every day. The war will end soon . . . the soldiers come back to their homes."

And why had she come to them?

TO ASK ALL TO AMEND THEIR LIVES. TO ASK PARDON FOR THEIR SINS. DO NOT OFFEND GOD MORE. HE IS ALREADY TOO MUCH OFFENDED.

The meaning was clear; the language simple and direct. Lucia understood.

In a familiar gesture of tenderness, the Lady leaned slightly forward, palms opened, from which again streamed that light which each time held them in a unique closeness to God . . .

The light rain was gone. The three watched the Lady disappear as they had five times before — her head first, then her back, and lastly her feet. As they looked, tensely watched by those able to see them, they saw her reappear. Mantle now blue, she stood beside a sun free of clouds, a sun which she outshone and which suddenly began to turn.

"Look up there!" Thousands of voices cried out. "The sun . . . my God, my God!" Amazement, fear, awe.

The sun, a silver disk, was revolving like a wheel, its edging of fire painting the landscape and every man, woman, and child, with shades of red, blue, and yellow. It stopped, reversed itself, doing a turnabout three times before gyrating across the sky (some thought it lasted ten minutes), plummeting earthward while a multitude of souls cried in terror, "Have mercy . . . we'll all be killed . . . forgive me my sins . . . it is the end of the world!"

Then just as the sun had seemingly detached itself from its orbit, so now it returned amid cries of: "Miracle, miracle." Men, women, and children wept openly and unashamedly. "It danced, it whirled," they told each other. "It zigzagged coming down. I could look straight at it . . . it didn't hurt my eyes . . . paler than the moon it was — silvery. It happened right after the rain stopped — no, while the

children were looking up, when the clouds parted like strips
of paper."

Still in shock at the spectacle of the "dancing sun" as so
many were now calling it, Maria Rosa lifted trembling hands
to her knitted kerchief, then opened wide her shawl. "Olimpia . . . can you . . ." she stuttered, "imagine this? I . . . I
am perfectly dry." So it seemed everyone else was. She
looked over at her husband staring with wide unseeing eyes,
pale but wordless while the world about him teemed with
wordiness. Her eyes took in the long *boné* in his hand, the
brown suit, the boots. Dry. Next to her on the bench, Olimpia patted her kerchief and the front of her shawl, pointed to
her feet. "Dry" her lips said. "Even my shoes." She exchanged glances with her sister-in-law, and their laughter,
half-tearful, joined as if this was the greatest miracle of all,
not the almighty one which they had just seen.

Blessing herself and shaking her head as some of Maria
Rosa's daughters and her own approached, Olimpia greeted
them with eloquent eyes and hands that said it all. She stood,
pushed her way as voices ebbed and flowed. Heads and
shoulders above everyone, the man who had rescued Jacinta
now held Lucia on his shoulder. Near them, Olimpia saw
Jacinta in her father's arms, pale and wan. Where, she wondered, was Francisco?

He was near and unnoticed, tight within a colony of
buzzing chatterers, for now it was not Francisco and the two
girls, nor even the Lady, which absorbed them. Their reac-
tions to the miracle transcended everything. But, for Francisco in this secluded bit of time, it was a different kind of
miracle which preoccupied him. Just as he had hoped, he had
seen the Child Jesus and Saint Joseph. In the sky, even as the
sun had whirled, he had seen them. Not a little Baby he had
been but a beautiful Child about two years old, dressed in
bright red like Saint Joseph beside Him. Our Lady had been
there, too, her mantle no longer white but blue.

He now heard his name, a faint, muted "Francisco" as

the group around him hurried off, drawn by the great voice of the man who had set Lucia on a rock, higher than the *azinheira* closeby. That man was calling: "Over here! Come over here." Ready to go, Francisco again heard his name, this time clearer. About thirty or forty paces away, a hatted young man standing on a high rock was furiously waving an umbrella. "Can you hear me?"

Hardly. He couldn't even see him now as people rushed past him toward Lucia and the man beside her. "Listen," his voice was booming; "Lucia is going to tell us what Our Lady told her today." The young man's moustache, like everything about him, was big. He was an attorney — Carlos Mendes — who today, against his will, had found himself near the tree with a brother recently returned from the French front.

Lucia stood composed, eyes downcast. The shawl that covered her white dress had fallen back from her shoulders. Both the dress and shawl, like the kerchief in her hand, were dry. Unlike Jacinta, lying still in her father's arms and looking out with dull lifeless eyes, Lucia looked fresh; there was color in her cheeks, and a vibrancy radiated from her as she looked down at the ring of quiet faces that also included her mother and father and many of her relatives.

She began, "Our Lady said that she . . ."

"Louder, speak louder," Carlos Mendes urged.

"Our Lady said — she told us that God wants people to amend their lives because . . ." She paused, her eyes on the sober upturned faces, "because He is already too offended. Everybody must ask pardon for their sins."

Many quietly blessed themselves, wiped their tears. Only moments ago they had witnessed, not only the warning might of God but also His loving compassion.

"And that sums up her message!" Carlos Mendes said firmly. In September, he had seen nothing extraordinary at the *Cova da Iria*. A brief encounter with Lucia had left him unimpressed. At that time he might have queried: Offended? How could the Creator be vulnerable? Hurt by his creatures? After what he had seen today there was no mystery. Christ's sufferings and death movingly gave the answer. For Him there was no time as humans knew it — no past, no future. It was *now*. And Christ to redeem man had died for man's offenses. "And that is why Our Lady has come here!" he added.

Lucia nodded, and nodded again as Jacinta said from her father's shoulder, "Our Lady said the war will end soon." Few heard her; the talk was on again; but again Francisco heard his name and swinging around came face to face with the young man who had waved his umbrella at him. A loose forelock over his forehead, the felt hat jauntily set, the stranger's laughing eyes drew a quick smile from Francisco. "I saw you on that rock — calling me," he said.

"Ah! Did anyone ever tell you what a wonderful, intriguing smile you have?" And such a charming voice he told himself.

"No."

"Well, you have! It's just great getting this close to you. I have something I want to ask you." Seeing the smile fade, he rushed on, "Nothing big, mind you. Just one little word!" His blue eyes teased. "Can you hear me?"

The smile was back in full force, the intrepid eyes looking straight into his. "Yes, what is it?"

"How old are you?" He was about to supplement his question with: "There's a boy who wants to know." But he was only able to catch the word "nine." A woman fashionably dressed had swept Francisco to her ample bosom. "My little saint!" Her friends took over but Roberto had what he wanted.

From Francisco's lips he'd gotten what Inácio wanted and he had seen Francisco at close range. Ah, Inácio, just wait until you hear what I have to tell you!

Remember what I said (was it only last night or was it this morning?) that the only miracle today would be a million bedraggled souls crying harder than the sky above? And, oh, how many other such things! He felt an immense urge to return promptly to Alburitel, but it was hours before he saw Inácio who also had something marvelous to tell him.

About seven o'clock that evening before Roberto hitched his horse and made ready to leave Fatima, a very solemn Father Formigão stood framed in the doorway of the Marto's parlor. His eyes followed an overtired Jacinta walking toward the kitchen where most of the family had assembled, still overawed by what they had seen in the heavens that day. He had just asked her to tell Francisco it was his turn, feeling a twinge of remorse at the utter weariness he had seen in the tiny, listless body. Yet he had not kept her long — just a fraction of the time he had questioned Lucia. In a few days he would return, but today while the present events were so vivid in their minds?

Stepping back into the cold room, he adjusted his glasses, examined some of the notes he had just written and noted that Jacinta's testimony was essentially the same as Lucia's. With two exceptions: Next to the sun, Lucia had seen a large figure of Christ blessing the people; she had also seen two portrayals of Our Lady similar to those of Our Lady of Carmel and Our Lady of Sorrows, as well as the Child Jesus and Saint Joseph, who were the only ones Jacinta had seen.

Had she seen these all at the same time?

No, one following the other.

Father Formigão glanced toward the door, went back to his notes. In all he had asked Lucia more than forty questions. Only at the end had he noticed the lassitude — her sudden fatigue — as she had sat back on the low chest like a sleepy tired child. She looked younger than her ten years. He looked toward the door again, thinking that he had heard a movement there. Francisco? No. Something must have detained him. It seemed quite a long time since his little sister had left. Ordinarily, he was a patient man, maybe not long suffering, a virtue often attributed to his countrymen, but today's happenings, which had borne out the children's prediction of a miracle — and what a miracle! — had taken the props from under him. Sitting closer to the lamp which Olimpia had earlier placed on the table for him — there was only one small window in the room — he began checking the answers Lucia had given him.

Did she expect to see the Lady in the *Cova da Iria* again?

No, had been her unequivocal answer.

Had the Lady made any signs requesting the people to look at the sun? Another steady "no."

Briefly, Father Formigão glanced at the open door. Had Jacinta been too tired to relay his message? He went back to his questions.

"Did the Lady want the people to do penance?" he read.

"Yes."

"Did she use the word 'penance'?"

"No, but she said to say the rosary, to be sorry for our sins and to ask pardon of Our Lord, but no, she didn't use the word 'penance'."

"Did you see the signs in the sun?"

"I saw it going around."

A shadow fell across the door. It was Francisco. He was bareheaded and wearing the short coat he had worn all day, buttoned up to the limp white collar of his shirt. His shoulders sagged a little.

"I'm sorry, Francisco," Father Formigão said warmly. "You are very tired and a little sleepy. *Sim?*"

With a faint smile, Francisco nodded. From his chair, the priest regarded him quizzically. In some inexplicable manner, it always seemed to him that this child was the most mysterious of the three. Certainly, the most reserved. Was it because he always said he didn't hear the Lady? He couldn't quite put his finger on it.

"Did you hear what the Lady said today?" he asked, eyes intent on the ones sleepily regarding him.

"I heard nothing."

"You heard nothing?" There was a long pause. "Wasn't it the Lady who once told you the secret?"

Francisco was puzzled. He had been sitting on the chest facing Father Formigão; now he pressed against the wall. Why, Father Formigão knew that he never heard the Lady. "No," he said, finally; "it was Lucia who told me." His eyes wouldn't stay open. The saints' pictures above the table were rocking, his head jerking. In a minute he was going to topple over, fast asleep. The next question brought him upright.

"Isn't it true that you won't tell the secret because you're afraid of Lucia. Afraid she'll hit you?"

"Oh, no!"

"Then why won't you tell me? Is it because you think it would be a sin?"

Francisco was wide awake now, poised on the edge of the wooden chest. "It would be — if I told."

"Would people be sad if they knew what the secret was?"

"*Sim.*"

Looking solemn, Father Formigão wrote slowly. Then: "When did the Lady appear most beautiful to you, today or . . ."

Suddenly, Francisco stood; he looked directly into the eyes of the priest who had also gotten to his feet. "Today, she looked as beautiful . . ." A shadow of a smile touched his lips, lingered while he considered, lost in thought and forgetting the crux of the question. As beautiful as . . . Now who could he compare her to? After all, he had told Father Formigão only a few days ago that she was the most beautiful person he had ever seen.

Father Formigão waited.

At last the answer came. "As beautiful as last month," he said quietly, for he could find no one — nothing — to whom he could compare her.

After Francisco's departure, the Reverend Dr. Formigão gathered his papers and slipped them into the flat leather case with unsteady hands. Why had he again asked Francisco about the secret, especially since he had not even included the question in his agenda. Sadly, he shook his head. Today of all days, when he had seen a celestial body fall — against all scientific laws. My God . . . to believe with the simple faith he had seen in the liquid eyes and reverent lips of thousands. Well, he did — he did.

On the last stretch of the road approaching Aributel, Roberto's churning mind still had not sorted out the answers he sought. It was possible that there was a scientific answer for such an extraordinary phenomenon, or was there? How, if so, had the children been able to predict weeks ahead such a fantastic miracle? Collective suggestion? His eyes just didn't play tricks like that, nor was he — ha! ha! — as cool as one certain Professor Garrett whom he had met the second time, this time in the crowded square of Fatima. Composed he had been, as if the sun danced every day of the year on its way to the earth!

Ah, yes, he had seen the sun pierce the clouds that had hidden it minutes before. "I turned toward the sun," he had said in his best matter-of-fact voice, "and I could see it, without risk of pain, like a disc with a clear-cut edge, yes, with a vivid rim — luminous, shining. It looked like a burnished wheel — iridescent — like mother-of-pearl."

The words had run like a lecture in the ancient halls of Coimbra. "The disc spun dizzily around . . . detached itself from the firmament, and advanced blood-red towards the earth." Then, with a grimace, the professor had remarked on the strange yellows which had jaundiced those around him, coloring his hands, too. The phenomenon from beginning to end, he had stated in the same unemotional voice, had lasted ten minutes. (Fifteen years later, these words with many more describing that eventful day would be recorded in a long letter of Dr. Garrett to Father Formigão.)

It was after nine o'clock when Roberto pulled in the reins in front of Inácio's house. The front windows faintly reflected the amber of candlelight, and in the garden people were talking and moving about, guided by a lantern and an oil lamp.

"Inácio!" Roberto whistled loudly as Inácio leaped out of the darkness. "Where did you come from?"

Inácio got into the cart with him. "We saw it here, too!"

"What are you talking about?"

"The miracle! Just like it happened in Fatima . . ."

"One minute, please! Do you mean — why, I can hardly believe . . ."

"We were still in school; it was almost lunch time when we heard yells and screams. 'Something awful has happened,' Dona Delphina said, running out the door. We all went, too, out in the street. Lots of people were there, too, waving their hands and pointing to the sky. 'Look at the sun!' I looked straight at it . . ."

"And it didn't hurt your eyes!" This time Roberto whistled softly. Check off the mass business hypnosis bit, which he already had.

"No, it looked like a great big ball of snow, turning and turning, and then after a while it came down fast — all fire. Even *Senhor* Fernandes was kneeling in the mud. 'Holy Virgin, Holy Virgin,' he kept groaning."

Roberto laughed gleefully. The picture of *Senhor* Fernandes, caped and kneeling in the street, praying, was the crowning point in a day of miracles. Both chapels empty, he had boasted. But then who was he to be throwing stones?

"Look, Inácio. I want to water this horse and then we'll have a good talk. I've got something to tell you, too."

"Wait a minute." In the darkness relieved by the approaching lamps, Inácio's black eyes gleamed. "Did you see that boy?"

"I did. I even talked with him."

"You did! They said lots of people couldn't even see those children."

"I was lucky . . ."

"What's his name?"

"Francisco Marto . . . a fine, wonderful, noble boy, just like you. And guess what? He's nine years old, too!"

"I just knew it! Is he going to be a priest?"

"I didn't ask him that . . ."

"I bet he is. I am. I've always wanted to be one."

(Years later when he had become a priest, Inácio Lourenço recounted the incident in the schoolhouse and the extraordinary solar phenomenon which the people in Aributel, about nineteen kilometers from Fatima, had seen that day.)

———

Chapter Twenty

Spring, 1918

Running toward one of the sheds, Olimpia caught up with her husband, hoe and shovel over his shoulder. "Francisco's done it again, and I tell you right here and now, I give up! I've just heard his catechism for the last time. I mean it!"

There was panic in her voice and the sound of anger, too, but he knew it was only worry clouding the words, and now he was afraid that he was beginning to feel the same way.

"And First Holy Communion tomorrow," she wailed. "I've told you before; he just closes his eyes every time, runs with the words of the Creed, paying no attention at all. He can't tell you what those words mean, not one!"

"Well, I wouldn't say that."

"If I stop him, no matter where, he doesn't know the next word."

"That's not too unusual. I've done the same thing myself."

"He does it every time, as if he'd gone off to the Lord only knows where!" She lifted a hand painfully to her forehead. "Ai, ai! When Father Ferreira quizzes him this afternoon the same thing is going to happen. I can hear the *senhor padre* already. 'Stop a minute, Francisco. If you please, eh? Can you tell me . . .' " She threw her hands up in despair at the evil image her mimicry evoked; a stern, reproachful Father Ferreira scowling at her poor, helpless, tongue-tied child.

"Try not to worry so much." Her husband shifted the tools on his shoulder. "Maybe it won't happen. I'm sure, in fact, I know that Francisco understands it all, every point in the Creed. Jacinta . . ."

"She's not my worry. You know I always prepare the children for their First Confessions and Holy Communions the best I can. If they're not ready, they just can't go, that's all. And that goes for Francisco, too!"

She was ready to burst. Well, he refused to believe that Francisco was not ready. A boy who had seen Our Lady six times, who wept in the middle of the night with compassion for his Savior. Not ready! "Look here, Olimpia. We both know how long he has looked forward to tomorrow. It just doesn't make sense that Father Ferreira . . ."

"Won't pass him? I wish I could say the same!"

Manuel Marto stood watching his wife dragging back to the house. His eyes shifted in the direction of the tiny acreage green with new alphalpha close to the rows of sprouting potatoes and dark green kale. At the timeless beauty of the hills and mountains he took a deep breath. Ah, a feathery greeness lay over the land again — like that spring evening a year ago when Francisco had leaned against his shoulder and said, "Papa, if I had put out my arm I could have almost touched her." No, no, it couldn't happen; Father Ferreira would not, could not . . . He would pass him. He started for the back field. The big boys were already at work. He stopped at the fig tree, noting the tangled limbs bursting at their ends with tiny clusters of leaves and tiny balls of fruit. There was no season more lovely than spring. He never stopped thanking God for His blessings. The war, too, was about over. That was the word each day . . . no sons wounded or killed. He began hoeing. As soon as he had finished these two rows he would go back to the house. Maybe there was something he might say to Francisco that would help.

Many months had passed since that memorable day of October 13, 1917, when 70,000 had witnessed the miracle of the sun. Shortly after that, a group of fanatics with the blessing of Artur Santos had hauled away Maria Carreira's arch with its cross and lanterns, broken the table and scattered into fragments the flower pots and pious ornaments, then mistakenly hacked down a full-blown *azinheira* near the real one. Undaunted, Maria Carreira had again arranged a small shrine. She was still the unwilling custodian of the purse, but knew from Lucia that some day soon a chapel would be built at the site of the beloved little tree. Perhaps, even some day a great basilica would rise to honor Our Lady of the Rosary whose presence she had felt so intimately as she had closely watched Lucia and her two cousins in ecstasy.

Pilgrims on their knees, kissing the ground, praying in groups, came in increasing numbers, especially on the thirteenth of the month and on Sundays. They were mostly Portuguese (the story of Fatima had been lost — shuffled to the back pages of a world press engrossed by the horrors of World War I).

Lucia's father still grumbled at his losses in the *Cova* as he saw more and more people stomping around, dragging their chattels over the land that used to bring him "fifty sacks of potatoes;" but like his wife he firmly refused the gifts and money often offered them.

A new dimension had also been added to Lucia's life and Jacinta's. An heretofore, unheard thing had happened, new to the parish of Fatima. A new school for girls had opened. Just as she had once wheedled her mother into letting her go sheepherding with Lucia over the hills, Jacinta now had her permission to accompany Lucia to school, with the added encouragement of a sobered Maria Rosa. When Jacinta had heard about the school she had said, "See, Lucia! I told you; some day you must tell everybody that Our Lord wants His mother really loved." The three had kept His mother's secrets inviolate, and to no one had they ever spoken of the Angel and his three visits. Only years later would Lucia reveal what had occurred in the spring, summer, and fall of 1916.

At the end of the row where he had been weeding, *Ti* Marto stopped, looked across the field where the boys' voices came to him in snatches. He held the hoe upright, glanced at the sun. He still intended to see Francisco. There must be something he could say, he wasn't sure what, but something that might help him when he stood before Father Ferreira. He turned, retracing his steps past the fig tree until he came to the rear of the yard. At the other end he saw Francisco at a chicken coop feeding the hen and her new baby chicks. He waited for a moment, then called, "Francisco! Come down here."

Francisco waved and sprinted toward him, frog-leaped over a rock as round as a toadstool. Happy as a lark, his father thought. Can I say? . . . Don't close your eyes when you're saying the Apostles' Creed. Don't go so fast. Keep your mind on the words so that when Father Ferreira asks you a question about such and such — Olimpia must have said all that.

"What did you want, Papa?"

The dark eyes were even brighter than usual it seemed to him — and the smile sweet and fresh as this morning's air. "Francisco, I was just wondering . . ."

"Yes, Papa . . ."

"Do you know — Francisco, do you know the acts of faith, hope, and charity?" Maybe this was the way to go.

Francisco nodded vigorously. Why would Papa ask him that? He knew all his prayers. One more day — tomorrow! — and at last he would be on his way up the aisle to receive the Hidden Jesus. "Papa, I can hardly wait!"

Ti Marto swallowed, pulled at his ear, then lightly putting his hand on Francisco's arm, he said, "How about the Creed? The *senhor prior* may — Mama says that you know it, but . . ." He couldn't go on; besides, Francisco had stepped back a pace, a bright confident look on his face. "Don't worry, Papa. I know it perfectly. See?" Blessing himself, he closed his eyes, and in those husky tones his father loved, began: "I believe in God, the Father Almighty, Creator of heaven and earth . . ." The words now began to take wings, "and in Jesus Christ His only Son Our Lord . . ."

Intent on the closed eyes and the face, serene and aglow before him, *Ti* Marto barely heard the rush of words ending with "Amen."

"See, Papa?"

Sim, sim, he saw. Ah, to be able to pray like that — with such love, such delight. Now he knew why Francisco's eyes were closed, as Olimpia had complained, why the words didn't mean so much to him. Maybe Father Ferreira would stop him as Olimpia feared, but not him — never.

Hours later — at the lean-to — *Ti* Marto caught a glimpse of Olimpia and their two youngest children. For the last hour, off and on, he had looked at the narrow road that came out of Fatima to their house. Putting down the thin strap of leather he had been mending, he craned his neck to see Francisco, suddenly dart from his mother's and Jacinta's side, dash past the big rock into the yard and straight into his bedroom at the front of the house.

Olimpia's "I told you so" expression confirmed his worst fears.

"So Father Ferreira didn't pass him!"

"True; it happened exactly the way I thought it would. He got mixed up in the Creed, so . . ." She stopped at the flare of outrage she saw in his eyes. "And don't go blaming Father Ferreira, either!"

Biting his lip, he mumbled, "He's never understood, not even after the miracle;" and in a lower mumble, "I thought he was leaving."

"Look, Manuel." Olimpia untied her kerchief, unduly creasing and folding it. "I saw many children today ready for confession from all over the parish, many of them older than Francisco. You know he won't be ten until next month." She looked directly into his eyes, her hands now busily unfolding the scarf. "He cried from the church door all the way up here. 'There's plenty of time,' I kept telling him."

She was just talking. She knew as well as he did how much tomorrow had meant to him. He looked down at Jacinta, standing so still beside them both, eyes big with sadness. He knew she was hurting for Francisco. Why, he should have been at the very head of the line tomorrow. Father Ferreira!

Hesitantly, *Ti* Marto leaned against his son's closed door, one hand on the latch, listening. Although the bed clothes muffled the sobs, he heard their anguish — but this time he turned away. This was not the time to go in there, not now. The bitter disappointment was a wound still too fresh.

The next morning, Saint Anthony's Church was filled with flowers and song and incense and all the happy excitement that came yearly when the hamlets of the parish celebrated the First Holy Communion of their *meninos* and *meninas*. Pale, Francisco sat close beside his father without tears. "He's used them all up," *Ti* Marto reflected, glancing sideways at him as the children sedately stepped by: first, the boys, hair straightly cut and neatly combed, wearing long suits like their fathers, the girls following them in soft white veils and dresses. He stole another look, just as Jacinta passed by, palms fervently clasped, eyes down. She was so little she was hard to see. He caught Francisco's quick smile. Jacinta's happiness is his, too, he thought, feeling for the fresh handkerchief Olimpia had slipped into his pocket that morning.

On the way to school the next day, Francisco tagged along with João, behind Lucia and Jacinta. As they went down the lane, he dropped farther and farther behind . . .

There was the church steeple. Why should he go to school today? It wouldn't be the first time he hadn't; besides, he would never have to read and write. Since the miracle, the professor paid little attention to him. Instead of slapping him and poking fun, he just acted as if he weren't there at all. He saw Lucia and Jacinta heading toward the church; they would make a visit to the Blessed Sacrament now, just as they always did after school.

"I'm not going to school today," he announced as they waited for him at the church door. They weren't surprised. "I'll wait for you here until you get out of school."

"Are you going to stay all day?" Now Lucia was surprised. She didn't think he'd ever done that before. He nodded; they went into the darkened church where a few women knelt in the shadows. His eyes on the tabernacle, his step quickened until he reached the front bench. He knelt on both knees and bowed his head. Not to have received the Hidden Jesus yesterday had been the greatest sacrifice of all — far more than being hungry, thirsty, wearing the scratchy rope . . .

It is for the love of You, for the conversion of sinners, in reparation for the sins committed against the Immaculate Heart of Mary.

Hours later — when Lucia and Jacinta entered the church — they knelt a few moments, then Lucia went to the front bench. "Francisco," she whispered. He didn't move. "You're still here!" He turned toward her, face slightly flushed, eyes shining, lips parted in a smile. She drew closer, peering at him curiously, then straightened and smiled, too. "Francisco!" she said again in a different tone. Silently, he reached for his cap. She followed him down the aisle, Jacinta trailing behind; short of the door he hurried and they saw him running through the square, homeward bound.

"What happened?" Jacinta asked.

Lucia made no answer.

At the top of the hill, near home, Francisco found him. "Papa!" He flung his arms around Papa's waist.

Eia! What had happened to his Francisco today to make him so happy? All the joy of this world was in his face, carved with the beauty of an angel. "You're so sweaty," he said, laughing and drawing back. "How did you get so hot?"

"Running . . ."

"You — did you go to school today?"

"No, Papa."

"Why not?"

"Because . . ."

"Because?" *Ti* Marto drew his arm around Francisco's shoulder and together they went into the yard.

"Papa, I'll never have to read and write — never."

Suddenly *Ti* Marto shivered; somehow the spring day was chillier than he had thought.

Chapter Twenty-One

Winter and Spring, 1919

"These shirts need buttons, and — and a few patches wouldn't hurt them, either!" Olimpia set down a small pile on the bench between Florinda and Teresa. "Do you girls know where Francisco is? Jacinta says he's been gone a long time. And in this weather!" There was a bright fire in the hearth, but all three were bundled in shawls, their slight figures swollen with petticoats.

Florinda shook her head negatively. With a languid air, she slouched out of the kitchen returning with a basket and a can rattling with buttons. "I feel shaky — after all this time," she said weakly, as if the few steps she had taken to the weaving room had drained her.

Olimpia sent her a sharp look, noting the sallow skin and lusterless eyes. "You do look a little peaked, but your cough is much better. Let me fix you a *gamada* — an eggnog would be good . . ." She stopped at Florinda's shudder. None of her daughters were as strong as she was; she had learned that when the whole family had come down with that terrible influenza. She looked hard at Teresa.

"I'm fine," Teresa said quickly, forestalling her mother's concern which she could feel was about to fall on her. Not that she wouldn't like a good hot eggnog. She threaded a needle and studiously inspected a faded brown shirt. Today she had coiled her smooth dark braids high on her head. That must be why she looked older than her sister, her mother decided, although she was only fifteen, a year younger. The planes of her face were rounded with a faint rosiness that gave her a blooming air of good health. Watching her reach for the can of buttons, Olimpia reflected that neither had Teresa been as sick as the others.

Glancing at the sunless gray patch at the window, Olimpia took the lamp from the shelf and after lighting it, set it on the table beside the green bottle with a handful of dripping candles. Nothing — measles, mumps, or anything else had ever been as bad as the "flu," she thought, her mind again on Francisco. Where was he? The rain had stopped for a while, at least; but the winds in February were still gusty and cold. And he had been one of the first to come down with it, just a few days before Christmas. One by one they had been strickened except Manuel. To this day she wondered how, besides all the outdoor work, he had ever managed the care of all of them.

Ai, Mother of God! Good news there had been last November and bad news, too. Through the *serra* the bells of Saint Anthony had echoed joyfully at the thrilling news that the terrible war had ended. Thanks to the good Jesus, they had cried. Our boys will be coming home. Like dew the happy tears had fallen. Then the same bells had rung again, this time tolling for their dead, as the world-wide Spanish influenza struck, taking many more than the war ever had. Surprisingly, Francisco had been the sickest in the family. She couldn't remember him ever having been sick before then; but the fever had finally left him not only pale and thin but with a hacking cough.

She heard that cough now. Flinging the door open, she cried, "Come in out of that cold wind." Anxiously, she studied the gaunt, flushed face. "Where have you been? No, don't tell me." His cap was low on his brow, the dark eyes too big, too bright. Reaching for the wet hat, she tried to feel his brow as he broke into a spell of coughing. "To bed," she ordered, the words rough with worry. So many, many people had died of pneumonia afterwards, even doctors. Not that they knew any; and the nearest hospital was in Vila Nova de Ourém where scores had died. The best medicine was bed.

She followed him into the small bedroom, her hands busy with his coat. "You ought to know better than to go out on a day like this, especially after you've been so sick," she scolded. This time she managed to get her hand on his forehead. Exactly as she had thought. Those pink cheeks didn't fool her any. "Francisco . . ." but now he was looking at her in such an odd way, not smiling as usual but with an unfathomable sweetness that suddenly made her draw him to her. Then holding him at arm's length, she said lightly, "Just for another day or two." She bent over the narrow bed and pulled back the covers. "I'll get the medicine and some hot milk."

Once under the covers, Francisco removed the frayed cord from his waist, shoved it deep under the covers. Somehow, he had managed to keep it out of sight all this time but one of these days he must get rid of it. He closed his eyes, felt a chill and then another one.

Those summer months of 1918, following Francisco's keen disappointment at not making his First Holy Communion, had seemed, comparatively speaking, uneventful. The Church interrogations conducted by Father Formigão had continued as well as the unofficial ones by hundreds seeking interviews and photographs of the three. "Try to look holy, keep your hands together like this, hold your rosaries high, be sure to look to heaven." (The children's distaste for this folderal and the camera is evident in all their frozen scowling expressions.) Their hidden life of prayer, penance, and fasting continued. In an emergency, Francisco still availed himself of the attic, or the back haunches of the big rock on the front road, as well as the hillside cave near at hand, where Jacinta sometimes joined him.

"I'm not going to run away every time," she told him one Sunday afternoon when a fine carriage had drawn up to their house. "I'm going to offer this one up."

Maybe he should, too, but what did he have to tell? He had said all he could, always adding, "No, I didn't hear her," which usually and happily, stopped more questions. Another thing that made him want to run faster than ten forks of lightning was worse than all the questions put together. It was acting like he was some kind of saint, pushing medals and rosaries and little bottles of water in front of him, begging for his blessing and even getting angry when he refused.

For Lucia the summer had been easier; she no longer was subject to the pique and ill-humor of her neighbors and family, although her father still bemoaned the loss of his crops and her mother continued to fret over a livelihood for the family. Outwardly, the trio seemed hardly different from other children. Asked about their behavior, Olimpia was wont to say, as she often had in the past: "They are like other children; Francisco still plays his *pifaro* and sometimes they sing and play." Listening, *Ti* Marto said nothing. In his eyes, they had never been like other children. A long time, he thought wryly, since he had seen his Jacinta whirling on her toes, dancing and snapping her fingers.

One day Francisco and Lucia had gone looking for honey. On their return they had found Jacinta sitting on the edge of the well, a strange look in her wide eyes. "Did you see the Holy Father?" she asked, staring beyond them as if she saw a picture. "Poor, poor Holy Father . . . kneeling and weeping with thousands of people around him, many throwing rocks." She had then turned to them, tears on her cheeks.

On another day they had seen the same thing. With fixed eyes, she had stared at a point far beyond the pines jutting out of the valley beyond. "Look . . . don't you see? All those fields with people crying with hunger, and the Holy Father praying before the Immaculate Heart of Mary."

This time Jacinta's vision had happened on the *cabeço* — at the threshold of the cave, isolated from the pilgrims who only a mile or so to the northwest swarmed over the *Cova da Iria*. Here on many days they prayed in reparation as they had done in the past, heads bowed to the earth, offering their prayers and penances for the conversion of sinners; the vision of hell, one part of their secret, had been indelibly stamped on their minds. For them the need for reparation was no problem; the crucifix on their rosaries and the sorrowful mysteries had taught and reinforced everything they had seen and heard. Love was the great heart of God, and the heart, too, of His mother which they had seen and which Lucia now knew that in some way, some day, she must find a way to make known and loved.

Here, in the solitude of the *cabeço*, they talked freely. The Portuguese words flowed fast and eloquent from Lucia's lips. Most of the time, Francisco listened. His thoughts moved in one direction; heaven for him had become more real than the vermillion reflections from Our Lord's Lamp which he had watched creep into the sloping sides of pebbly hills. He still expressed no curiosity when Lucia talked about the Lady's return to ask for the consecration of Russia and for communions of reparation.

But Jacinta whose natural curiosity never left her had questions. "When will Our Lady come? After Francisco and I go to heaven?"

"I don't know." The future seemed far away, like a fog beyond the mountain tops.

The chills had left him; he just felt hot. Looking up, Francisco saw his father rubbing his hands, the thick brows raised in mock surprise. *"Eia!* A great big boy like you in bed — this time of the day, too." He bent over the patchwork quilt and patted the thin hand, then moving closer and with a deepening frown, he asked, "Does your chest hurt?"

"Not unless I cough."

"Mama thinks you have a little fever; she's worried about that cough, but I'm not. In a few days you'll be up, faster than last time. You'll see!"

"Papa, this time . . ." He had tried to tell Papa before, but each time Papa changed the subject or else managed to do something else. Now he was up tall, tugging at his ear and backing toward the door. "Did you know that after getting you to bed, Mama did the same to Jacinta? She wants to be sure nobody gets worse this time!"

But Francisco didn't leave his bed in a few days as his father had hoped. Eventually, for short periods, he did get up, but never to leave the house. The sturdy figure that once had been so robust now looked fleshless and by the latter part of March he was back in bed, too weak to stay up for any length of time. Without complaint, he took his mother's thin soups, hot milk, eggs, the bitter medicine.

"He gets thinner and thinner; he's all bones," Olimpia wept in despair to her tight-lipped husband. Jacinta, too, was running a fever, and while not as sick as Francisco, was back in bed after a short respite.

She was sitting up in bed today, waiting for Lucia to stop on her way home from school. All day long she looked forward to these visits. Today she would tell her, "You know something? I wanted to sneak into Francisco's room, but I offered it up and I didn't go." And now here Lucia was at last. She could hear her voice in Francisco's room.

"Lucia, I've got something I want to tell you." Francisco looked toward the open door. "Is anyone? . . ."

"No, I came through the kitchen; I didn't see anyone;" but quietly she closed the door.

"I can't wear it anymore, and I'm afraid someone might find it." He reached down under the covers and handed her the strip of rope.

She wound it around her hand and slipped it into her pocket, then opened the door. Keeping her voice low, she said, "I'll burn it; I'll get Jacinta's when I go in to see her. Do you have much pain?''

"Yes. My head hurts, everything hurts, but I don't want Mama and Papa to know. Lucia . . ." he paused, his eyes on hers.

She came closer to his bed.

"Sometimes when you're coming home from school I can hear what some of those girls are saying . . ."

Lucia frowned. What did he mean? "They live near me . . ."

"I know where they live. Look, be very careful of who you play with, what kind of friends . . . remember this after . . ."

"You were going to say 'after I am gone'."

"Sim."

She was twelve years old now, but in some ways Francisco seemed older, no longer the little boy she used to boss around. "Don't you worry, Francisco. When school is out, I'll make a longer visit to the Blessed Sacrament. And now before anybody comes in I'll get Jacinta's rope, too."

That cord had three knots and was blood-stained.

On another day, she found Jacinta sitting up in bed, finger at her lips, eyes wet and clouded with mystery. "I thought you'd never get here," she whispered. "Oh, Lucia!"

"What's happened?"

"Our Lady — she came today to see me and Francisco."

"Our Lady! Here?"

"No, in Francisco's room."

"How . . ."

"Mama wrapped me in a shawl and a blanket. I had asked if I could see Francisco, so she put me at the other end of his bed. As soon as she left, there was Our Lady beside us." Suddenly, Jacinta fell back on her pillow, coughing and trembling, both hands tight on her cheeks.

"Don't talk now . . ."

Jacinta shook her head, slipped her hand under her pillow and blew her nose on a cotton remnant that served as a handkerchief. "I — I don't want to cry."

"But you said you saw Our Lady!"

"Yes, and she was just as sweet and beautiful."

"So?"

Jacinta sat up again. "She is taking Francisco very soon, but not me, not yet."

Lucia waited, dark eyes on the small tearful face.

"She asked me if I wanted to convert more sinners, if I wanted to suffer more . . ."

Lucia was silent, not quite understanding. No sacrifice ever seemed enough for Jacinta: being hungry, thirsty, or like the bloody rope she had secretly burned with Francisco's . . . And after the Lady's first visit she had never danced again, except when that prisoner had swung her into the fandango.

"I'll tell you why I'm crying."

"It's not because you don't want to suffer more . . ."

"No, that's not it; it's because you won't be with me, not you or Mama. I'm going to two hospitals, and then I'm going to die in one — all alone. Oh, Lucia, isn't that a very dark place where you can't see anything?"

"No, no, it's not like that at all. Look, Jacinta — listen. You won't be alone, you know that. Our Lord and Our Lady, they'll both be with you." Lucia wheeled toward the door, her head turned to hide the flow of tears. "I'll be back . . ."

When she walked into Francisco's room she immediately saw the deep smile in the large hollowed eyes. "She came again," he whispered.

"I know."

"Lucia, I've been thinking since she left. Will you do something for me?"

She nodded, still fighting tears.

"Find Papa. I would like him to . . ." but before he had finished Lucia had left the room.

She lingered at the door as her uncle stood beside the bed, the shoulder-length boné as usual squarely set above the shaggy brows.

"What is it, Francisco?"

"Papa . . ."

Ti Marto knelt beside the bed the better to hear the low husky tones. His Francisco, once such a strong boy, now but a shadow; yet always with fearless eyes that even now shone with a tranquil certainty that the grave shadow about his lips could not disguise. He had a sudden feeling that something had happened today — in this room?

"Remember, Papa, a long time ago when I thought I was going to make my First Holy Communion?"

"Sim." How could he ever forget that morning?

"I told you that . . . that I could hardly . . ."

"Yes, yes. 'Papa,' you said, 'I can hardly wait.' See? I remember." What was Francisco trying to tell him? That he could hardly wait to go to heaven? With other words, he well knew, he had been trying to tell him that for some time.

"Will you go to the priest's house?"

"Oh, that's why you wanted to see me! You mean right now?" But he knew without asking.

"Yes, I want to go to Confession and Holy Communion."

Not daring to let himself touch the thin hand so near, *Ti* Marto rose from his knees, the white gray of the plastered wall in front of him suddenly blurred. This would be Francisco's First Holy Communion and, perhaps, his last. Why hadn't he thought about going to see the priest before this? There was a new one now at Saint Anthony's — Father Morreira. Aloud, he said, "I'm on my way!" He rubbed his hands. "And now you can hardly wait!" The words were gruffly said but their inflection brought a quick gleam to the dark eyes and a small assenting nod.

As soon as his father had left, Francisco motioned to

Lucia. "I want to ask you something before Papa gets back with the priest."

"What?"

"I've been thinking about my sins, but maybe I've forgotten something. Do you remember?"

Lucia lowered her head, the straight dark brows caught in thought. "Sometimes you ran away when your mother told you not to leave . . ."

"That's right — what else?"

"Let's see. No, I can't remember anything more."

"Please ask Jacinta."

Lucia returned immediately. "She says that you once stole a *tostão*, " a coin worth a few pennies.

"I've already confessed that . . ."

"And that you threw stones at the boys from Boleiros . . ."

A long time ago . . . he remembered. When he opened his eyes he saw that she was gone, but he heard voices. Mama and Florinda and Teresa were back, and there were footsteps in the parlor right next to his room. Father Morreira had arrived. In the late afternoon the bedroom was darkening; yet he could plainly see the crucifix above the long crack on the wall next to the wooden shutter without louvers. He put out his hand to the table beside his bed, then took it back as Father Morreira smiled down at him, waiting for a chair that Olimpia was bringing from the parlor.

The priest's visit didn't last long. After absolving his penitent, he promised to return the next morning with Holy Communion. Again he must wait.

The next morning he heard it — the little bell ringing to announce the arrival of his Hidden Jesus. His heart was beating, thumping fast in his chest and in his ears. He tried to sit up, but his godmother, lighting a blessed candle, whispered, "You can receive Him lying down." She propped his pillow, then stepped back to make room for the priest and the acolyte who, with the small bell, had accompanied him.

Francisco closed his eyes, heard the Latin words above him: "Corpus Dómini nostri Jesu Christi custódiat ánimam tuam in vitam aetérnam. Amen. May the Body of Our Lord Jesus Christ preserve your life unto life everlasting. Amen."

Now looking up at the small host in the priest's hand, he opened his mouth and again closed his eyes . . . He was back on the heights of the *cabeço* where the Angel had offered him the Cup, filled with that same sweet fire.

It was still with him hours later when Jacinta, wrapped in a shawl, was carried to the foot of his bed. There was now a look of new strength that showed in the lift of his head, the movement of his hands. The skin that had been sallow had lightened and even the hollows in the flat cheeks seemed fuller, as if to make room for the smile that now regarded Jacinta happily.

"You're better! At last you received . . ." Her voice trailed off as she looked at him. So many times she had seen the longing in his face before she had gone to the altar. Now very soon he would be going to heaven.

"Look, Jacinta, don't look so sad. When I get to heaven, I will ask Our Lord and Our Lady to bring you up right away."

They heard running footsteps, and at the door Lucia stood for a moment. "You received Him!" she said, touching his bed. Except for looking so thin . . . "You are sitting up!"

They began talking in low tones and laughing softly. After a few minutes Olimpia appeared, alarmed by Francisco's coughing. He was lying back on the pillow, his breathing labored.

"I'm leaving now, Aunt," Lucia said worriedly, moving closer to Francisco. His eyes were closed; the cough had left him ashen, he lay so still that she bent over him.

"Lucia?" He was looking straight at her now.

"If you go tonight, Francisco, don't forget to pray for me."

"Lucia . . ." His eyes like hers were filmed with tears. "I won't forget . . . never." The hand on hers felt suddenly strong. "Till heaven," she whispered, and breaking away, she ran blindly past Jacinta barely visible under the shawl, and her aunt, white-faced, standing at the door.

Late that night, a flickering candle in her hand, Olimpia found her husband still undressed, on his knees against the bed, both arms cradling his head, a rosary twined in one hand. He was so still, she wondered if he slept.

"Manuel?" she said softly.

He raised his head, got heavily to his feet. Olimpia placed the candle on the table. "He couldn't swallow the milk, but he never complains. Finally, he took a little water. Then I think something happened . . ."

"Happened?"

"Just as I was leaving his room I think he saw someone. His eyes got so bright — no, no, not feverish. He seemed so — so alive, like this morning after Holy Communion. He sat right up in bed. 'Look, Mama, there by the door — a beautiful light.' I looked but I couldn't see anything. I felt his forehead; it felt cool. Manuel, maybe, you know sometimes after receiving the Viaticum the very sick take a sudden turn . . ."

Maybe, her husband thought, tiptoeing into Francisco's room early the next morning. He saw that he was asleep, his face slightly turned. The cheeks didn't seem so thin that way. Both arms were under the covers. Still on his toes, he reached up to the small window and quietly opened the solid wooden shutter. Let the April sunshine come in and warm the cool night air. Spring was early this year, already gladdened with the song of the big larks and the impatient fury of birds in search of new homes — a new life. Spring — his favorite season. He paused beside the bed wanting to stroke the light brown hair that had grown longer. Certainly long hair would make a face look thinner . . . maybe Olimpia was right. After Viaticum . . .

Feeling his gaze, Francisco opened his eyes, smiled. He raised his hand and felt it clasped in two strong ones.

"Eia! I woke you up; go back to sleep."

When *Ti* Marto returned to the house to see how Francisco was — it was about ten o'clock that morning of April fourth — he heard the sounds of heartbreak: Mama, Florinda, Teresa, and Jacinta. No boys yet. He knew before be entered the bedroom. For a moment he stood at the door, then took one step into the room. Why, his Francisco was still smiling — that sweet beguiling smile! — just as he had left him. He took another step and bent over Olimpia, lifting her into his arms.

"He was almost eleven," she sobbed.

"Look, Olimpia," he said, holding her close. "See how happy he looks!"

Ai, Jesus and Mary. How was it that right now, suddenly at this very moment, he could feel singing all through him a little of the joy and glory already Francisco's. New life, my dear little son — no more waiting.

"Mama, Mama, don't be too sad; he is where he's wanted to be for a long, long time."

And the thought brought deep comfort to the heart of Francisco's father.